a&b

Flawed

Jo Bannister

First published in Great Britain in 2007 by
Allison & Busby Limited
13 Charlotte Mews
London W1T 4EJ
www.allisonandbusby.com

A CIP catalogue record for this book is available from the British Library.

10 9 8 7 6 5 4 3 2 1

ISBN 0 7490 8149 X
978-0-7490-8149-2

Typeset in 11/16 pt Sabon by
Terry Shannon

Printed and bound in Wales by
Creative Print and Design, Ebbw Vale

The author of over twenty acclaimed novels, JO BANNISTER started her career as a journalist after leaving school at sixteen to work on a local weekly newspaper. Shortlisted for several prestigious awards, she was editor of the *County Down Spectator* for some years before leaving to pursue her writing full-time. She lives in Northern Ireland and is currently working on her next novel. *Flawed* is the seventh in a series featuring Brodie Farrell, Daniel Hood and Jack Deacon.

Also available from Allison & Busby

In the Brodie Farrell series

Flawed

Requiem for a Dealer

Breaking Faith

The Depths of Solitude

Reflections

True Witness

Echoes of Lies

Other titles by Jo Bannister

The Tinderbox

The Lazarus Hotel

The Mason Codex

Mosaic

A Cactus Garden

The Winter Plain

The Matrix

In the Rees series

The Fifth Cataract

The Going Down of the Sun

Gilgamesh

Striving with Gods aka *An Uncertain Death*

In the Mickey Flynn series

Death and Other Lovers

Shards aka *Critical Angle*

In the Castlemere series

Changelings

The Hireling's Tale

Broken Lines

No Birds Sing

A Taste for Burning aka *Burning Desires*

Charisma aka *Sins of the Heart*

A Bleeding of Innocents

In the Rosie Holland series

The Primrose Switchback

The Primrose Convention

CHAPTER ONE

Miracles happen every day. They happen in classrooms.

Every day children of four and five, and occasionally twelve, look at the same white page covered with black symbols that they've been poring over bemusedly for almost as long as they can remember, and suddenly it means something. Yesterday it didn't, today it does. It might only mean *The cat sat on the mat*, but the cat's there and the mat's there, and this time they can see the relationship between the two because of the words in front of them. Because they read it.

They read it aloud, in tones of wonder – twice, to make sure it wasn't a fluke. But it wasn't. The brain has finally hardwired the connection so that the mind can hear what the eyes are seeing. Revelation glows like sunrise in the child's face. It had seemed impossible, remembering what all those little marks were supposed to sound like: huge double-handfuls of them, covering the pages – and somehow you were supposed to make sense of them. It simply wasn't reasonable. Yesterday the child knew for a fact that he was stupid, that he would never be able to do what other people could do. But today he's doing it. He's reading. And the whole world opens up before him.

Compared with that miracle, thought Desmond Chalmers,

keeping 3c from putting their fingers in the pencil-sharpeners and stabbing one another with their compasses was nothing, a mere reflex action. Any teacher worthy of the name could do it without thinking – like breathing and keeping the heart beating, not so much an achievement as a habit. But teaching your first child to read is a hard act to follow. After that you tend to use the word *miracle* sparingly.

Chalmers had been a teacher for fourteen years, a head teacher for eight of them. He hadn't lost his sense of wonder – some mornings it was all that got him out of bed – but he wasn't easy to impress any more. He'd seen most things that children were capable of, good and bad, and most things that teachers were capable of. In fact, he'd seen most things that people are capable of. Before he went into teaching he was a Royal Marine commando, possibly the ideal preparation for running Dimmock High.

He hadn't seen anything quite like this before.

God knows he'd seen courage – on the battlefield, and also in places where the issues aren't quite so clear-cut, where excuses are more acceptable and cowardice goes by politer names like expediency and pragmatism. He thought that perhaps heroism in such circumstances – where it wasn't expected, where it might easily go unnoticed – might be of an even higher order.

He was aware that almost no one else standing in this corridor, watching through the glazed portion of the door, would see anything remarkable. A class of twelve-year-olds learning maths. Quiet for the most part, engaged, even interested, which suggested a certain quality of teaching. But even today, even in Dimmock High, that wasn't so unusual as to invite comment.

But Des Chalmers had been here – in this very corridor, as it happens – the last time Daniel Hood returned to the school where he once taught. It had ended, quite literally, in tears. It had ended with a terrified Daniel running wildly through the building because he needed to get out and couldn't find the door. It had ended with Des Chalmers taking him down in a rugby tackle and holding his shaking body still until the panic ebbed, making way for a soul-deep humiliation.

Then he'd taken Daniel home to his odd little shack on the shore, and made tea, and watched his trembling hands fill the saucer, and suggested quietly, 'Maybe a bit too soon?' But what he'd thought was, This young man is never going to stand in front of a room full of children again.

Whether you called it post-traumatic stress disorder or shell-shock, it was as real and crippling a catastrophe as anything that starts in a shatter of blood and bone. Chalmers knew the story, of course, heard most of it soon after it happened. Daniel told him the rest this morning when he came to ask for his job back. He wanted the Principal to have the full picture before he decided whether to trust him with thirty of his pupils. He had trusted him implicitly once. Daniel had worked in the maths department at Dimmock High for twelve months before...

Before. All discussion of the subject tended to end with that word and a row of dots. People were kind, didn't want to embarrass him. They tried to skirt around the issue, leave the man to deal with his pain in privacy.

Sometimes it was the right thing to do. Daniel Hood was a

private person, had always dealt with his problems alone, even before… But this was different, and both men knew it. If Daniel returned to work, whatever problems remained with him would cease to be his alone. They would inevitably be shared, not just with colleagues but with the pupils. Children. He wanted his job back – desperately, teaching was all he'd ever wanted to do – but not at any price. He didn't want Des Chalmers to feel sorry for him and make allowances, and let him fail the children he was there to serve. They needed to be honest with one another. Painfully, brutally honest.

'I was tortured,' said Daniel quietly. 'It was a misunderstanding – I hadn't done anything: nothing I want you to know about, nothing I *don't* want you to know about – but for most of that weekend someone was stubbing out cigarettes on me. Then I was shot and dumped in a rubbish skip. But it was a cold night and you know what they say – you're not dead till you're warm and dead. After a week in hospital I was on the mend.'

'No, you weren't,' said the Principal, his voice hollow.

'Well, no,' admitted Daniel, 'I wasn't. My body was healing: the psychological damage was harder to handle. I'd lost my equilibrium. I had mood-swings that hit euphoria and despair, and everything in between, sometimes quicker than I can say it. I was bursting into tears for no reason.'

'No,' said Chalmers again, 'you weren't. You had *every* reason. Of course your balance was shot. Neither minds nor bodies are designed to cope with what was done to you. You survived it; more than that, you've managed to move on. But these are still recent events. Don't expect to put them behind you in a couple of years. It's amazing what a human being can recover from, but the healing takes time. What makes you think you're ready to work again?'

It was a legitimate question. Chalmers was responsible for the well-being of everyone in his school, adults and children alike, but the children took precedence. He wouldn't let Daniel back into a classroom, even if it was what Daniel needed, if there was any danger that his pupils would be harmed or frightened.

'I'm better,' Daniel said simply.

'How much better?'

'Lots.'

'Enough?'

When Daniel Hood smiled, suddenly you realised his fairy godmother hadn't after all been on a sloe-gin blinder behind the Christening cake. She might not have given him much stature – half the third year were taller than him, including some of the girls. She might not have given him much in the way of looks – the sunshine yellow hair was the only memorable thing about him. She managed to equip him with an impressive intelligence, though if she'd tempered it with a little more tact he would be less prone to irritating his friends with a quite unconscious arrogance. And his pale grey eyes were so weak she must have found them in the reject bin after the eye factory closed for the weekend.

But his smile made people who'd never met him before warm to the world. There was a simple sweetness about it that made them forgive his gaucheness, his obstinacy, and that way he had of caring so much about big issues that the nuances most people live by – the shades of grey, the concept of *least worst* and *the lesser of two evils* – were like a foreign country to him, full of signs he couldn't read, where even if he asked directions he couldn't understand the replies. In his twenty-eight years Daniel Hood had annoyed a lot of people, but only the ones who hadn't seen him smile managed to stay annoyed for long.

'I don't know,' he said honestly. 'I hope so.'

'Only you remember what happened last time you were here,' said Chalmers gently. 'And you were only using the library.'

Daniel would never forget. 'I'm better now in a lot of ways. I can deal with people. I can even deal with crowds. As for teaching, I don't know any way of finding out except by trying.'

'And if you freak out again?' It wasn't tactful, or very kind. But there were higher priorities than Daniel's feelings.

The younger man shrugged. 'The flying tackle worked pretty well.'

Finally Chalmers agreed, with a caution. 'I'll be no distance away. You start to lose it, you get out. There's enough mayhem in an ordinary school day without you going ape-shit.' Des Chalmers wasn't a typical head teacher. His days in the Services, which had equipped him with many skills he now found tremendously useful, had also left him with a vocabulary he had to edit in polite company.

Daniel had been away from Dimmock High for two years: most of its twelve-year-olds had no idea who he was. Chalmers introduced him without much explanation then left them to it. But he didn't go far. He checked out Daniel's progress five times in as many minutes; three in the next ten; and then, with no sign of problems, ventured as far as the staff room for a cup of tea.

When he got back this was what he saw: Daniel with his jacket off and his shirt-sleeves pushed up, expressive hands helping to tell the story, calculations and a diagram of the Solar System up on the board, and thirty-odd children vying to answer questions.

'Oh yes,' Des Chalmers murmured to himself, 'you can still do it.'

Afterwards, back in his office, he asked Daniel how the lesson had gone.

The smile stole across his face again, touching his homely features with pixie-dust. 'I've missed it so much. Even when I knew I couldn't do it, didn't even want to try, I always missed it. Teaching is like learning afresh every day. I love maths – but I only remember just how much when I try to pass it on to someone else.'

Chalmers thought for a few moments before he said anything more. But only a few. 'Are you ready to come back?'

'Yes,' said Daniel immediately.

'I told you your job would be here when you wanted it. I meant that. You know I can always use a decent maths teacher. Start on Monday if you want. Just a couple of classes a day, if you like, to see how you get on.'

'I can do a full week. I don't need protecting any more.'

Chalmers chuckled at the glow in his face. 'Of course you do, Daniel – you're a national treasure. Tell me: what does Mrs Farrell think about you coming back to work?'

The merest flicker of uncertainty crossed the pale eyes behind Daniel's thick glasses. 'Ask me again on Monday. I haven't told her yet.'

'She'll be thrilled,' Chalmers predicted confidently. 'Of course she will. Why wouldn't she be?'

'Yes, of course she will,' nodded Daniel. 'But first she'll be surprised.'

'She doesn't think you're ready?'

'Oh yes – she thought so before I did. She'll be surprised I didn't consult her before coming to see you.'

It wasn't a criticism. It was a little glimpse for Chalmers, as through the window of a moving train, into the heart of other people's lives. Like the past, like a foreign country, Daniel Hood and Brodie Farrell did things differently. 'She's been a good friend to you,' commented the Principal. 'She cares what happens to you.'

'She *has* been a good friend,' Daniel agreed warmly. 'I don't think I'd have survived without her. But…'

Chalmers thought he understood. 'It's time to stand on your own two feet?'

Daniel considered. 'In a way. Hell's bells,' he snorted in exasperation, 'this is nothing to do with what I came here for. But you've been a good friend to me too, Des, and maybe I don't owe you an explanation but it's good to confide in someone. Things are a bit different between us now. Things I would have said to her, only a few months ago, now… It's different. Not in a bad way. Just…'

Chalmers had his head cocked like a curious parrot. 'Daniel – are you trying to tell me you two are now an item?'

'No,' Daniel said quickly. 'I mean, if it was up to me… But no. Only…'

'You're in love,' said Chalmers plainly. Nothing in his tone or his eyes suggested this was as absurd as all Daniel's instincts told him it was. Of course, Des Chalmers was a head teacher – he was good at hiding what he thought.

Daniel gave a little lop-sided shrug. 'I suppose so. Yes, I think that's what it is.'

The older man grinned broadly. 'Well, you may have been off work but you've not been wasting your time. Can we expect to hear wedding bells?'

'I shouldn't think so,' said Daniel glumly. 'What I want and what Brodie wants aren't the same thing. I want to marry her. She wants to know that I'm eating enough and not reading *The Astronomer* under the bedclothes when I'm supposed to be asleep.'

Chalmers laughed out loud. 'I always say, a man can never have too many mothers. Hang on in there, stud, you'll work it out.'

Never in his entire life before had Daniel been addressed as Stud. 'Of course we will.' And he knew that they would, just not necessarily how he hoped. 'At least now I can support a family.'

'Go tell her,' advised Des Chalmers. 'And if she allows you, I'll see you on Monday.'

CHAPTER TWO

Detective Superintendent Jack Deacon, alone in the quiet of his office at the top of the police station in Battle Alley, had women on his mind. Two of them, and he didn't know what either of them wanted. This made him very uneasy. He was not now, at the age of forty-eight, and never had been a ladies' man. They really were from Venus, so far as he could work out. There was no metaphor involved.

He'd been married to one once, but all the experience had taught him was how deep was the well of his incomprehension. Every time he thought he'd learnt something, finally got something right, fresh enigmas rushed to fill the vacuum. She left him, ostensibly, because of the strain his work put on the marriage. When he'd got over the shock, and found out how the washing-machine worked, and tracked down suppliers of non-trendy, non-healthy, non-PC food and drink, in the privacy of his own skull he was glad she'd gone. He faced puzzles all day, every day: he didn't need them waiting at home as well. At least there were answers to the ones at work, and he was paid to look for them.

So for fifteen years now he'd lived alone, and for much of that time his closest companion had been the world's most evil cat, a devil-eyed, cauliflower-eared tom who never answered to the name of Dempsey. But for something over a year there'd been a woman as well, and he didn't understand her any better than the first but he did like having her around. And for a lot of that time the feeling seemed – inexplicably – to be mutual.

Then once again fate had wee'd in his slippers. Things had come between them that could not be resolved and could not be ignored, and they'd gone their separate ways. This time Deacon had nothing but regrets, and knew he always would. Because he couldn't see them getting together again, even though he had and would have no one else and, so far as he knew, at least in the conventional sense, neither had Brodie. Toying with the memo on the pad on his desk, he still doubted that a reconciliation was her reason for asking to see him.

He didn't know why Alix Hyde wanted to see him either, but he knew it was business and therefore firmer ground for him. She was Detective Inspector Hyde, of the Serious Organised Crime Agency, and whatever it was she wanted to talk about it wouldn't be her feelings, his feelings, or how doing the right things for the wrong reasons is worse than doing the wrong things for the right reasons. In short, Alix Hyde might be a woman by accident of birth but she was a police officer by definition and that made her someone he could work with.

When the front desk phoned to say she'd arrived he went downstairs to meet her. He didn't have massive expectations. TV drama was, in his experience, unrealistic about how much glamour can be fielded with the time and energy left to a police officer of either sex at the end of the working day. In practice, male detectives tend to look as if they've slept in their clothes – often because they have – and their female colleagues as if their priorities are comfortable shoes and washable trousers.

For all Deacon knew, Detective Inspector Hyde's shoes were supremely comfortable and her trousers could be boiled if the need arose. It didn't matter: no one would be looking at her feet.

She came forward like a man, handshake first. 'Alix Hyde. Good to meet you, Detective Superintendent Deacon.' There was something mannish about her voice too, pitched half an octave below where you expected. It was probably no more than a reflection of her body type, as tall as Brodie and more sturdily built – but it was unusual, unsettling even, and...what was that word?...Deacon knew it as well as he knew his own name...hell, lots of people thought it *was* his name... Ah yes. Sexy.

He took her hand and by now was unsurprised by the strength of her grip. It went with the height, the voice and the short, ruthlessly styled hair, somewhere between brown and blonde and flecked with grey. She might have been forty, and she didn't dye the grey hairs because she didn't care who knew. Deacon found that reassuring in a woman. It spoke of the triumph of confidence over anxiety, of someone not so much growing older as growing up.

He realised he was still holding her hand and dropped it abruptly. God knows what kind of a rube she took him for. He'd heard of a thing called a practised smile and tried for that; but he hadn't had enough practice so it came over as a leer. 'Anything for SOCA, Inspector.'

All the way up the stairs, and there were four flights, he was fighting the urge to make the obvious comment. She must have heard it so often. She must be ready to deck anyone who thought it was original and clever and too good to keep to himself. And he almost made it. But the silence stretched, and you have to say something, and Deacon was never any good at small talk. As he opened his door for her he did the crocodile smile again and said, 'And are you, Inspector? Serious and organised?'

Somehow she refrained from kicking his shin. But he heard the disappointed sigh. 'Not particularly,' she said. 'And hardly at all.'

'Me neither,' admitted Deacon, though she might have guessed from the state of his in-tray. Not because it was overflowing: it wasn't. The papers in it were surprisingly tidy, either sorted into files or held together with bulldog clips. What was significant about Deacon's in-tray was not its contents but that it balanced precariously on top of four or five others in a stack half a metre high, like ancient cities built each on the ruins of the last. Tel Deacon. Detective Sergeant Voss, who kept the habitation level in order, declined responsibility for excavating the foundations, some of which had been here longer than he had. He said it was a Health & Safety issue and would require pit-props.

Deacon moved another pile of papers onto the floor to enable his visitor to sit. Though it wasn't a huge office it would have been big enough for anyone else. But Jack Deacon took up a lot of space, physically – he was both tall and heavy – and also psychologically. When he walked into a room he filled it. He had the same kind of presence as a bull or a bear

– indeed, colleagues referred to him, with varying degrees of affection, as The Grizzly. Even when he wasn't doing anything, he wore the potential for explosive action like a cloak. Riotous assemblies quietened down when he walked past. Having fists the size of butchers' hams didn't hurt.

'Sorry,' he said belatedly. 'Around here, that's what passes for wit.'

She grinned at that. 'Here, and every other police station I've been in this last twelve months.'

To be fair, she wasn't a beauty, probably wasn't even as a girl. Perhaps she was handsome; perhaps it would be more accurate to say that she was attractive, because attractiveness goes beyond appearance and speaks also of the personality, the intellect, even the soul. Deacon couldn't put his finger on what it was but – like the joke – he knew he wasn't the first man to spot it.

He gave himself a mental shake. This wasn't why either of them was here. 'So how can I help, Inspector Hyde?'

'This is a courtesy call,' she said, 'in a way. I'm after one of your local villains and it seemed only polite to let you know. And also…' And there she stopped.

Deacon frowned. 'What?'

The strong lines of Alix Hyde's face twisted momentarily in a gargoyle grimace. 'It might be awkward. You know the man.'

'I should hope I do,' grunted Deacon. 'I should hope I know every villain within a thirty mile radius who's big enough for SOCA to have got wind of.'

'Yes, of course.' But there was something she wasn't saying, something she felt the need to be tactful about. 'I mean personally. Don't read any more into this, and don't think I'm reading any more into it, but you personally know him personally. I wanted to be sure that wasn't going to be a problem.'

Now Deacon knew what she was pussy-footing around. 'You're talking about Terry Walsh.'

She nodded. 'I'm told – and I may have been told wrong – you were friends once.'

For a moment Deacon didn't react, left her guessing. Then he sniffed disparagingly. 'You weren't told wrong. You may have been misled. I knew him when we were boys. His family lived in the next street to us. We went to the same school, played for the same football team – it was that sort of friendship. Long but not particularly close. I moved down here – what? – ten years ago now. A few years later Terry bought a site up on the Firestone Cliffs and built that damn mansion of his. I think he was as surprised to see me as I was to see him.'

'He's done well for himself,' said Inspector Hyde guardedly.

Deacon gave a sharkish grin, at once more honest and more attractive than his Cary Grant impression. 'No, Inspector, *I've* done well for myself. Terry has made more money, but he hasn't done it legally. There's a difference.'

She nodded appreciatively. 'Indeed there is. About eight years, with good behaviour. I take it, then, you've no problem with me going after him?'

'Of course I haven't,' he assured her. 'We could have been a lot better friends and I'd still help you bust him if the evidence was there.'

Alix Hyde raised an eyebrow. 'You're saying it isn't?'

'I'm saying Terry Walsh is a clever man, and a careful man.

I know he didn't make that kind of money by diligent endeavour. A lot of police officers have reached the same conclusion over the years, but none of us has been able to bring him down. I'm not saying you won't, and I'm certainly not saying you shouldn't try, but don't think it'll be easy. Terry came from nowhere with nothing. Even then he could outsmart just about anyone else. Imagine how much better he is after thirty years' practice. Good luck to you, Inspector – you'll need it.'

She rocked a broad, perfectly manicured hand. 'Well – I have some ideas about that. This isn't just housekeeping. I didn't get a memo from Head Office telling me it was time someone had another go at Terry Walsh. I wouldn't be here if I didn't think I had a good chance of getting him. I think this time he's going down. But I would appreciate your support.'

'You have it,' replied Deacon, a shade shortly. She hadn't exactly asked if he meant to shield Walsh, but clearly that had been her worry. Deacon wasn't new to this job, and he hadn't been a starry-eyed idealist when he was. He knew that police officers were flawed individuals like everyone else and that things like that happened. And he didn't know Alix Hyde and she didn't know him: she was entitled to wonder if he could be trusted. It still felt like an insult.

'I wasn't expecting anything different,' she said. 'Before I talked to you I talked to people about you. At Division, and other places. A lot of them thought I was crazy targeting Walsh, but none of them thought I'd have a problem with you.' And then, just as he started to blossom in the warmth of the compliment, she added in an undertone: 'At least, not in that way.'

Deacon blinked. 'What way, then?'

Alix Hyde laughed out loud. 'Superintendent, you don't need me to tell you what kind of a reputation you've got at Division. I assumed you'd spent the last ten years cultivating it.'

The slow, bashful grin made him look like a schoolboy caught out in a bit of surreptitious intelligence. 'I can't imagine what you mean,' he lied.

She didn't elaborate. There really was no need. Both of them knew that Detective Superintendent Deacon's superiors had him down as a hard, difficult, occasionally unpredictable, wholly ungracious man who – regrettably enough – was very good at his job. And both of them knew that Deacon would be content with that on his tombstone.

Hyde sat back in her chair. 'Fine. Well, there's one more thing to settle, and I've one more favour to ask you. How closely do you want me to keep you informed as the inquiry proceeds? And, can you spare someone to help me?'

Mercurial was not a word commonly associated with Jack Deacon. He was a big, heavy man now well embarked on middle-age, and he tended both to move and to think ponderously. Except in absolute need, when he could still move like the county-class rugby player he once was and think with both speed and precision. By the time she'd finished the questions he knew the answers, and the same answer served for both. 'I've got just the man for you. Charlie Voss, my sergeant. He's smart and he's sharp, he knows this town inside out, and he's as straight as a die.'

What he thought and didn't add was, And he'll keep me as closely informed as if it was me doing your legwork.

CHAPTER THREE

Daniel walked home through the park. A scant three days before the winter solstice – and coincidentally, or possibly not, his birthday – the light had gone from the afternoon by three o'clock and by four it was dusk. Street lamps glimmered like a string of beads along the Promenade, and on the shore the three black fingers of the netting-sheds were silhouetted against an English Channel bright with moontrack. The one nearest the old pier was his home.

From the outside, all that distinguished it from its sisters were the gallery he'd built at upper-storey level and sometimes a couple of milk-bottles waiting politely at the foot of the iron steps. But inside he'd got as much space and comfort as a single man needs, and when he took his telescope out onto the gallery the night sky was a perfect dome above him.

But though it was almost dark enough for astronomy he had something to do first. He walked on another hundred yards, then turned left up Fisher Hill and left again into Shack Lane.

When he first came here from Nottingham three years ago, Shack Lane was about as salubrious as the name. There were boarded-up windows and lock-up garages, and an Anglo-Chinese takeaway whose *tour-de-force* was sweet-and-sour chips. But about the same time he was moving into the netting-shed – and it was still a netting-shed then, complete with ancient lobster-pots in the boathouse underneath – still unknown to him, Brodie Farrell was setting up her new business round the corner.

It was two rooms and a broken window, and the day she went to look at it someone had been sick on the step. But it was central, it was cheap, and it was just enough off the beaten track to be discreet, which mattered because some of her clients would be shy of seeking her out.

She called it Looking For Something? She'd had it inscribed in dull gold lettering on a classy slab of slate, painted the new front door a glossy burgundy, replaced the broken glass in the boxy little bay-window and hung burgundy velvet curtains to protect her callers' privacy. Word raced up Fisher Hill that she was a high-class prostitute, and immediately property prices began to climb.

Once upon a time the misunderstanding would have caused her deep embarrassment. But Brodie Farrell wasn't at all the woman now that she'd been a few years ago, and her business was a big part of why. Five years ago she was a wife and mother who hadn't gone out to work since the birth of her child. Four and a half years ago her husband left her for a librarian, and at first she didn't know how she'd survive. After she worked it out, she vowed never to be that dependent on anyone ever again, and she put her divorce settlement into buying a flat for herself and Paddy and setting up a business to maintain them.

Before she married John Farrell she worked for him. As he was a solicitor, a lot of her time was spent on research. She was very good at it. John swore she could get information out of a paving-slab. Maybe she couldn't do that, but if it was recorded anywhere, officially or unofficially, if mention of it had ever been committed to print, or if someone remembered his uncle saying something about it fifteen years ago, Brodie Farrell would run it to ground. She could find almost anything for almost anyone. She'd always thought she could make a living doing it. Looking For Something? had proved her right.

Growing success meant that the business had really outgrown her office. But she was reluctant to leave a spot where she was just the right degree of known. She was trying to buy the building behind, to expand out that way. Three years ago she could have had either of the adjoining properties for a song, but even after the nature of her trade was better understood her presence had had a knock-on effect. One was bought by a jewellery designer, the other by a financial adviser. Today Shack Lane was an up-and-coming address.

Perhaps he was biased, but Daniel thought the burgundy livery and slate shingle, and the door that remained closed until you rang the bell and – if it suited her – she answered, still made Looking For Something? a cut above its neighbours.

It had taken him fifteen minutes to walk here from the school. With every step he'd felt the crazy happiness within him swell until breathing became an effort. He didn't care, would have continued on his hands and knees if need be. This was a day he'd despaired of seeing. Maybe it wasn't everyone's idea of a victory, being able to return to full-time, nose-to-the-grindstone, proverbially stressful work, but it was Daniel's. And maybe no one else he knew would understand that, but Brodie would. Understand what it took to get here; understand what it meant to him. Understand and rejoice with him. He couldn't wait to tell her. He had his hands fisted in his pockets, physically restraining himself from shouting it through the letterbox.

He couldn't tell from the street if she was in, or if she was alone. That wasn't accidental: she'd planned it that way. There was no glass in the door for a shadow to fall on, so the first indication was the lock turning. Pleasure made him grin like an idiot. It wasn't that his news was urgent, or even important except to him. But everyone needs someone to share their triumphs and disasters with, and that was one of the things Daniel and Brodie did for one another. They could talk about their achievements without embarrassment. They could be honest about their fears.

So when she opened the door what Brodie Farrell saw was a grin wearing Daniel's glasses. It was a sufficiently diverting sight to distract her from her worries, and she glanced up and down the street in search of an explanation.

'I've got something to tell you,' he confided happily, his face aglow.

'You'd better come in then.' She stood back to let him pass and closed the door behind them.

'You're not too busy?' Even today he couldn't shrug off the habit of consideration.

'Busy beating my head on a brick wall,' Brodie replied grimly. 'I could do with cheering up.'

And when he looked again it was obvious she wasn't having a good day. In fact, now he thought about it he suspected she hadn't had much of a week. She'd been quiet and withdrawn for at least that long, the spring gone from her step and the colour from her cheek, and if he hadn't had the meeting with Des Chalmers on his mind he'd have noticed before now. She didn't look well, and she hadn't for a while.

The reason for his visit side-lined, Daniel peered anxiously into her face, noting the tiredness in her dark eyes, the fine worry-lines around them, the pallor of her skin against the extravagant cloud of curly black hair. 'Brodie, what's the matter? What's happened?'

'Nothing's happened,' she said, waving him to the compact sofa, herself slipping into the generous chair behind her desk. 'At least...'

She was five years older than him. Compared with all the other complications in their relationship it was a mere bagatelle. Besides which, Daniel was oddly ageless. Sometimes he was offered cheap fares and asked for his student pass; or you could look into his eyes and glimpse millennia. 'Come on,' he said softly, 'tell your Uncle Daniel.'

She managed a smile at that. 'I've got a problem.'

'A big problem or a little problem?'

She considered. 'It's a little problem now. But there's every reason to expect it's going to grow.'

In spite of that, he never saw it coming. Whatever he was expecting, it wasn't this. Brodie watched those mild, weak, infinite eyes and knew he had no idea what she was trying to say. For an intelligent man he could be infuriatingly dense at times. Finally she despaired of dropping hints, blew out a gusty sigh and slapped it on the desk between them. 'I'm pregnant, Daniel. I'm going to have a baby.'

For long seconds his expression didn't change. As if she'd

suddenly switched into Urdu, or produced three fish-heads and started juggling to the strains of a rugby song, he was waiting for normal service to be resumed.

And she knew how he felt, because she'd felt very much the same way when the doctor – following a check-up for something entirely different – dropped his casual bombshell. She hadn't known she was pregnant. She hadn't known she *might* be pregnant. She hadn't wanted another child. And she'd just sat staring at him, waiting for him to slap his thigh and admit he was joking. When he didn't, she imagined she looked pretty much like Daniel looked now.

'Daniel?' she said softly. 'Did you hear me?'

He blinked. He swallowed. 'I think so,' he said carefully. His voice was flat with shock. 'You said you're going to have...?'

'A baby, that's right. You know, a little person? Bald, pink, no sense of responsibility at either end? A baby.'

Still he didn't know what to say. Nothing in her manner suggested that the usual congratulations would be in order. 'Jack's?'

It would probably have been better to stick with the shocked silence. Anger sparked in her eyes like firelight on diamonds. 'Of course it's Jack's. What do you think – I was seeing someone behind his back?'

'I thought you two were finished,' Daniel mumbled lamely. 'I thought it was over between you.'

'It *is* over,' agreed Brodie sharply. '*Now*. It wasn't when this baby played contraception roulette and won, three and a half months ago.'

'Then...you didn't mean...'

'*No*, Daniel,' she said heavily. 'Oddly enough, with a six-year-old daughter and a one-woman business, and a relationship that was looking rocky even before it hit the rocks, I never actually said to myself, "What I really need right now is a baby!" It just happened. It shouldn't have done. I wasn't trusting to luck. I suppose, even something that's 99 per cent effective still has a failure rate.'

Daniel could hardly have been more stunned if someone had told him *he* was pregnant. Of course, for a lot of his life surprises had been something that happened to other people. That had changed rather since their orbits crossed, but spontaneity still wasn't his strong suit. And then, he'd had two minutes to absorb the idea. Brodie had had six weeks.

He was still stumbling round for the right thing to say, and still getting it wrong. 'What are you going to do?'

The firelight in her eyes flared as if someone had added petrol. 'Do you mean, am I planning to get an abortion?'

'No!' he exclaimed, horrified. And then, because telling the truth was important to him, he amended that. 'I suppose it's an option. For some people. I don't know if it's one for you.'

'Then I'll tell you,' she said fiercely. 'It isn't. It's damned inconvenient, it couldn't have come at a worse time, but that's not a good enough reason to kill it. I'm not sure it would be if it was a puppy, let alone a baby. Of course I'll have it, and of course I'll raise it. Just, right now, I have no idea how.'

At last Daniel was getting to grips with the situation. He knew he hadn't distinguished himself, wished he could have slipped more smoothly into support mode. But perhaps having reason to snap at him made it easier for Brodie. 'We'll find a way,' he said firmly, 'or make one. Whatever you want, whatever decisions you take, you're not on your own. You have me. You also have Jack.'

'I *had* Jack,' she corrected him, not without a hint of bitterness. 'I let him get away.'

Daniel smiled at that. However things between them rested, it was impossible to imagine Brodie Farrell as the hunter and Jack Deacon as her elusive prey. So it was a joke. It was a good sign, that she was up to even a rather sour little joke. 'I don't think he'll have gone far. I take it you haven't told him yet?'

Her wide brow furrowed. 'Why do you say that?'

'Because if you had you'd have a different set of problems.'

Brodie snorted a rough little laugh. 'I'm going to tell him, of course. He's entitled to know. I kept putting it off, trying to decide how to handle it. I don't want him talking me into something I don't want to do. But I'm going to have to tackle it. I called him this morning, asked him to pop round when he has the time.'

'What are you afraid he'll try to talk you into?'

She rolled her eyes. 'For one thing, marrying him to give the child a name.'

It took an effort for Daniel to keep his tone even. 'Is that such a bad thing?'

She nodded emphatically. 'If we'd wanted to marry we'd have done it. We wouldn't just have split up. It's not much of a kindness to a child, that he pops into the world and you hand him the job of patching up his parents' relationship.'

'Nevertheless, he'll need a name.'

'He'll *have* a name,' said Brodie sharply. 'He'll have my name.'

'John's name,' Daniel reminded her.

'Then he can have two – mine and Jack's. Daniel, it's not about names. It's about...expectations. Jack's going to be over the moon when he finds out. But the coming of a baby doesn't alter the fact that we as a couple had been failing for months. We'd reached the point of hurting one another. You can't go on like that. It was better to draw a line under it before we ended up hating each other.'

'You could try again,' murmured Daniel, watching covertly to see if he needed to duck. 'Try harder.'

But Brodie had had six weeks to review everything she and Jack Deacon had done, everything they could have done differently, and what were realistic options and what weren't. If they'd had this conversation a fortnight ago she might well have bitten Daniel's head off, but not now. It was one reason she'd delayed telling him.

She shook her head, the dark curls tumbling on her shoulder. If there was regret in her voice there was also acceptance. 'We did that already. It didn't help. It was time for a strategic withdrawal. We both felt the same way. We didn't storm out in a temper: we talked about it and thought about it, and reached a mature and mutual decision. The right decision. That doesn't change because there's a baby on the way.'

'And yet,' said Daniel quietly, 'it *will* change things. It'll change your life, and Jack's. It'll create a whole new set of circumstances. Would it be so unreasonable to review the situation in the light of that?'

Logically, he may well have been right. But Brodie's instincts told her he was wrong. 'You shouldn't use a child as glue. He – or she, I don't know it's a boy – will have a full set of parents whether or not they live together, whether or not they're married. I've no intentions of robbing Jack of his child. But I don't think he and I can make a go of things now, and we'd only make ourselves – and Paddy, and the baby – unhappy trying.' She shrugged in that way she had when she was trying to look tougher than she felt. 'I've been a single parent before, I can do it again.'

'Then why are you so worried?' asked Daniel softly.

She never could get things past him. She looked around her. On the face of it, it wasn't much – a small office, mostly filled with filing-cabinets, a miniature kitchen and cloakroom behind, a slate on the wall. It wasn't what it was so much as what it represented. Three years of hard work. Two years of success. Two years of people she'd known, and one she'd been married to, looking at her differently because they hadn't guessed she had it in her.

'Mostly, about this,' she admitted. 'Babies take a lot of time. I can put the business on hold while the baby grows a bit, but I'm not sure it'll be here to come back to if I do. So much of my stock-in-trade is confidence. If I'm not here when people need me, they'll find someone else. I've worked so hard, Daniel! And I think I'm going to lose it.'

'You need someone to keep it ticking over until you're ready to come back.'

'Yeah, right,' Brodie retorted sarcastically. Not because it was a stupid idea but because she'd already considered and dismissed it. 'The job centres are bursting with people qualified, competent and trustworthy enough to do this job! And kind enough to do it for a year or two and then hand it back because I ask them to. Who wouldn't think of using what they've learnt here to set up in competition. Tell you what: you put together a shortlist and I'll interview them.'

They'd known one another too long now, and too well, for Daniel not to recognise her waspishness as a guise for fear. He reached across the desk and took her hand. 'There'll be an answer,' he promised. 'We'll find it.'

She appreciated that more than she could say, or would have done if she could. Of everything he meant to her, everything he'd done for her, this uncritical faithfulness was the thing for which she'd been most grateful. She held onto his fingers as if she was teetering on the edge of an abyss.

'Maybe. I hope so. But that's not it. It just isn't practical. I could afford to employ someone, but who? I could spend months finding a suitable person, and then I'd have to train them. This isn't wholesale grocery: you know, better than most, there are complex issues to negotiate. You couldn't expect someone who'd only been doing the job a few weeks to make the right calls. To see the problems coming and steer round them. To know when to walk away, and when to run.'

'How long have you got?'

'The baby's due at the end of May. Training someone to a level where both they and the business would be reasonably safe would take a minimum of six months. It's a non-starter.'

'Could you run it from home if you had someone to do the legwork?'

She'd dismissed that too. 'I wouldn't want to hire anyone who'd be prepared to work like that. Think about it, Daniel. Who's going to leave a responsible job for a short-term contract with questionable security, some personal risk and a back-seat driver for a boss? The only people who'd apply would be cowboys, and they'd ruin the business even faster than me neglecting it. I don't think I have a choice. I have to go on as long as I can, then shut up shop and start from scratch in a few years' time. And just hope there's some goodwill left to draw on.'

Every time she'd thought about it, and she'd thought about it a lot in the last six weeks, she'd come to the same conclusion. This was the least worst option. It might take her years to get back to where she was today, but she saw no alternative.

Daniel said nothing, and finally it struck Brodie that this wasn't the conversation he'd bounced in here expecting to have with her. She squeezed his hand. 'Sorry. I didn't mean to dump all this on you. Just – the opportunity was there and I went for it. I've been needing to talk to someone, and you're always my first choice. But there was something you wanted to tell me. What was it?'

There was a stillness in his face that meant the cogs were working overtime, spinning and meshing and producing something intricate and valuable. When he had all the pieces in place he blinked and came back to her. 'What? Oh – yes. Sorry – just thinking.' He smiled. 'I'm going back to work. It's time, and I'm ready.'

To her credit, all her own worries were not enough to sully her delight. He'd thought she might be hurt that he hadn't discussed it with her first. Of course, sitting on an enormous secret of her own for the last six weeks rather limited her scope for indignation. Delight painted her face like sunrise.

'Daniel! That's terrific. When? Where? How long have you been planning this?'

'As soon as possible,' he said. 'And, for a little while. I've known I was ready, I just needed to do something about it. This is it.'

'What is?'

Daniel met her eyes as if he'd been a liar all his life. 'Actually, it's quite a coincidence. Because obviously I'd no idea what you were going to say when I got here. But what I came to say was, can I work for you?'

Des Chalmers understood. Or he understood that this was what Daniel needed to do, even if he didn't entirely understand why. 'The offer's there, any time you want to take it up.'

Daniel hoped the man didn't know how close he was to tears. 'Des, that's too generous. You can't keep a place for me.'

'I don't intend to,' said the Principal. 'I have an adequate maths department now. But when you change your mind, or your circumstances change, I will expand it by one. You're a fine teacher, Daniel. Quite apart from anything that's happened, any school with its pupils' interests at heart will always have a vacancy for a good maths teacher. There aren't that many around.'

Daniel made himself meet the older man's gaze. It wasn't that he expected to see contempt there, or pity, or any of the tacit criticisms he felt were due. Experience had taught him that usually people treated him better than seemed altogether reasonable. Of course, every so often someone levelled the score, but still on the whole he found the world was good to him. He just wished he understood it better. Understood why people who owed him nothing went out of their way to help him. He said levelly, 'You think I'm making a mistake, don't you?'

Chalmers shrugged. 'I think you're doing what you feel is best. I just wish I thought it was *you* you felt it was best for.'

'I owe her so much...'

Whatever he hoped, Chalmers could hear his heart breaking in the plangent note of his voice.

'You're a young man, Daniel,' he said firmly. 'This is not your last chance. I will see you again.'

They shook hands and Daniel left, closing the door quickly behind him so Chalmers wouldn't hear him sniff. There were things he'd confided in Des Chalmers that he wouldn't have told even Brodie, but he didn't want anyone to know the pain this was giving him.

He could do it. He could put his body and soul into being Brodie Farrell's gopher, because she needed him and that mattered more than anything else. But no effort of will that he was capable of would stop him regretting the turn events had taken, or feeling trapped by the solution he'd found. What he wanted almost more than anything else had been within his grasp, and he'd thrown it away because of the one thing he wanted more.

And it wasn't that he thought of it as an investment – that when she realised what he'd sacrificed for her Brodie's fondness for him would turn to love. He knew as he hurried down the school corridor, busily polishing his glasses as displacement activity, that she must never find out. That she would never forgive him if she did.

CHAPTER FOUR

Deacon was still thinking about Alix Hyde when he went to meet Brodie. On mature reflection he decided this was probably not a good idea. One of the few things he reckoned to know about women was that they could read your mind. He made a point of clearing his before rapping on the burgundy door in Shack Lane.

When she'd called, for a minute they couldn't think where to meet. Lunch didn't feel appropriate for two people who'd split up, so that ruled out the French restaurant which was Deacon's preferred venue. His office was too public, her home too personal, a park bench too absurd. There was baggage associated with Brodie's office too, but it was the least worst option. It was private if they ended up arguing, and small enough to facilitate a swift departure. Deacon had slammed that burgundy door behind him a few times in the last six months. Once Brodie had stalked out, and had to come back later to lock up.

She met him at the door. He could read nothing from her expression, but she ushered him in with a kind of careful politeness, as if he were a wealthy but unpredictable client. Inside his own head Deacon gave an ironic snort. One out of two ain't bad.

'Jack.'

'Brodie.'

'You're looking well.'

'You too.' He thought that was probably safe enough.

'I'm fine,' she agreed. 'Well – in the circumstances.'

He didn't know what circumstances she meant, except that he didn't think for a moment she was pining for him. If she had been she'd have died rather than admit it. He wouldn't have told her how losing her had felt like having his legs hacked off, and he wouldn't have asked precisely what she meant except that this appeared to be why she'd brought him here. 'What circumstances?'

In the tiny kitchen the kettle was boiling. Brodie made coffee and put a cup – he noted the use of the good china – into his hands before answering. Even then she built her reply carefully, foundations first then one brick at a time.

'The first thing I want to say is, I don't see this as changing how things are between us. I don't expect you to do anything. I don't want anything and I don't consider that you owe me anything. At the same time, if there are things you want we can discuss them. You have certain rights and I've no wish to deny them.'

She saw the puzzlement in his craggy face but didn't stop to explain. If she kept going, a minute from now he'd know all there was to know. 'I hope we can handle this in a civilised fashion, because whatever we decided two months ago, what it means in practice is that we're going to remain part of one another's lives for the foreseeable future. How big a part is for us to decide – mainly, for you to decide. I'm fine on my own, I don't need any help, but the child I'm carrying is yours as well and if you want to be involved with it you can be. We'll work out how.' She watched him over the safety barrier of two coffee cups, waiting for him to react.

For most of Jack Deacon's career the police had been considered a Force rather than a Service. Perhaps that coloured his attitude. Perhaps if he'd been a young PC today he'd have learnt an entirely different approach. Or perhaps he'd have been rejected as unsuitable and the many strengths he brought to the job would have been lost. He wasn't tactful, courteous or in any obvious way caring. Old ladies never asked him to see them across busy roads and small children would rather stay lost than seek his help. He was not a people person.

But though he didn't like people very much, he took his professional obligations to them seriously. Several times in the course of his career he'd put his life on the line for them. Much more frequently he'd worked himself to exhaustion in their interests. He routinely gave everything he had in the way of physical strength, intellectual commitment and sheer bloody-minded persistence to keep them safe. But anyone asking him the time would get told to buy a watch.

So Brodie had a pretty good idea how he was likely to take the news. She knew it was totally unexpected, that it would take time to absorb. Part of him would be thrilled. But a big part, possibly the majority shareholder, would feel that it was a damned nuisance, an unnecessary complication in an already full life. Something that had never been part of the deal. She didn't expect to hear his reproaches, but she did expect to feel them.

But she also expected that he'd shoulder his responsibilities, not because she needed him to and not because she'd ask him to but because what he lacked in grace he made up for in honour. He cared about doing the right thing, and not letting people down. It was almost the only thing he had in common with Daniel. Jack Deacon was a good man. He just wasn't a very nice one.

She expected to have to repeat her news, maybe a couple of times, before she got any reaction at all. Or else that he'd respond angrily, before he had time to think, and be forever haunted by how badly he'd handled this first encounter with his child.

What she didn't expect was that his body would react to her news quicker than his mind, as if somewhere deep in his genes he'd been waiting for it all his life and the details of how and why and what next were exactly that – details. His eyes filled with wonder and then tears.

'Jack?' murmured Brodie, amazed and touched.

He didn't even pretend to have a smut in his eye. His voice was hoarse. 'You're not joking?'

'Of course I'm not. You think it's something...?' She stopped herself from snapping at him. 'Look,' she said quietly, 'I think you need some time to take this in. Why don't we talk again later? Tonight, or tomorrow if you like?'

But Deacon shook his head roughly. 'Just...stay where you are. You say that, and then try to throw me out? I don't think so.' His breathing was unsteady, as if he'd been running.

Brodie spread an accepting hand. 'I'm not trying to get rid of you, Jack, I just don't want to rush you. I know I've sprung this on you. I couldn't think of a way of telling you that *didn't* seem like springing it.'

'How long...' It caught in his throat so he had to try again. 'How long have you known?'

'Six weeks.'

'And how long has it been on the way?'

'About three and a half months.'

She saw him doing the math. Three and a half months ago they were already having problems, but neither of them had been ready to call it a day. Three and a half months ago...

Deacon's eyes flashed suddenly wide. 'I suppose you're sure it's mine?'

All Brodie's instincts were to slap him. Inside her shoes her very toes clenched with the effort to remember that what she'd known for weeks he'd learnt in the last couple of minutes. Of course he was off-balance. And he wasn't diplomatic even when he hadn't just had his world turned upside down. And, in fact, he was entitled to ask.

'Yes, I am,' she said levelly. 'We can get a blood-test to confirm it once the baby's born, but barring delayed implantation like you get in badgers' – she had *no* idea how she knew that: from Daniel, probably, he was a mine of useless information – 'it's yours. Biologically,' she added, because she didn't want him to feel she was dumping a problem on him. 'If you want, that can be the extent of your involvement. We don't need to put your name on the birth certificate.'

His eyes were hot. 'I don't know how you have the nerve to say that to me.'

Patience was never Brodie's strong suit and she felt it stretching, like a rubber-band just before it pings in your face. 'Jack, I'm not trying to upset you. In fact, I'm trying quite hard *not* to upset you. If you insist on being upset anyway I shall stop trying.'

Struggling to control his feelings, for a moment he shut his eyes. 'I'm sorry if I'm not doing this very well. I've never been in this position before – I'm making it up as I go along. I'm not upset. I'm – gob-smacked. You've changed my world with a couple of sentences. I don't know what you expect of me. I came here thinking we were going to talk about who keeps which CDs, and I find you've changed my life forever. How do I feel about that? Stunned. I'm sorry if that isn't what you were expecting.'

'OK,' said Brodie sharply, 'two things. First, I don't expect anything from you. I've already said that, but I'll say it again as often as it takes for you to believe it. I can imagine this has come as a shock. Now *you* imagine how I felt.

'Because secondly, this isn't something *I* did. I didn't change your life a fraction as much as you changed mine. Neither of us wanted this, and both of us thought we'd guarded against it, but the reality is that it happened anyway, and you have a choice about what you do next but I really don't. With or without you, I'll be dealing with the consequences for the next twenty years. So don't tell me I've turned your world upside down. It wasn't a case of immaculate conception, and I sure as hell didn't rape you!'

Deacon sucked in a ragged breath as if it had been a while since he'd thought to. By degrees, hand over hand up a greasy pole, he was catching up with developments. The possibility of intelligent thought and rational decision-making drifted nearer. Finally he met Brodie's gaze and held it steady. 'Tell me,' he said in a low voice. 'Tell me how you feel.'

And she nodded slowly, and flicked him a brittle smile. 'Gob-smacked,' she admitted. 'And worried sick. And kind of happy.'

When Daniel smiled it was like sunrise flooding a valley. When Deacon did, it was more like melt-water pouring off a glacier. He was megalithic in construct and craggy of mien, and there was a touch of the mountain in everything he did. 'I'm glad. Not so much about the worried sick bit.'

Brodie grinned. She'd been dreading this. Time and again she'd got to the point of calling him and put the phone down as if it had grown hot in her hand. In the event it hadn't gone badly. They hadn't ended up shouting at one another. They hadn't sunk to recriminations. 'Less worried now than I was an hour ago.'

'Why did you wait so long? Before telling me?'

She shrugged. 'A couple of reasons. Not every pregnancy goes to term. If this one hadn't there'd have been nothing to gain by telling anyone, even you. I'm thirty-three now, and you tend to hit more problems as you get older. And then, it didn't get the best start in life. I don't know what effect veterinary tranquilliser is likely to have on an embryo, but I can't believe it's good for it.'

It wasn't that he'd forgotten, more that he'd thought she'd got away with it. She'd cornered a manufacturer of designer drugs and he'd tried to kill her. But he'd failed. The chemicals had cleared her system and Deacon had thought that was the end of the matter. Now he realised he should have been more concerned. Brodie's fondness for meddling in his job had almost cost her her life. It could still cost her the baby.

'Have you? Hit problems?'

'Not so far. A bit of morning sickness, nothing dramatic. I feel fine. And, three months in, the odds improve. I thought it was time to let you in on the secret.'

'Do you know what it is yet?'

Brodie blinked. 'I think it's a baby.'

Deacon breathed heavily at her. 'Boy or girl?'

'Don't know. Do you mind?'

He shook his head decisively. 'Not as long as it's healthy.'

Brodie laughed aloud. 'People always say that. But I want to be there when the midwife hands you a little bundle of joy and says, "We don't know what sex it is but by God it's healthy!"'

Deacon didn't think that was funny. But then, this whole business was new to him. Brodie had a child already: Deacon, as far as he knew, hadn't. Had never wanted one; had never understood how you were meant to fit one in with everything else that needed doing. But a couple of sentences, and all at once finding time to wash the car and getting a bit of sleep in what his job left of the night were the last things on his mind. You make room in your life for what you want. The CPU in Deacon's brain was defragmenting in order to make space on the hard disk for a *baby.exe* file.

He realised that Brodie would have done a lot of thinking in the last six weeks, and almost certainly had an answer to any question he might ask. But he wanted to make sure. 'Have you thought how you're going to manage? What you're going to need? I don't need to say, do I, that any problems that money will solve, I'll take care of.'

She touched his hand, the briefest butterfly kiss that left his skin tingling. 'Thanks, Jack. That's nice to know.'

'What about this place?' He looked round him critically. 'Can you keep it going *and* look after a baby?'

'Now there,' she said, 'I was lucky. I've taken on staff. Daniel's going to come and work for me – keep things ticking over until I'm ready to come back. It was the most amazing thing. He came to me for a job before he even knew I was pregnant.'

Deacon went on watching her steadily. But if she'd been paying attention, had not still been enjoying the sense of relief that came with getting this said, Brodie would have heard the creak that was the melt-water turning back to ice. 'Before he knew.'

Brodie nodded cheerfully. 'Coincidence or what?'

'So Daniel knows you're pregnant.'

Again she nodded. By now, though, her brows were gathering in a perplexed little frown.

'You told Daniel Hood that you're carrying my baby before you told me?'

Perhaps that had been less than tactful. But it was too late to deny it, even if Brodie had felt the need. 'He asked me for a job. It was a God-send – I jumped at it, and I told him why.'

'And now you're telling me.'

She wasn't going to apologise. 'Don't be like that. I had to explain the situation. I wasn't going to lie to him.'

'Of course not,' said Deacon, with a tiny growl like a cat who's been stroked long enough. 'He's your friend.'

'That's right, he is.'

'And I'm your baby's father!'

Brodie felt her own hackles rising now. 'Yes, but you're not my husband. You're not my partner any more. You're my ex.

You have rights in relation to the baby: you have none in relation to me. That's the reality, Jack, get used to it. When I was expecting Paddy, John and I talked endlessly about what we should do and agreed things down to the tiniest detail. This is different. I'm a single woman. I'll keep you informed, I'll listen to your opinions, but I'll make my own decisions. When to inform my closest friends of my pregnancy is one of them. I don't need your permission.'

'And this,' said Deacon softly, 'is *why* we're ex-partners. Because of how you set your priorities. You want it all, don't you, Brodie? You want the relationship, but you also want the freedom of being single. You want to make all the decisions. And one of them – one of the big ones, the ones that got in the way of us being a success – was that you were never prepared to forsake all others and cleave only unto me. Not for as long as we both shall live – not for a few years – not at all.'

Anger brought the blood to her cheeks. She might have given him reason once, but she'd thought – and he'd said – they'd got beyond the brief madness of her infidelity. 'That's not fair, Jack. I'm sorry about what happened with Eric Chandos, but I'm not going to spend the rest of my life saying so. I wouldn't have done if we'd stayed together – I'm damned if I'm going to grovel for forgiveness now!'

'I wasn't talking about Chandos,' growled Deacon. 'It wasn't him who split us up. I was talking about Daniel.'

Outrage and genuine astonishment clashed in her voice like cymbals. 'Daniel didn't split us up!'

'Yes, Brodie,' Deacon retorted forcefully, 'he did. I don't think he meant to, but that's what happened. He took things out of our relationship that it needed to survive. But I don't blame Daniel. He didn't steal those things, he was given them. You gave him parts of yourself that you owed to me. I knew from the start that you weren't a free agent. I knew you had a child who would always come first. Of course Paddy has first claim: on your time, on your love. But I expected to be next in line. I wasn't prepared to come third.'

'I am not in love with Daniel Hood!' shouted Brodie, furious with exasperation. 'I never was, I'm not now, I'm never going to be. He's my best friend. I care about him, and he cares about me. None of which is any threat to what you and I had. If we couldn't make a go of it, you need to look elsewhere for the reason. Keep blaming Daniel for everything that goes wrong with your life if you must, but it isn't just me who's starting to find that pretty pathetic!'

Men in positions of power – and being senior detective in even a small town qualifies – need families. They need people around them who aren't intimidated by their status, who'll tell them when they're being stupid or paranoid or are just plain wrong. Without that reality check they start to feel self-important, cocooned from the rough-and-tumble of everyday argument, invulnerable to the forces that moderate other people's actions. It's a dangerously short step from being master under God to thinking you're God.

Before he knew Brodie, Deacon had never had that. There were arguments enough in his short marriage but it was easier to walk away than to resolve them. They finally stopped the arguments by not giving a toss, and the marriage ended soon afterwards.

There were no children, and Deacon had no close friends, so until he met Brodie he had a simple rule-of-thumb for dealing with the world. Criminals, suspects and police officers of lower rank he shouted at; witnesses he listened to with frank incredulity; and the same for police officers of higher rank except that he tried to hide the incredulity. The system served well enough but left him almost totally ignorant of the language of personal intercourse. He spoke a kind of pidgin version, and never got enough practice to improve his accent.

He'd been called all sorts of names in the course of his career, many of them unprintable, but before Brodie no one had looked at his six-foot frame, his traffic-stopping shoulders and his riot-quelling fists, and come up with the word Pathetic.

Not that Brodie was a shining example of how to run a mature relationship. She was selfish. She admitted as much quite freely, even proudly. She hadn't always been. She'd been most men's idea of the perfect wife: attractive, attentive, admiring, clever but not too clever, an efficient housekeeper and devoted mother. She'd *worked* at being a good wife. She'd thought she had a happy marriage.

But when John Farrell fell, inexplicably but hard, for a pleasant, slightly plump librarian, the rule-book went on the fire. What emerged from the ashes was Brodie Farrell as she was today – still a devoted mother but also a sharp businesswoman, a hard negotiator, a clear-eyed pragmatist, a bit of a cynic. Someone who was quick to identify what she wanted and prepared to tread on toes to get it.

She was, in fact, a more socially adroit and easier-on-the-eye version of Deacon himself. Perhaps that was the real reason for their unlikely partnership, and also why it ended. Neither of them was good at compromising. They never saw why they should.

'I don't have a single problem with Daniel!' snarled Deacon. 'He might be peculiar but at least he's honest. He doesn't say one thing and do something else. He doesn't pretend that you aren't the most important thing in his life. And he doesn't think he can run another relationship alongside that without a conflict. That's why he's always on his own. If he can't be with you, it's the only honest way to be.'

All the expression had fallen out of Brodie's face and her eyes were still. Her voice was low and rigidly controlled. 'And what do you know about it?'

Deacon was reckless with passion, too angry to heed the warning signs. 'I know he's in love with you. He told me as much. He begged me not to tell you but, hey, this is a day for sharing secrets! Why don't you admit you're in love with him too?'

If they'd been standing up, making it less awkward, Brodie would probably have slapped him. Her temper was like a tiger caged within her. Most of the time it was pretty quiet but every so often someone left the latch up and then it was just a question of whether the beast was hungry or not. Today she knew as if she'd seen it that if Deacon said one more thing, took one more snipe at her, the tiger would rip his throat out.

She said, 'Did you think I didn't know? Did you think I'd be shocked? That I'd be so unnerved I'd beg you to take me back? Is that how you think, Jack – that you can scare people into doing what you want? And that there's no difference between that and them wanting what you want?

'I know Daniel's in love with me. He told me so. He knows I'm not in love with him: I told him. Do you know something? I wish I was. I wish I could marry him with a clear conscience.

He'd never hurt me; he'd never use my feelings against me; and I don't think he'd let irrational fears of the future spoil the here-and-now. I think I could be happy with Daniel. I think, if he mattered just a little less to me, I'd take the chance.'

Her voice was calm now but Deacon could hear the regret in it. 'But I'm not going to. He deserves better. Actually, so do I. Nobody needs to be stuck in a relationship where one party is trying to do enough loving for both. We could make it work, for a year or two. But long-term we'd end up resenting one another. I'd feel guilty, he'd feel used. I'm not going to risk our friendship when I know it would end like that. He understands. Do you know why? Because he listened when I told him, and he believed me.

'That's the bit you and I never managed to get right, Jack.' An edge was creeping back into her voice. 'Not even the listening but the believing. I told you over and over that Daniel was no threat to us, that the only threat to us was *us*. But you couldn't believe me. You kept looking for the wedge that would force us apart. Well, you look that hard for anything, you're going to find it – hell, you're going to *make* it. We all create our own demons. You were so obsessed with my feelings for Daniel that you managed to strangle what we felt for each other. God knows I haven't always behaved well, but I wanted this to work. I tried to make it work. Daniel was never the obstacle. Your fear of Daniel was.'

For a second, denial was on the tip of his tongue. He almost said she was crazy, he was never afraid of anyone, if he was *going* to be afraid of someone it wouldn't be a neurotic maths teacher who shaved maybe twice a week. Some impulse of honesty stopped him. Actually, she was right. He *was* afraid of Daniel Hood. Because Daniel stood, and had always stood, between him and what he wanted most, and he could never find a way of moving him that wouldn't mean immediate and total defeat. Now the game, or perhaps it was a war, was over he could afford to tell the truth.

But now it was over he didn't need to. 'Do you know something, Brodie? I don't care. You want to play house with Daniel, you go right ahead. I hope you'll be very happy together. Tell you what: why don't you tell people it's his baby? Give them a laugh.'

Brodie clung onto her temper only because there were important decisions to be made here. She was astonished at the turn the conversation had taken. For once, she really didn't think it was her fault. Of course she'd surprised him. But he was a grown man and a detective superintendent: it couldn't be the first time he'd heard something unexpected. She said through her teeth, 'Are you seriously telling me you don't want to be this baby's father?'

He seemed incapable of damming the bitterness long enough to see the implications of his words. 'Now? What's the point? Six months ago I'd have given my right hand to be having a baby with you. But now? You've already made it clear there are too many compromises involved in sharing your life with me. You don't want to live with me, you don't want to be with me, and you don't want me muscling in on the decision-making process. I'll meet whatever legal and financial obligations there are, and if you need anything more from me, call. But in all the circumstances, Brodie, I'm finding it hard to see this baby as mine. There isn't enough of it left over from being yours.'

Angry as she was, she was also on the brink of tears. The steel in her voice was to stop it cracking. 'You don't want to give it your name?'

Deacon stood up abruptly, filling the little office, and reached for the door. 'Call it what you like, Brodie. Let me know what you decide and I'll send it a birthday card.' Then, leaving the door quivering on its hinges, he was gone.

CHAPTER FIVE

Daniel started work on January 1st, which seemed somehow auspicious. A new year, a new beginning. But for a month, every time he looked round Brodie was hovering behind his shoulder. She told him how her filing system worked, then checked that he was doing it right. She wrote out a list of questions to ask when he phoned round the south coast antiques shops, and she had him tick them off when he'd asked them. She let him sit in on a couple of meetings with clients, but when the meetings were over she told him what to do next.

This was not in itself unreasonable. She was the expert, the one with the experience, the one with the name, and he was the rookie. But for all the sense he got of her preparing to pass over the reins, he might as well have been a dog trotting at her heels – amiable, good company, someone to fetch things, but no more capable of managing Looking For Something? than a Springer spaniel.

In other circumstances, even the famously equable Daniel would have started to grow testy. Would have reminded her that four months from now, ready or not, like it or not, he'd be running this business so it was probably time she trusted him out in the big wide world. Of course he would make mistakes.

But if he started small they would be small mistakes. The longer she kept him tied to her apron strings, the bigger the mistakes would be when she had no choice but to cut him free.

But the stakes were high. If he questioned her judgement, in a fit of pique she was as likely as not to sack him, and while that would be no disaster from his point of view it would be from hers. It would leave her where she was six weeks ago: trying to ignore the inevitable although its shadow – like hers – loomed larger every day. So Daniel held his tongue and hung onto his patience, and ticked the little boxes and sat quietly through the meetings, and knew that his time would come.

It came when Brodie had an ante-natal appointment at Dimmock General at ten o'clock one Friday morning in February. She considered leaving the office shut until she could get there. But Daniel's expression said that, if she did that, she could open it on her own.

'What do you think?' she said doubtfully. 'Will you be able to manage?'

'Gee, Brodie, I don't know,' he replied. 'What if someone comes in? I might have to talk to them.'

She knew he was teasing, she even knew that she'd given him good reason, but to Brodie this was no laughing matter. This was her business, that she'd built from nothing against heavy odds and whose continued success depended absolutely on good judgement. Daniel was a good man but she wasn't sure he always showed good judgement. Of course, who did? And she only had two choices: entrust it to Daniel or throw it to the wolves.

'I know I'm being stupid,' she admitted. 'But I wasn't this nervous when I lost my virginity.'

'Well, if you keep lurking in the background I'll never get the chance to lose mine,' said Daniel firmly. 'Plus, you need to go to the clinic. I can run your business for you. What I can't do is deliver your baby.'

She chuckled at that. 'All right, I'll go. But...'

'No buts.'

'If someone asks...'

'If someone asks me a question I can't answer, I'll take his number and promise to get back to him. Then I'll write the question down, taking great care over spelling and punctuation, and when you've decided what we should do I'll call him back *and then I'll tick it off*. All right? Go. Keep your appointment. Lie back and think of England.'

'If...'

'Go!'

So Friday morning came round, and Daniel opened the office and opened the post, and did some filing, and phoned some dealers in case anyone had something Brodie was looking for; and by then it was eleven o'clock and still there were no hordes of frustrated searchers with bulging wallets beating a path to his door. He sighed and made himself some coffee. It didn't look as though he was going to get the chance to fulfil Brodie's worst fears after all.

He never quite knew what made him go to the door just then. There was a knocker and a bell, but neither made a sound; and the burgundy velvet curtain in the window that stopped the curious looking in stopped him looking out. But he knew there was someone there. He waited for a minute, expecting them to get up the courage to ring. When they didn't he waited another minute, wondering what he should do. Perhaps nothing: when they were ready to see him they'd let him know. Brodie had warned him about twitchers – people so nervous about whatever brought them to her that they would ring the bell and run away, or phone her three or four times before managing to say a word. It wasn't a routine service she offered, and people hesitated to put themselves in her hands.

It may have been intuition, it may only have been eagerness to see his first client, but after five minutes, with his coffee going cold and still the sensation of someone waiting just a few feet away, Daniel got up from the desk and opened the door.

At first he thought he'd been wrong and there was no one there. Then he looked further down and saw it was a short person. Not just short but shorter than him. It was in fact a child.

'Hello,' he said.

It was a boy of perhaps twelve years old, in the grey and red uniform of Dimmock High School, still waiting for his pubescent growth spurt and the deepening of the voice that would come with it. 'Hello,' he said back, warily.

'I wasn't sure if I heard anyone or not,' said Daniel.

'I didn't knock,' said the boy quickly, as if he'd been accused of something.

'OK.' But Daniel didn't go back inside and close the door. He stood on the step, hunched against the cold, looking up and down Shack Lane as if there was something to see.

After a minute the boy said, 'I've seen you before.'

'Yes?'

'At school. Before Christmas. You took a maths lesson.'

Daniel smiled. 'That's right. Were you there?' The boy nodded. 'What did you think of it?'

'It was interesting.'

'Do you like maths?'

'No,' said the boy.

'OK,' Daniel said again.

'I might have got to like it. We all thought you were going to be teaching us.'

Daniel gave a sad sigh. 'That was the idea. It didn't work out.'

'So you work here instead.'

'That's right. My friend runs it. I'm her assistant.'

'What do you do?'

'I make coffee,' Daniel answered honestly. 'I've just made some. Do you want a cup?'

The boy thought for a moment. 'All right.'

Thank God for that, thought Daniel, who'd been about to freeze to the step. 'I'm Daniel Hood, by the way.'

'I know. I'm...' He stopped.

Daniel didn't press him. Handing the boy a steaming mug he seemed to change the subject. 'It's a funny business, this. No two days are the same. Mrs Farrell – my friend – always said that, but I didn't understand until I started working here. You never know what you're going to be asked next. You can be looking for a house on Monday, a vintage car on Tuesday, a piece of china to make up a damaged tea-set on Wednesday, researching the history of a valuable painting on Thursday, and on Friday...'

He let the sentence hang for a moment, hoping the boy might finish it. But he didn't. Daniel carried on. 'Whatever.

People come here with all sorts of requests. Most of them we can meet. Even the ones we can't, usually we can tell them where to go instead.' There was perhaps no one else in the English-speaking world who could have said that without a trace of irony.

'Can I tell you a secret?' he asked. The boy nodded. 'My friend thinks we're here to make money. I haven't told her yet, I'm not sure how she'll take it, but I think we're here to help people.'

'People who're looking for something,' offered the boy.

Daniel smiled. 'That's right. People who're looking for something. Even if, sometimes, they're not quite sure what it is they're looking for.'

The boy frowned, considering. Wispy brown hair was trimmed midway between a high forehead and intelligent brown eyes. 'You mean, things that aren't real?'

Daniel demurred. 'Things that aren't concrete – solid – perhaps. Anything that's important enough for someone to want help finding is real. Even peace of mind. Especially peace of mind.'

'I didn't knock,' the boy said again. 'But I wanted to.'

'Then tell me how I can help.'

Charlie Voss wasn't quite sure what to make of Alix Hyde. When Deacon told him his services had been requisitioned, he was neither pleased nor dismayed but intrigued to meet a female inspector from the Serious Organised Crime Agency. He was expecting something like Deacon but with lipstick.

And at first glance, that was roughly what he got. She was big-framed without being heavy, and she wore a checked jacket, tailored trousers and brogues. In point of fact, she didn't wear lipstick. On a girl of twenty it might have been hailed as the next big thing: on a woman of maybe forty the effect should have been inescapably butch. Instead it was just a different sort of femininity – strong, unconventional, idiosyncratic even. But Voss doubted anyone ever took her for a man.

Anyone who's worked in a police station will know what conclusion the pundits in the canteen came to. 'Of course, she's a lesbian.'

'Oh yes, she's a lesbian. Not even hiding it.'

'Definitely a lesbian.'

'My mum had one once.'

'Hardly seems fair, does it? When they're at it with one another, that's two less for the rest of us.'

'*What*?'

Detective Constable Huxley, who'd made the last contribution but one, realised he was the object of everyone's attention. He looked mildly surprised. 'It was only little but boy, was it hairy!'

He was doing nothing to shift people's gaze off him, or even make them blink. He breathed at them in exasperation. 'You know – one of those spaniel things. Tibetan. Isn't that what they call them?'

Voss considered. 'I think they call them Lhasa Apso, Hux.'

'Isn't that what you said?' Huxley hadn't been listening.

Voss made an effort to move on. 'Do you talk about me when I'm not here? Wondering whether I'm queer?'

They were positively affronted. 'Of course not. You've got a fiancée.'

This was true. It was one of the life-altering decisions he'd made in the year of his thirtieth birthday. That, and buying a flat. As a single man he'd happily rented bedsits at some of Dimmock's least glamorous addresses, on the basis that working as a policeman – and particularly working for Detective Superintendent Deacon – didn't leave him time or energy enough to care about the décor. Being engaged to a charming but strong-minded Chinese nurse gave him a new set of priorities.

Which didn't invalidate his point. 'Jack Deacon's middle-aged and unattached. Do you sit here discussing his sexuality when he's safely out of earshot?'

A wave of fear swept through their eyes. 'Christ, no!'

'Then maybe we shouldn't be discussing Detective Inspector Hyde's. Because (a) it's none of our business, and (b) who gives a shit?'

'She had one of those, too,' Huxley muttered darkly. 'My mum.'

'A Shih Tzu?' hazarded Voss patiently.

'No, it was a Pekinese.'

Deacon wasn't in the canteen when all this was going on. Somebody told him about it later. It was all he could do to hold himself together until he was alone. Even so, people who heard him laughing in the privacy of his office were reminded irresistibly of Mrs Rochester in the attic. Deacon had been twenty-five before he worked out what a lesbian really was. Until then he thought the word for women who wouldn't sleep with him was Discriminating.

Later, finding Voss alone in the office that had been cleared for Alix Hyde's inquiry, he asked how it was progressing.

'You know what these things are like,' said Voss, wrinkling his freckled nose, 'it's all paperwork at the start. Collating files. We've been to see Walsh a couple of times. He was very polite – well, he didn't laugh in our faces. He just kept insisting the rumours about him weren't true.'

'He said he was keen to cooperate,' guessed Deacon.

Voss nodded. 'He said the sooner he could satisfy us, the sooner he'd get us off his back.'

'He offered to give you access to his accounts.'

'He did. He gave us written authority...' Voss was an intelligent and astute detective. He didn't believe in lucky guesses. 'You mean, these are not necessarily the actions of an innocent man?'

Deacon chuckled. It sounded like the rumble of a distant avalanche. 'What I told DI Hyde, I wasn't making it up. I really have tried to nail Terry myself. I found him enormously cooperative, and his accounts a model of bookkeeping practice, and he may not have laughed in my face but he nearly had a stroke not doing. Don't let me put you off, Charlie. Nobody's fire-proof: keep plugging away at it and you may well get a breakthrough. We all know he's as bent as a dog's hind leg: nothing would give me greater pleasure than visiting him in Pentonville. But it isn't going to be easy and it isn't going to be quick. He likes being a rich crook. He isn't going to give it up without a fight.'

'You can't think of any angles I could try?'

Deacon regarded him. 'If I could, don't you think I'd have mentioned it?'

Voss hastened to apologise. 'I didn't mean...'

'I know. You've got to remember, Charlie Voss, this has

been tried before. More than once. He won, we lost. That means we go into the rematch with him confident but us hungry. That's the only edge you're going to get. Now you've started, go into everything. Take nothing on trust. Try to find a way of turning his confidence into a weakness.'

Voss was nodding slowly, taking mental notes. 'One more question. How hard can we push before he turns violent?'

Deacon shook his head. 'I don't think he will get violent. I think he'll get very, very sneaky. Let me tell you a story. When Terry was fifteen he invented what he called the *doppelgänger* scam. You know how some things come in pairs, and lose most of their value if one piece gets lost or broken? He'd find someone with a pair of Ming vases, or garden urns, or crystal chandeliers – anything. Then he'd find a reason to visit the house – as a gardener or decorator or something – and accidentally damage one of the pair. Profuse apologies all round, the householder's insurance will pick up the tab, but he's left with one piece that's comparatively worthless.'

Deacon watched to see if Voss was anticipating where this was going. But there was no sign of it yet. 'In an effort to make amends, the remorseful gardener or window-cleaner or whatever says he knows a man who does restoration work, and he'd like to pay for the damaged piece to be patched up – just for the look of it, it'll never be worth anything but it'll stop the place looking lop-sided. And after the loss adjuster's been he takes the broken bits away.

'About now an accomplice, someone with a posher accent than Terry's, calls on the mark with a proposition. He heard about the recent misfortune because he's in a similar position. He too has lost one of a pair of Greek urns/Wedgwood vases/you name it of the same pattern, and he offers to buy the mark's surviving piece in order to restore his own set. But he's only offering what the single piece is worth. The mark figures that if he offered a bit more, *he* could have the pair, he'd be back where he was and he'd still have change from the insurance. They dicker a bit, but in the end the mark offers enough and they make the deal.'

'And there isn't another piece?' puzzled Voss.

'Of course there is. He's not stupid, he's not going to buy sight-unseen. He has an expert verify its authenticity. Money changes hands and our man spends a week admiring his new acquisition.' Deacon gave a sombre smile. 'Only then does he notice that his own urn has been in the wars. Whole chunks have been broken off and glued back. It's a neat enough job but it wouldn't pass as perfect. But then, it didn't have to. That one was never going to get the microscope treatment from the expensive expert.'

Then Voss understood. 'He switched them,' he breathed, awestruck. 'At some point he switched the broken one that he'd had restored for the intact one. Then he sold the mark his own urn.'

Deacon nodded. The story obviously afforded him some satisfaction. 'Terry Walsh won't get violent if you back him into a corner. He will get inventive. You really don't want him getting inventive.'

CHAPTER SIX

'I have a friend,' said the boy.

Daniel nodded encouragingly. 'Yes?'

'He's worried about something. He wanted my advice. I didn't know what to tell him.'

'So you thought you'd look for someone who might. That's good thinking.'

Abruptly the boy changed the subject. 'I've been to the dentist.'

Daniel blinked. 'Yes? Painful?'

'Just a check-up. But that's why I'm not in school. I don't skip school. If my father thought…' The sentence petered out in a crackle of alarm like static.

'I'm with him,' Daniel said firmly. 'But if you had to take the morning off anyway, it was a good chance to check things out.'

'That's what I thought.' Relief worked on the small body like a muscle relaxant.

'So you were wondering how best to help…' Daniel gave the odd little shrug that was the last memento of a broken collar-bone. 'You don't have to tell me his name. You don't have to tell me *your* name. But it would help if I had something to call you.'

This made sense. 'You can call me Tom.'

'You can call me Daniel. And what shall we call your friend?'

The fractional hesitation confirmed what Daniel already knew, what anyone who'd worked with children would have known. 'Zack.'

So Tom just might be called Tom, except that his parents probably insisted on Thomas, but Zack was a figment of his imagination. Or rather, a device. He could say things about Zack's situation that he would never volunteer about his own.

'And Zack's got problems. At school?'

'Oh no,' said Tom, with an unwitting arrogance that would have reminded anyone else of Daniel himself.

'At home, then.'

'I suppose.'

'Brother, sister, mother, father?' Daniel marked the precise moment at which the brown eyes blinked. 'Zack's worried about his mother?'

'He wants to help her,' ventured Tom in a low voice. His eyes dropped too, and he picked nervously at a scab on the back of his wrist.

'Of course he does,' agreed Daniel. 'If something's troubling her, naturally he wants to help. As long as he doesn't get the idea that looking after adults, even parents, is the responsibility of kids. It isn't. It's the other way round. They look after you, and in due course you look after your kids.'

'They shout,' the boy mumbled. 'All the time.'

So that was it. Daniel nodded sympathetically. 'It's pretty scary, isn't it? You just have to remember that it may not be as serious as it sounds. I dare say a fair bit of shouting goes on between you and your friends as well. It doesn't mean you don't like one another. Sometimes it's like that with parents. It sounds worse than it is.'

Tom didn't contradict but Daniel didn't think he was buying it. 'Tom – is anyone getting hurt?'

'No!' The promptness of his response should have been reassuring. Somehow it wasn't. It was too immediate, too dogmatic. As if he'd rehearsed. As if he'd known this was one question he'd be asked and was ready for it. 'No. Just shouting. But it's getting worse. They're both great people, you know? They both have really important jobs. I think that's part of it. They're so tired when they get home that anything sets them off.'

'Sounds about right,' murmured Daniel. 'And I guess Zack thinks that maybe two people with important and tiring jobs shouldn't have to worry about him. But Tom, you tell him from me that raising their children is the most important job either of his parents have – and they'd be the first to say so. I think you're right. I think they're too tired to see how difficult things are getting. I think if they knew how it was affecting Zack, both of them would want to quit their important jobs and take up road-sweeping or shelf-stacking or anything that would leave them time to make him happy.'

This child had spent too long keeping his feelings to himself to burst into tears now. But Daniel was pretty sure he wanted to. 'You think so?'

'A fair bit of time, effort and money goes into raising kids. And it's not compulsory. All the same, most people do it. Do you know why? Because most people love their kids to bits. It's just that, sometimes, when they're tired, they forget to say so. They may even forget just how important their families are to them. Sometimes it takes a bit of a crisis to remind them.'

Tom managed a shy smile. 'You think I should start sniffing glue?'

Daniel laughed out loud, and didn't draw attention to the fact that Zack had quietly disappeared. 'Not quite what I had in mind.' He thought for a moment. 'Do you know what I'd do if it was me? I'd write them a letter. That way I could take as much time as I wanted putting down exactly what I wanted to say, and there'd be less chance of us all getting upset and saying things we didn't mean, and it would give us all a focus to start talking about the problems. What do you think? Could you write them a letter saying how much you care about them and how much it upsets you to see them angry all the time?'

The boy was nodding slowly. 'I guess I could.' But when he looked up the shadows were still in his eyes. 'What if it makes things worse?'

'It won't. Trust me.'

'You don't know them. What if it does?'

It was a reasonable question. Daniel considered. 'Well, maybe that would be the time to get another adult involved. What about your grandparents? Would they help?'

Tom shook his head disconsolately. 'My dad's parents live in Spain. My mum's dad is dead and her mum's in a nursing home.'

'What about aunts and uncles?'

'Not that we're still talking to.'

'How about a teacher?' suggested Daniel. 'Would they discuss this with one of your teachers? It must be affecting your school-work.'

Tom gave an awkward little shrug. 'They're all right,' he

said doubtfully. 'My teachers. They're all right at teaching. They know about punctuation and algebra and stuff. I don't think any of them would help with this. I don't think I'd want to ask them.'

And strictly speaking it was no part of a teacher's job. Perhaps, if they managed to teach them punctuation and algebra, they'd done as much for their pupils as could be expected, especially in today's climate of mistrust. Almost the first thing student teachers learn now is how not to leave themselves open to violent confrontations and allegations of impropriety. Why would anyone who'd completed his classroom hours, and done his night's marking, then troop round to Tom's house to tell his parents that their inability to manage their own workload was making an intelligent, caring and sensitive boy miserable? Daniel might have done it, but that was getting to be a while back…

Daniel would have done it. Daniel would do it again if he had to. 'Tell you what,' he said, looking the boy squarely in the eyes. 'You write them a letter. Be as honest as you can, and tell them what you need them to do to make things better. I think that'll solve the problem. But if I'm wrong, come back to me and we'll talk to them together.'

Detective Inspector Hyde picked up Charlie Voss as if he'd been a warm coat, threw him into her car and took off at speed. They were climbing the back of the Firestone Cliffs, heading east along the coast, before he got over the surprise enough to ask, 'Where are we going?'

She looked at him as if, for a moment, she'd forgotten he was there. 'Oh – yes. Sorry. Dover. We've got a witness against

Terry Walsh. I think we've got the bastard.'

In the three years he'd worked with him Voss had never heard that note of triumph in Jack Deacon's voice. It raised hairs on the back of his neck. 'Who? What?'

'A woman called Susan Weekes. Until recently she worked as a croupier at The Dragon Luck casino on the Brighton Road. Walsh's wife is a major shareholder. Weekes has known Terry for years.'

'Known, as in…?' Voss raised a surprised eyebrow as Hyde nodded. 'I had the impression he was very much a family man. Devoted husband and father.'

Hyde shrugged. 'I suppose, if he can keep a whole criminal enterprise where you couldn't find it, one little mistress wouldn't pose too much of a problem.'

Voss said nothing. He'd noticed that Hyde had a tendency to criticise Deacon, however tacitly; and of course Deacon was never shy of criticising anyone. It left Voss feeling a little like a tug-of-love child.

Hyde glanced at him as she drove, realised he wasn't going to react and, with a little secret smile, continued. 'She says he used the casino for business meetings. I'm not talking here about the bulk paper business, you understand. Weekes claims she was present on numerous occasions when the real source of his wealth was discussed. She says she heard enough and saw enough to put him away.'

It occurred to Voss to wonder why Susan Weekes was offering to do this now when she never had before. 'And do we believe her?'

Hyde grinned at him. She might be new to Dimmock but she wasn't new to this job. Nobody gets to be a detective inspector at SOCA by believing everything they're told, even when they very much want it to be true. 'Couldn't say, Charlie, not yet. I haven't spoken to her myself. I got the heads-up from Customs. It seems Miss Weekes was found in possession of slightly more cocaine than most people would have for personal use. In fact, a suitcase full. She was looking for something to trade it down and this is what she came up with. She was there when Terry Walsh met with other non-law-abiding citizens to plan their non-legitimate business activities.'

Voss pondered. 'Even if she's telling the truth, won't it be her word against his? If she's willing to grass him up, I'm guessing the affair is over. Courts tend to be pretty sceptical of the motives of former mistresses.'

'Understandably,' nodded Hyde. 'To be honest, I'm not sure how good a witness she'll make. Maybe terrible; maybe so bad we'd be crazy to use her. That doesn't mean we can't use what she tells us.

'Walsh is a clever man, Charlie, he must be to have got away with this for so long; and what he's been cleverest of all about is keeping his head down. Never giving us a handle on him. We *know* he's a crook, we know that's where his money comes from, but we've never had facts and figures – who, what, where, when, how much. What I need – maybe all I need – is a way in. Like one of those little silver gismos that let you open an oyster. If I can crack open the shell I can get at the good stuff inside. That's what I'm hoping to get from Susan Weekes. Some facts I can check, some names I can lean on.'

'Is she in custody?'

'With a Louis Vuitton full of crack? What do you think?'

According to the custody record, Susan Weekes was thirty-six. Maybe, on a good day, she could pass for thirty. This was not a good day. Tears had wrought havoc with the expert make-up. She wasn't crying now but her eyes were hollow with despair.

Yesterday she'd had breakfast in Paris with a man called Michel, who helped her pack the results of a shopping spree into her car and bade her a safe journey as he waved her off. It was a sunny February day, she was looking forward to the drive. She had all her life ahead of her, and a nice little earner to help her enjoy it. She had lunch in Calais, and afternoon tea on the EuroStar, and everything went smoothly right up to the point that she left the train.

She had supper in a back room of the Customs shed in Dover.

Today she'd spoken to a solicitor, and to a number of different police officers, and for the last couple of hours she'd been waiting for a detective inspector from the Serious Organised Crime Agency. She didn't know exactly how much trouble she was in. She knew they'd been ready to throw the book at her when they opened her suitcase, but she'd been given to understand that the weight of the book might be negotiable. It might be a family bible, it might be a Booker Prize contender, it might be an airport lounge paperback, all depending on what she could offer in return.

What they expected, what they wanted, was that she'd give them Michel. But that was more than her life was worth. He was a charming and attentive companion, handsome, urbane and knowledgeable on the fine arts; but Susan Weekes knew that if she so much as nodded a traffic warden in his direction he'd have her killed. In France, in England, under an assumed name, following plastic surgery. He'd do it from a prison cell if he had to. To make a point; like his fellow-countryman Napoleon, who liked to shoot a general from time to time *pour encourager les autres*. So Michel was safe. She'd spent a desperate hour looking for something else she could trade with.

And now here were two new police officers, one of them a woman. 'Tell us about Terry Walsh.'

The big hair had gone a bit flat over the last twelve hours. The mascara had run and the eyes were scared. 'What do you want to know?'

'What he's up to,' said Hyde. 'How he does it. How I prove it.'

'What do I get?'

'Friends at court,' said the Inspector judiciously.

'It's not enough.' She was so scared Voss could hear her rings rattling on the table-top. But instinct told her this was the best chance she'd have to hold out for a better deal. 'I want to walk.'

Alix Hyde laughed out loud, a musical tone like a bell. 'Susan! You know I can't do that. I could get you Cowes Week on the Chief Constable's yacht before I could get you free and clear. You were caught with a suitcase full of crack cocaine! You hadn't even bothered disguising it.'

'There didn't seem any point,' mumbled Weekes. 'I knew if they opened it I was up shit creek. It seemed better to stuff it full and never have to do it again.'

'You mean, this was your first time?'

'Yes.' The woman looked up with hope-haunted eyes. 'The

money was just too good. I thought, Just once. People do this all the time and get away with it. I can get away with it just once.' She gave a minimal shrug. 'You know the rest.'

Hyde shook her head decisively. 'Sorry, Susan, I'm not buying it. That business of filling the case – that wasn't the action of a virgin. She'd have put little packets into her underwear and little packets into her wash-bag, and spent hours squeezing tiny little quantities into her toothpaste tube. And it would all have been wasted effort because you're right, the moment you were challenged you were lost. Whatever you were carrying, however well you'd hidden it, they'd find it and then you'd be past all help.'

She pursed her lips. 'Except mine. I can help you, Susan, and I'm probably the only one who can. Because there's something I want even more than I want you behind bars, and luckily enough – and you'll never know *how* lucky you've been, this isn't an offer I'd be making in any other circumstances – you're in a position to help me get it.'

So far as Voss could judge, Hyde had made the perfect pitch. Brisk, matter-of-fact and determined, she'd given Weekes the impression that all the cards were now face-up on the table. That there was a deal to be made, but only one and only once. Either she took it or she let it go. Nothing in the DI's voice or manner held out any hope that the pot could be sweetened so there was no incentive for Weekes to spin this out. At the same time, Hyde appeared to be sure of her authority to make a deal stick. It was this or nothing, now or never. Whatever Weekes could get for her information, now was the time to take it.

'So what *can* you do for me?'

Alix Hyde smiled, not unkindly. 'I can pretend to believe you when you say you've never done this before. That you were stupid and greedy, not a professional drug-runner. That's probably worth about four years to you. Two hundred weeks. One thousand, four hundred days. Three hundred and...'

'All right!' exclaimed Susan Weekes quickly, desperate to stop the parcelling up and throwing away of large chunks of her life. 'All right. I'll tell you what I can.'

'You'll tell me everything you know,' Hyde corrected her, 'or we've nothing more to talk about.'

'All right! That's what I meant. All right.'

'She's good,' said Charlie Voss, leaning on the bar of The Belted Galloway later that night. 'She got what she wanted, she got it pretty well immediately, and she didn't even...' He stopped dead, waiting for the smoke-blackened roof-beams to fall on him.

Deacon looked up slowly from his pint of shandy. Apart from a bottle of wine with a sit-down meal, this was as close as he got to serious drinking. And Voss knew, and the publican knew, and that was all, so if the secret got out he'd know exactly where to start his inquiries. 'Didn't what, Charlie?' His voice was the soft purr of a tiger tucking in its napkin.

Like Susan Weekes the moment someone in a Customs uniform beckoned her, Voss knew exactly what the future held for him. He might as well open the suitcase right away and put his hands up. Only some primitive survival instinct made him wriggle. 'Um...'

Deacon wasn't an angler. He got all the excitement he

needed catching criminals. But he didn't need actual experience to know this was what it felt like when a nice big fat one was flapping round on the end of the line. 'Didn't even shout? Didn't swear a lot, and stamp up and down, and loom in a threatening manner? Didn't lean on the Police & Criminal Evidence Act until it screamed for mercy? Is that what you were going to say, Charlie?'

Voss tried to make the best of a bad situation. 'Horses for courses, chief. Everyone finds what works for them. I didn't say your methods *wouldn't* have got the job done.'

'Just that hers are more – elegant?'

'Ladylike,' said Voss, inspired. He thought he'd somehow stumbled onto safe ground.

'Well hell, Charlie Voss, I wouldn't want anyone accusing *me* of being ladylike.'

'Course not, chief.'

'So she coughed? Your drug-smuggler – she dished the dirt on Terry Walsh?'

Voss nodded. 'Names, places, dates. It'll all need checking, of course, and guess whose job that's going to be, but it sounded authentic.'

'Who is she? What do you know about her? Is she reliable?'

Voss found himself caught uncomfortably between conflicting loyalties, reluctant to answer. This wasn't Detective Superintendent Deacon's case, it was Detective Inspector Hyde's, and he didn't want her thinking that everything she said to him was going straight to Deacon. He prevaricated. 'Of course she isn't reliable – she's a drug-smuggler! But she says she knew Walsh, professionally and personally, for years – and if that's true then she was in a position to know the rest. If she knows even half of what she says she knows, it's worth working with her. That's what Alix reckons, anyway.'

'Alix?' echoed Deacon, deadpan.

Detective Sergeant Voss blushed to the roots of his sandy hair. 'She told me to call her Alix.'

When he smiled like that, there was something of the night about Jack Deacon. A hoot of owls, a whisper of vampire wings. Something fundamentally evil. 'I can see I'm going to have to up my game if I'm not going to lose you to the serious and organised Detective Inspector Hyde.'

And while Voss was trying to convey the notion that the thought had never occurred to him – without, and this was the hard bit, actually lying – Deacon got up from the bar, shrugged his coat on and, chuckling bleakly, left to go home. Voss picked up the tab without complaint. Partly because it was a small price for ending the conversation, and partly because he always did.

CHAPTER SEVEN

'So how did things go?'

Brodie got it out first, by a millisecond, so Daniel felt obliged to answer first. 'Very quiet. I did the phone-arounds – somebody needs to run over to Brighton, a couple of bookshops and antique dealers had items on your list.' He paused hopefully, in case she said, 'You'd better go this afternoon, then.' But she didn't, and really he'd known she wouldn't. She still wasn't resigned to sharing this business with anyone, was clinging onto every aspect of it with a grip like a hawk's.

Daniel sighed. 'The only soul I saw all morning was a boy I taught once who dropped in for a chat.' That was perfectly accurate, but the twinge of his delicate conscience warned him it was not totally honest.

'Not a client, then,' said Brodie. She had a regrettable habit of pigeon-holing people according to whether or not she could make money out of them.

Daniel smiled. 'Not yet.'

When she returned from the hospital they'd shut up shop and repaired round the corner to The Singing Kettle for lunch. They'd always met up for lunch two or three times a week – sandwiches on a bench on the Promenade in summer, something hot at The Singing Kettle or in the netting-shed when the weather turned cold. It struck both of them as slightly odd to go on doing it now they were working together, but even odder to stop.

'Your turn,' said Daniel. 'Anything new?'

Brodie shrugged. 'There's a baby in there, but we knew that.'

'And once you've had one you've had them all?'

'What can I tell you?' she said plaintively. 'They poke you, they prod you. They smear your belly with jelly and expect you to coo lovingly over a screen full of static. It's a pretty surreal experience.'

'Any pictures?'

Brodie shook her dark head. 'Nothing worth keeping. Everybody else seemed to think it showed a baby. To me it really did look like a bun in the oven.'

Daniel had known Brodie Farrell long enough and well enough to know that her manner wasn't always the best guide to how she was feeling. This slightly world-weary cocktail of coolness and flippancy just might have been a cover for an excitement she wasn't ready to admit to. But he didn't think so. 'What's the matter?' he asked quietly. 'Not getting the same buzz this time?'

She glanced at him gratefully. He'd summed up in a sentence things she'd been fretting to make sense of. 'I guess. When Paddy was on the way…'

'…It was different,' said Daniel. 'You were twenty-six years old, you hadn't been married long, the pair of you were happy, a baby was the next step. Of course it was exciting. This time it wasn't what you'd been hoping and planning for.

It took you by surprise. And then, you've other things to worry about now. Paddy for one, the business for another. Even if you and John had stayed together, you can't hope to capture the same thrill about a second pregnancy that you had with your first.'

His earnestness, and the way he could talk authoritatively about things he knew nothing about, always made Brodie want to giggle. She felt her mood lightening. 'I suppose that's it. I expect the whole maternal instinct thing will cut in when it arrives.'

'Of course it will. And probably long before that. Are you still feeling sick in the mornings?'

'A bit queasy sometimes. Nothing dramatic.'

'You'll be better disposed towards it when it stops making you want to heave.'

Brodie nodded, hoping he was right.

'Have you given any thought to names?'

She shook her head. 'Doesn't seem any point till I know what sex it is.'

Daniel's pale eyebrows arched in a surprise that amounted to criticism. 'There's only two options. You could be ready with alternatives.'

'I'll call it Danny.'

'Don't you dare,' he said, and meant it. 'How did you settle on Patricia?'

'It's John's mother's name,' Brodie said, with an unconscious little scowl. 'I never liked it. That's why I called her Paddy from day one.'

'It didn't occur to you *not* to call her Patricia?'

She gave a fierce little grin. 'You should have known me

then, Daniel. I'd go along with anything anyone suggested rather than make a fuss.'

He thought about that. 'No,' he decided, 'I'd rather know you now. So what kind of names do you like? English classic? Biblical? Trendy?' He couldn't have made it clearer with a placard that Trendy was the wrong answer.

She considered. 'I suppose good, strong, non-frilly, non-twee, non-clever names. John-and-Jane sort of names.'

'John?' he echoed doubtfully.

'Good point,' she conceded. 'I don't really want people wondering if it's named after my ex-husband or my ex-lover.'

'David, Mark, James. Mary, Elizabeth, Amy.'

'Shane,' she postulated, to annoy him. 'Jordan.'

'Abednego,' he countered. 'Berengaria.'

'You made that up!' said Brodie accusingly.

He shook his yellow head. 'Richard the Lionheart's wife was called Berengaria. You can't get better provenance than that.'

'Beyoncé. Dylan.'

'Noah.'

Brodie blinked. 'Yeah, right. Let's go the whole hog and call him Jonah.'

But it wasn't Daniel's suggestion, and he was looking round to see where it had come from. It was a coincidence. A big man in an expensive suit and a boy in the grey and red uniform of Dimmock High were settling themselves at one of the tables. 'Noah, what do you want?' asked the father. 'We'd better order if we're going to get you back in school on time. And if you keep scratching that it'll never heal.'

Daniel's gaze was returning to Brodie when suddenly it flicked back as if on elastic. So he wasn't even called Thomas.

And it wasn't his scabbed wrist he was scratching. He was absent-mindedly rubbing the top of his left arm while he studied the menu.

Brodie noticed where he was looking. 'Do you know them?'

He shook his head. 'I had the boy in a class once.'

'Oh?' She looked again, closer. 'I wouldn't have thought he was in secondary school when you were teaching.'

Sometimes telling the truth was a minefield. 'It was just one class. I didn't even know his name.'

Fortunately she didn't pursue it. 'I'm surprised they sent him to Dimmock High. I'd have thought they'd hold out for Eton and Harrow.'

'Why, who are they?'

Brodie indicated the man with a nod of her head. 'He's a solicitor. Adam Selkirk. John knows him. Actually, Jack does too.' She leant forward conspiratorially. 'Jack calls him a high-priced mouthpiece. I'm not sure he means it as a compliment.'

Daniel chuckled. Then he glanced back at the table behind them. 'Selkirk. Where have I heard the name?'

'You're probably thinking of his wife. Marianne – she's big in the world of Good Works. She makes a lot of speeches, cuts a lot of ribbons. She always gets an honourable mention at Women of the Year luncheons. Daniel, if you keep staring like that I shall have to introduce you.'

'Sorry,' he said, chastened. 'It's just, when you're teaching you think you know the kids – but what you know ends at the school gates. Somehow it comes as a surprise that they have homes, families, dentists…'

Brodie's shapely eyebrows arched. '*Dentists*?'

'Sorry,' he said again, waving a hand dismissively. 'Thinking of something else.'

'Well, think me up some more names. Because Berengaria isn't going to cut the mustard.'

'Ignatius?' he hazarded. 'Igraine? Isadora?'

'A witness against me?' said Terry Walsh with a puzzled frown. 'What witness? A witness to what?'

He was Deacon's age, rather shorter but with the same heavy frame, running a little to fat now a lot of his business was conducted by mobile phone. But his hair was still black, with a crinkly wave running through it, and his keen intelligent eyes held a subversive hint of humour. Even in winter his skin never quite lost the tan that came from close proximity to the English Channel. When he wasn't making money, honestly or the other way, he was commonly to be found on his boat.

It wasn't sailing weather today. It wasn't garden weather either, but his conservatory commanded spectacular views of garden and Channel both. When he took them there, Voss wondered if he wanted to show the police officers his rolling acres – well, acre – or to keep them out of his office.

'Someone who was pretty close to you at one point,' said Detective Inspector Hyde. 'Close enough to see you doing the sort of business you don't declare to the VAT-man. You might as well give it up, Terry. You're not going to talk your way out of it this time.'

Walsh shook his head bemusedly. 'I'm sorry, Inspector, none of this is ringing any bells. If you've got some allegations you want me to answer, you're going to have to give me a clue.'

'All right. That casino you're involved in, The Dragon Luck. There's a safe room there, where they keep the takings and monitor the tables. Because of the sums of money involved, the security is massive. No intruders, no surprises. Which makes it an excellent venue for the kind of meeting you don't want witnessing with the kind of people who don't want to be overheard.'

Now Walsh was nodding thoughtfully. 'I can see that it would.'

'We have someone who was at some of those meetings. We have dates, times and the names of other people who were present. We know what you discussed and what decisions you reached.'

'Goodness,' said Walsh mildly. 'That really would be quite worrying, wouldn't it? If we'd been discussing anything I didn't want you to know about. But how many secrets do you suppose a man amasses in the bulk paper trade?'

Alix Hyde laughed. The pair of them were enjoying the encounter like a couple of chess players, appreciating one another's strengths, ready to exploit the first sign of weakness. 'I can think of one. How much space is left inside a shipping container when it's packed with rolls of newsprint.'

Walsh shrugged negligently. 'Rolls are round, containers are rectangular. But I've never thought of anything useful to do with the space left over.'

'Gee, Terry,' smiled Hyde, 'I bet you could squeeze something in there. If it was small and not too delicate, and sufficiently profitable to be worth the trouble.'

'Oh – I know,' said Walsh, as if it was a quiz and he was going to win the washing-machine and the cuddly toy. 'You could smuggle drugs in there. Little packets of drugs squeezed into all those corners. You could make a fortune. If,' he added, 'you weren't an honest businessman.'

'Quite,' said Hyde.

Walsh was still thinking about it. 'You know, it's a wonder Customs & Excise haven't thought of that. They're usually pretty sharp with these things.'

'Yes, they are,' agreed Hyde.

'No, wait,' remembered Walsh, 'they *did* think of it. They had those containers of mine back to bare steel. Can you guess what they found?'

'Nothing?' murmured Alix Hyde.

'That's right,' said Walsh, nodding enthusiastically. 'The first time. Of course, that's several years ago now. So they did it again. Stripped it right down, took out everything that would move. Guess what they found that time.'

'Nothing.' Detective Inspector Hyde wasn't smiling any more.

'Well,' Walsh said expansively, 'they always say third time's a charm. So a couple of months after that...'

It didn't take a clairvoyant to see where this was going. 'All right, Mr Walsh,' Voss interjected hurriedly, 'we get the point. You've been subjected to a number of Customs searches and they haven't found anything that wasn't on the manifest. But you know, and I know, and Inspector Hyde knows, there could be two quite different explanations for that.'

'I'm an honest businessman.' Walsh's eyes were merry.

'That's one of them,' agreed Voss. 'The other is that you're a clever crook.'

Terry Walsh beamed. 'It's good to see you again, Charlie Voss. I've hardly seen you since that business with Joe Loomis. I haven't seen Joe much either. How's he doing?'

'I believe the inflatable cushion's a great help,' said Voss with restraint, and Walsh roared with laughter. Joe Loomis's discomfort would always be a source of joy to Terry Walsh, and vice versa. They were rivals. And not in the bulk paper trade.

Hyde was drumming her fingernails on her chair's arm. 'When you two have finished with the jolly reminiscences, could we get back to the point?'

'Sorry,' said Walsh, still chuckling. 'What was the point again?'

'The safe room at The Dragon Luck, and the secret business you did there. On…' She got out her notebook. 'Would it be helpful to have the dates?'

'What would be *more* helpful,' said Walsh pensively, 'is a bit more information about your supergrass.'

'Oh, come on…!' began Hyde indignantly, but Walsh interrupted her.

'Because I can't quite see what anyone at a secret meeting to discuss illegal enterprises could possibly gain by telling the police about it. I mean, if you're hoping to arrest me for being there, presumably you think you can charge *everyone* who was there.'

Hyde tried a lazy smile. 'Come on, Terry, you know how these things work. Someone finds themselves in trouble and tries to make it go away.'

But Walsh still wasn't convinced. 'I don't know, Inspector. The kind of people who attend that kind of meeting don't usually get themselves into that kind of trouble. Unless…' An idea dawned in his face like sunrise. 'Inspector Hyde – we're not talking about *Susan*, are we?'

Alix Hyde wasn't in the least concerned that Terry Walsh had guessed the identity of her witness. Being in custody was no guarantee of the woman's safety, but even that was a minor consideration. Susan's information was always going to be more use than her testimony, and Hyde already had the facts.

'That's right. Susan Weekes, the croupier at The Dragon Luck. Who was also your mistress, and in that capacity was present on a number of occasions when you'd have been better sending her back to the tables. It's time to get serious, Terry. You're going down. The only question in my mind is how much work it's going to be pulling it all together. You could make it easier. It's not in your interests that I'm tired and bad-tempered at the trial.'

Walsh was regarding her calmly, still smiling though now the smile had a different quality. It had teeth. 'Let me get this right, Inspector. You think I'm some kind of criminal mastermind. You think you've found someone who's willing to testify against me. And it's a woman I'm supposed to have had an affair with?'

'In a nutshell,' said Alix Hyde, 'yes.'

He shook his head. 'I've never had an affair with anyone.'

Hyde considered. 'Nobody's memory improves with age. Maybe we should ask your wife.'

The sheer effrontery of it startled Voss. Trying to blackmail the man – *this* man: this strong, clever, unflappable man – in his own conservatory. For half a minute no one spoke, no one moved; if anyone breathed they did it quietly. Voss didn't know what to expect.

Then Walsh moved so quickly Voss saw Hyde flinch. But he was walking to the door. 'Good idea.' He raised his voice. 'Caroline? Have you got a minute?'

Anyone, and anything, which has hunted a prey as powerful as itself knows that moment when the roles – and the rules – change. That dark dappled moment in the jungle when you're almost close enough to catch your tiger by the tail, and then you hear the crack of a twig behind you. The heart and the world both lurch, and after that it's anybody's guess who's going home to the wife with a trophy.

('Ooh,' she says, 'that'll look nice on the floor.' 'Just a minute,' he says, 'let me skin it first. These safari suits are the devil to get off.')

And Charlie Voss, who'd never hunted tiger in his life, who'd never hunted anything except men and done it with nothing but his own wits for a weapon, felt that little lurch as the world changed gear.

Caroline Walsh may have been a gangster's moll but nothing in her demeanour suggested it. She was a few years younger than Walsh, and half a class-system above him socially, and she greeted the police officers cordially, as if the Widows & Orphans Fund was the charity she'd graciously consented to support this year. She had to know she was living on the proceeds of crime, but she was supremely unconcerned by the presence of detectives in her house. Everyone's job has a down side: this was his. She had no doubt Terry would deal with it.

'How are you, Charlie?' she said with a smile – and that was clever too, because while she knew Deacon a little she'd hardly met his sergeant. It was simply a device to put the senior officer at a disadvantage. It didn't help that she was a notably handsome woman.

'This is Detective Inspector Hyde, of the Serious Organised Crime Agency,' said Terry Walsh, expressionless. 'Go on, Inspector – ask your question.'

Alix Hyde didn't fluster easily. She wasn't flustered now. She regarded Walsh levelly. 'Are you sure this is what you want?'

He nodded. 'I think it's best, don't you? Cards on the table and all that. I'm a plain man, Inspector, I like to keep my dealings with people straightforward and above board. What it is, darling,' he said, turning to his wife, 'the old rumours have surfaced again and Detective Inspector Hyde thinks I'm a crook. She has a witness who heard me planning capers – that is what you call them, capers?' he asked Hyde, but then didn't wait for a reply – 'in the back room of The Dragon Luck, and that's not quite as silly as it sounds because she was my mistress at the time.'

There were three seconds of absolute silence. Then Caroline Walsh was laughing immoderately, tears filling her eyes, one hand on the back of the sofa for support. And Walsh was laughing too, something between a rumble and a cackle, vastly amused.

Voss dared a glance at Alix Hyde. She was trying not to react, to wait until the merriment died down and she could find out what was so funny. But she couldn't pretend this was the response she'd expected.

Finally Caroline wiped her eyes with a fine lawn handkerchief and said weakly, 'I take it this is Susan we're talking about?'

Walsh nodded. 'Apparently.'

The woman patted his hand. 'You certainly made an impression there, dear. That woman's been carrying a torch for you for years!'

'Well, I wish she wouldn't. It's damned inconvenient.'

'What's she said now?'

'The same thing. I'm the Godfather of the south coast, she was my mistress, I ran half the crime in England from the safe room at the casino and she saw me do it.'

'It's true what they say,' said Caroline fondly. '*Hell hath no fury like a woman scorned.* There's one thing about this fantasy of hers – it's easily disproved. At least, it was before.' She held Inspector Hyde with a gaze of calm challenge.

Hyde was still blanking her expression. 'You mean, you've heard these allegations before?'

'Inspector, *everyone's* heard these allegations before. Well,' Walsh amended that, 'everyone from round here. You're new in Dimmock, aren't you? Maybe you should have run this past Jack Deacon before you put too much faith in Susan's delusions. He caught wind of what she was saying a few years ago and, old mate or not, he felt he had to look into it. But he's got a lot of experience in these matters. He quickly realised that Susan's story wasn't credible. It was just a rather lonely woman trying to impress people.'

Voss felt the searchlight of Hyde's gaze turn slowly his way. But he hadn't known either. Of course, Deacon had had a lot of sergeants before Charlie Voss drew the short straw a couple of years ago. He had a reputation for eating them.

Until this moment Voss had never felt in danger from him. Certainly he'd felt the rough edge of Deacon's tongue – when he deserved it, when he half-deserved it and when he didn't deserve it at all, so often he'd come to the conclusion there wasn't a smooth edge – but this was different. They'd talked just last night. All Deacon had to do was warn Voss where this line of inquiry was leading. And he'd said nothing. He'd hung him out to dry. Voss felt betrayed.

Hyde said carefully, 'Just for the record, then, perhaps you'll disprove it again. For the benefit of us out-of-towners.'

Caroline Walsh nodded pleasantly. 'Of course. You know I'm a partner at The Dragon Luck? I inherited my shares from my father fifteen years ago, and naturally I keep an eye on my investment. Terry and I spend an evening there maybe once a month. But it's me conducting business there, not my husband. He whiles away an hour or so at the tables while I disappear into the back room with the Manager and the other partners.'

She smiled. 'He's a charming man, my husband – you may have noticed this. He caused quite a flutter among the female staff. I'm afraid poor Susan mistook a bit of good-natured flirting for something more and started telling people she was Terry's bit on the side.

'The Manager asked if I wanted her dismissed. But it was more funny than it was offensive. No one who knows Terry, who's seen him with his family, was ever going to believe her, and I didn't think it mattered what people who don't know him thought.'

'But she was dismissed,' said Hyde. She wasn't sure what she was hearing – the truth, a lie, or the kind of half-truth that's harder to unravel. She needed to ask more questions. But police officers don't like asking questions until they have a good idea what the answers ought to be. 'Six months ago.'

'Yes, she was,' agreed Caroline. 'She was boasting more and more, in front of people she hardly knew. We weren't concerned about the police: they knew her story for what it was. But sooner or later someone was going to believe her and it was going to matter. Being called a philanderer wasn't going to do Terry much harm but being accused of criminal activity could. He's a businessman, his integrity is important.

'I was on the point of doing something about it myself but the Manager beat me to it. He has a licence to protect, he couldn't have people talking about The Dragon Luck as if it was a den of vice. Susan lost her job for lying, Inspector, not because she was having an affair with my husband.'

'I see.' Alix Hyde spoke carefully, as if through a mouthful of broken glass.

'Yes?' said Caroline Walsh coolly. 'I hope so. I really hope we don't have to go through all this again. Of course you have your job to do. But it's just plain silly to keep covering the same ground.'

Walsh saw them to their car. Until they got there Voss entertained the faint hope that Alix Hyde might yet produce a rabbit from the hat and dissipate the aura of smugness that surrounded him like cigar-smoke. But she'd been wrong-footed too, and had enough experience to know that now – undermined and uncertain – wasn't the time to take him on. She held her peace until Walsh insisted on helping her into her own car.

Then she smiled tautly at him. 'I feel absolutely sure, Terry, that this is *au revoir* rather than goodbye.'

Walsh leant closer to her. His voice was so low even Voss strained to hear. 'I'm counting on it, Inspector. But next time you come to my house to accuse me of everything from drug-running to marital infidelity, remember your manners. Call me Mr Walsh.'

CHAPTER EIGHT

For once, the raised voice crashing down the stairs from the CID offices on the top floor of Battle Alley was not that of Jack Deacon. However, the general feeling was that it was only a matter of time, so everyone who wasn't pressingly engaged elsewhere – and right now an axe-murderer would have been asked to come back later – kept busy within earshot. There's plenty of free entertainment to be had in a police station at any time, but senior officers publicly tearing strips off one another is a rare joy. Sometimes protecting and serving the community just has to wait.

'You assured me of your full cooperation,' snarled Detective Inspector Hyde. 'I counted on it. You said you'd lend me your best officer. I counted on that too. What I didn't count on was having your old mucker Terry Walsh laugh in my face as I worked my case on the basis of evidence that you knew was flawed! That you personally had investigated and dismissed as unsafe and unsatisfactory! *Why didn't you tell me*?'

Deacon was still sufficiently amused to be holding onto his temper. 'It's your case, Inspector. You didn't tell me who your new witness was or what evidence they were offering. If either you or Sergeant Voss had had the wit to pull the back-files *before* you went to see Terry, you might have heard the gentle trill of alarm bells ringing.'

'You talked to Charlie in the pub last night! Would it have cost you blood to warn him off? To say you'd already looked at Susan's claims and they didn't stand up?'

'Two things,' rumbled Deacon. 'Charlie Voss *is* my best officer – you're lucky to have him. But he's a sergeant, and the reason for that is he still has things to learn. I lent him to you because I hoped there might be things you could teach him. I'm regretting *that* already.

'And the other thing is, he's not my spy. He doesn't come running to me to report everything you've said and done. Yes, I bought him a beer' – this was an outright lie and Deacon knew it – 'and he said you'd been to Dover. He said you had a new witness, someone involved in the drugs trade. He didn't give me the name and I'd no reason to associate Susan Weekes with drug-smuggling. Despite what you might have heard, Inspector Hyde, I'm not psychic. But everything she told me when I interviewed her was in the file. If you'd looked you'd have known it was the same story from the same woman. And you'd have seen that it fell apart when I leant on it.

'Anyone can make a mistake, Inspector. But try not to make stupid ones.'

Brodie always did the Saturday morning trawl of the Brighton antiques scene with Paddy. It was an outing they both enjoyed, and there weren't many weeks when their efforts went unrewarded. But since they had different ideas of what constituted a find, the crates in the back of the car were frequently packed with an egalitarian mix of Georgian lead crystal, broken china horses patched with Araldite, Victorian linens, toy tractors, almost complete Worcester dinner services and plastic frogs that made a rude noise when squeezed. Paddy Farrell, now nearly seven, had inherited her father's kindness and her mother's determination but neither of them admitted responsibility for her sense of humour.

With the boss and her car on the road, Daniel was left to his own devices. Brodie had made it clear that, barring emergencies, she didn't expect him to work weekends, but actually he had nothing better to do. He walked up Fisher Hill to pay a visit to Edith Timoney. He didn't yet know enough about antiques to risk buying much on his own, even with Brodie's list of watch-out-fors to guide him. But he could scrutinise the stock and report on it when he saw Brodie this evening. If there was anything promising he thought Miss Timoney would put it under the counter for him. Miss Timoney liked Daniel.

Daniel liked Miss Timoney too. He liked her honesty. In these days when every plaster duck was a Fabergé swan, Dimmock had antique shops, antique fayres and even an antiques emporium, but Miss Timoney's at the top of Fisher Hill was the only honest-to-God junk-shop left. The fact that, in an uncharacteristic moment of trying to move upmarket, she'd had the words *Ye Olde Junk Shoppe* written in a curly cod-medieval script over the top of the cobwebbed windows only endeared her to him more.

The dirty windows might have been a clever business ploy – it was impossible to see through them, if you wanted to know what she had for sale you had to go inside, at which point she considered you fair game. But they also made it impossible to see who else was in the shop, so opening the door was a little like opening Pandora's Box.

Today what came out as Daniel was going in was Noah Selkirk.

The thing about a black eye is, it's impossible for people to look at anything else. They try not to stare, then they worry that by ignoring the patently obvious they're actually drawing attention to it, then they avoid the issue entirely by being somewhere else. Usually; normal people.

Daniel's eyes widened behind his thick glasses. 'Good grief, Noah, where did you get the shiner?'

The boy reddened and wouldn't look at him. He mumbled something about a swing.

'Somebody took a swing at you?' said Daniel, astonished.

Unseen behind the dirty glass, a woman was following the boy onto the pavement. Not Miss Timoney; not by any means Miss Timoney. A woman in her late thirties with a mane of curly ash-blonde hair just about tamed in a rough chignon – which, as Daniel would have known had he known more about women, took much longer to achieve than a perfect one because the escaping tendrils didn't fall into that charming portrait of mild abandon without a lot of artistic encouragement. A small woman – not just smaller than Daniel but small for a woman – and neither thin nor plump but with just the right sort of curves in just the right places, just about visible through a straight, beautifully tailored, long wolf-grey coat buttoned up to a high stand collar under her chin. She had sea-green eyes, and when she smiled she showed small perfect teeth.

'He said, he was hit by a swing. In the playground.'

Daniel had seen a lot of playground accidents. He'd seen

children floored by the recoil of a swing going for the Olympic record, and the catalogue of possible injuries certainly included black eyes, as well as broken noses and broken cheekbones. There was nothing about the marks on Noah Selkirk's face that called his mother a liar. And yet...

Childhood is a steep learning curve. You learn not to run down stairs, not to touch the pretty flames and not to headbutt the patio doors mostly by doing it once and not liking the consequences. And yes, you learn not to stand behind a swing to see how high you've managed to push it this time. Most childhood injuries are accidental. Even kids who seem to spend every Saturday afternoon in A&E, whose parents know all the hidden parking spots and which vending machines make a decent cup of tea, who've already run the gamut of emotions from fear to embarrassment to grim resignation, are mostly just excitable and clumsy and brilliant at thinking up new stunts on a trampoline.

But hidden among those, sometimes quite well hidden, are a few whose injuries are ambiguous. Who might have walked into a doorknob, who might have trapped their fingers in a drawer, who might have picked up a lit cigarette, but who might not. Hospital staff develop an instinct for which they might be. So do teachers.

It was one of those crossroads moments. He could choose to believe a plausible explanation. He could express sympathy, advise caution in future, exchange a friendly nod with Noah's mother and go about his business; in which case he would probably never know the truth. Not about the grazed wrist; not about the black eye; and not whether it ended there. Noah Selkirk would never be taken into care because his drunken father laid into him in Woolworths one day. Nice prosperous middle-class families like the Selkirks don't wash their dirty linen in public. They may be no better at managing their anger but they can always control themselves until they're safely behind their large solid oak front doors. Children like Noah may be as likely to suffer violence as their friends from the sink estates, but the abuse is much less likely to be recognised. People can't quite believe it happens at the nice end of town.

If Daniel did nothing, probably no one else would either.

He put on his most ingenuous smile and didn't look at Noah again. 'You must be Mrs Selkirk. I'm Daniel Hood. I'm a maths teacher. I taught your son – rather briefly, events took an unexpected turn – at Dimmock High.'

So far, so truthful. He spared a moment to congratulate himself before continuing.

'I'm glad I've seen you, actually, I've been wanting a word. Not just with you – there were a number of children in that class that I felt showed real promise with mathematics. Can I walk you to your car? I'd like to make you aware of some of the options for children with a feel for the subject.'

It was a gamble. In truth, Daniel didn't remember anything about Noah except his face. He might have been a mathematical genius in the making; he might still have been counting on his fingers. If Marianne Selkirk had said, 'But Noah's *terrible* at maths!' he might have been hard pressed to continue the conversation. Fortunately, two truths are almost universal. Most people's abilities, at any age, fall somewhere in the middle; and most people's parents want to hear that their children are smart. However scant the evidence, if you tell them their offspring have talent they want to believe you.

As soon as Mrs Selkirk smiled, Daniel knew he was in business. 'Actually, we were going for a coffee now. Would you like to join us?'

They ended up back in The Singing Kettle. It wasn't the only café in Dimmock, but perhaps it was the most genteel.

Gentility wasn't something that mattered much to Daniel. Usually he used it because it was across the road from his house. Today he'd have picnicked in an abattoir if that was what it took to make the acquaintance of the Selkirk family.

Perhaps what he was doing was dishonest. He was ingratiating himself with the woman in order to gain her confidence. Only his purpose went some way towards justifying his actions. If he was right about what was happening to Noah, and if he could find a way of helping this family before the situation deteriorated beyond the aid of a well-meaning busy-body, it would have been worth it. If not, he'd be left feeling like a pimp.

But Daniel would always take risks himself that he wouldn't countenance in others. And once he had an idea in his head it was almost impossible to shift it. Certainly neither the fear of embarrassment, nor fear itself, would do the trick.

As much as he could he avoided looking at Noah. He knew the boy had been terrified, from the moment they met in Edith Timoney's doorway, that he was going to blurt out an account of their last meeting. He wasn't, and by the time they reached The Singing Kettle Noah seemed to understand that he wasn't, but the boy still needed leaving alone to steady his nerve. So Daniel did what he never did, and talked over his head as if the child wasn't there.

'I was pleased at how well that whole class were able to grapple with mathematical concepts. You may be aware, there's real concern in education circles that too many children of perfectly adequate intelligence are leaving school without a grasp of the fundamental skills. So I wasn't expecting to find myself talking astro-physics with a bunch of twelve-year-olds.'

Marianne Selkirk smiled. 'Noah told me about that class, Mr Hood. He said it was the first time he realised maths could be interesting.'

Daniel demurred with a modest little shrug. 'To be honest, Mrs Selkirk, I'm a maths bore. I bang on about how fascinating it is and never notice people's eyes turning glassy. But kids at that age, they're open to the wonder of it. They *want* to hear about how stars form, and how the cosmos formed, and how we *know*. They're the perfect audience.'

'That doesn't seem to be the universal experience of maths teachers,' observed Mrs Selkirk dryly. 'I suspect you're rather good at it. So what was it,' she asked then, putting him on the spot, 'that you wanted to talk about? You're not telling me Noah's the next Steven Hawking?'

Daniel laughed dutifully, using the time to think. 'Who knows? I don't expect they thought Steven Hawking was, when he was twelve. But actually, it's not geniuses – genii? – that I worry about. If you have that kind of remarkable mind, you're always going to make use of it. If a rather moderate education leading to an appointment as a patent clerk wasn't enough to stultify Einstein's mind there's no reason to suppose other geni— ...clever people spend their lives sweeping floors because their talents go unrecognised.

'No, what worries me is when ordinarily bright kids decide they can't do maths because it's obscure and difficult and unrewarding. Because a GCSE in History of Art might be easier to get but it won't open the same doors. This is an increasingly technological world, and it's not going to get any simpler. We're already at the point where people who understand the technology have the world at their fingertips. Yet fewer kids, not more, are studying maths and the sciences. We're going to end up with a real skills shortage. And people like Noah, and the other kids in that class, could fill that gap and end up running the world because of it.'

Every word of it was true, and it was a cause that Daniel believed in passionately. But today he didn't care about Noah Selkirk's future. He could be an art historian if he wanted; he could publish religious pamphlets or play piano in a bordello. Right now all Daniel cared about was what the boy was going home to tonight.

It's a tricky business, interfering with a family dynamic. There are more ways of making things worse than making them better. Probably the only reason even a determined do-gooder should get involved is to protect someone who can't protect himself and who can't leave.

And he knew that if he asked Noah outright whether his father was hitting him, the answer would be no. Because the heartbreaking fact is that there is almost nothing a parent can do that will stop a child wanting his love and approval. Another blow, another kick – that's something he's familiar with. Breaking up the family is the unknown, and that really scares him. He would genuinely rather suffer in silence than face the unknown.

Daniel realised Marianne Selkirk was watching him, curiously, her head a little on one side like a bird's. 'Where's this going, Mr Hood? It wouldn't be that you give lessons in maths and you just happen to have a vacancy?'

Daniel coloured so violently that, outside, he'd have confused low-flying aircraft. 'That isn't what I was saying. I just wanted…'

Seeing his embarrassment, Marianne thought she'd misjudged him. 'I'm sorry,' she smiled. 'I asked because, if you're willing to tutor Noah, I'd be interested.'

Which was exactly what Daniel had been hoping for. He hadn't expected to feel so humiliated by his success. He didn't know what to do now, what to say.

But the bottom line was the same. He thought the boy needed his help, and this was a way to give it without anyone knowing that Noah himself had made the first move. If that meant being taken for a snake-oil salesman, Daniel didn't suppose that in the grand scheme of things it was too high a price to pay.

Mrs Selkirk was waiting for a response. He'd have to say something. 'We've been a little at cross-purposes. It's my fault: I have this habit of expecting people to read my mind. No, I wasn't really suggesting that Noah needs a tutor. He's smart, and he gets good teaching at school. I just wanted to encourage him, and you, to see that maths could offer him a good future, to keep it up and keep his options open while he thinks about a career.

'But if you want to get him extra help, that's not a problem. I used to do a bit of tutoring. If you like, I could come to your house for a couple of hours some evening and let's see if it does any good.'

Marianne Selkirk looked at her son. 'What do you think?' But the boy wasn't volunteering an opinion. Perhaps volunteering an opinion wasn't a wise move in the Selkirk household.

The woman smiled back at Daniel. 'It's a good offer, Mr Hood, and we'd be foolish not to take advantage of it. I'll be going up to town on Monday. Would you be free tonight?'

CHAPTER NINE

'Al Capone,' observed Detective Inspector Hyde, entirely out of the blue so far as Voss could judge, 'went down for tax evasion.'

'Did he?' said Voss carefully. Caution was his default position when he didn't know where something was leading.

Hyde nodded. 'The dogs in the street knew he was a gangster, but the authorities couldn't prove it. But they *could* prove he fiddled his income tax.'

Voss supposed there was a moral to the story. 'Honesty is the best policy?'

Alix Hyde chuckled. 'Indeed it is, Charlie. And the other thing to remember is, there's more than one way to skin a cat.'

Voss considered. 'You mean, if we can't get Terry Walsh through the front door we should see if he's left a back window open?'

Hyde liked that. 'Exactly. It's no use sending the cavalry after him if he's going to see them coming a mile off. But maybe an Indian scout could sneak up behind him without being noticed.'

Voss had seen that film. He remembered what happened to the scout. 'It could be risky. He's an affable villain, but maybe only when he's got nothing to worry about. Maybe not so much if he's cornered.'

'Then we'd better be ready for him,' said Hyde briskly, 'because one way or another I intend to corner him. Front door, back window, Indian scout or Inland Revenue, I mean to have his head on my wall.' She paused a moment, frowning. 'Where the hell did all these metaphors come from?'

'A metaphor shower?' murmured Voss.

Hyde wasn't listening. She was planning. 'So we can't use Susan Weekes. What *can* we use?'

It needed saying, and Voss was the only one who was going to say it. 'The one who knows him best is Superintendent Deacon.'

Hyde's jaw rose in a way that, in a man, would have been described as pugnacious. 'He might know, Charlie, but can we count on him to share his knowledge? I think we're on our own.'

There were drawbacks to working for Deacon. Voss had been warned of every one of them when he drew the short straw. But there were advantages too. The man was a damned good detective, and someone wanting to learn the trade could do worse than watch him closely. And Voss had always felt he knew where he was with Deacon. That he could be relied on. Yes, he could be relied on to shout a lot, and be inventively unpleasant at the least provocation. But also to hold the line between good and evil if it took every ounce of strength and every drop of courage he possessed. He didn't tolerate laziness, sloppiness or lack of commitment in others because he'd have quit the job rather than do it that way himself. No one believed him, but Voss felt privileged to work for someone who in so many ways – just not in all of them – was an outstanding police officer.

Now, almost for the first time, he wasn't sure where he stood with Deacon. He found it hard to believe the Superintendent was putting a childhood friendship ahead of his duty, but to someone who didn't know him – to Detective Inspector Hyde, for example – it could have looked that way. And Voss felt like a toy they'd been told to share nicely by an adult who had then left the room.

Hyde went on: 'What I know about Terry Walsh is what's on the record, and if it wasn't enough before there's no reason to suppose it will be now. But you're the local man, Charlie. Everything you've heard about him won't be on the record. It won't seem terribly relevant, some of it – off-the-cuff things Walsh has said, things people have said about him, maybe some things Deacon has said – not even about his activities so much as the man. I can't tell you what I'm looking for because I don't know what there is. But you have an instinct for this job, I know that already. The sort of thing I'm looking for, you'll know it when you see it. Think, Charlie. What can you tell me about Terry Walsh that might give us a way in?'

Voss knew a few things that weren't on the record. The problem was, most of them were to Walsh's credit. When he wasn't being a crime magnate he was a good husband and father, a good employer, a good neighbour. And at least once he'd put himself out to help Deacon in a personal crisis, one man to another. Part of Voss would be sorry when Walsh finally got his comeuppance. Though it wouldn't stop the rest of him joining the celebrations at The Belted Galloway.

He said slowly, 'There's one thing. A scam Mr Deacon told

me he used to pull when he was starting out.' And he explained the *doppelgänger* fraud.

Like Deacon, like Voss himself, Alix Hyde had a struggle to contain her admiration. 'So he went round selling people their own goods. That was...'

'Reprehensible,' said Voss, straight-faced.

'Yes. Thank you, Charlie, that's exactly the word I was looking for.' She thought about it. 'And – in a reprehensible sort of way – witty. I'm not sure how it's going to help us. But one day it may. One day it very well may.'

He was on his way back to his own office when he heard the sudden laugh behind him and turned back, startled, to see Alix Hyde grinning at him. 'A metaphor shower indeed, Charlie Voss!'

Marianne Selkirk was waiting with coffee and homemade buns when Daniel arrived at the big house on River Drive at seven o'clock. She showed him into the sitting room. There was no sign of her husband.

'This is very good of you, Mr Hood,' said Noah's mother. 'I'm afraid I rather hijacked you this morning. We still have to come to a proper arrangement.' She meant talk about his fees.

Daniel shook his head. 'This one's on me. If you want to do it again, I can quote you some figures. I'm not expensive. I love maths and I love teaching. Events have conspired to keep me from doing it at the moment but I hope to get back to it. In the meantime, I'm glad of the chance to keep my hand in. And please, call me Daniel.'

She did the bird-like tip of the head again. 'Not Dan?'

He shrugged, self-conscious. 'No one's ever thought I *looked* like a Dan. All the others are six feet tall with Army boots and tattoos.'

She laughed, a light sound like the tinkling of little silver bells. 'Danny, then.'

Daniel restrained himself. 'Do you know what it was that set Napoleon on the path of world domination? It was people calling him Nappy.'

Half-hidden behind a blueberry muffin, Noah was starting to relax. His nerves had been screwed as tight as wire when Daniel arrived. But these easy, friendly exchanges were reassuring him. Daniel thought he'd been dreading this all day, and now he was beginning to enjoy it.

'Did you mind?' asked Daniel when they were alone. 'Being button-holed outside the junk shop? If you did, if you want me to mind my own business, I will. But I thought I saw a chance to help so I went for it. *Did* you mind?'

Noah had closed the study door as soon as they'd gone in, shutting out the rest of the house. It was his father's study: the boy had permission to use it for serious purposes only. And you can't get more serious than doing extra maths on your own time.

'No,' he said after a moment. 'I did at first. I thought you were going to get me into trouble.'

'That's the last thing I want,' Daniel said quietly.

'I know. I figured it out. You made friends with my mother so you could talk to her without it seeming like it came from me.'

Daniel nodded, impressed. 'That's pretty sophisticated thinking for a twelve-year-old.'

Noah gave a solemn smile. 'My dad says I'm only twelve on the outside.'

Daniel laughed. 'Do you want to know something? I'm *still* twelve on the inside.'

He wanted to ask about the bruises but knew it was the last thing he must mention, that there was no surer way of making the boy clam up and never trust him again. 'Is your dad still working?'

'A client needed him.' The reply was at once so grown-up and so wistful that Daniel felt the words in his heart.

'I suppose it goes with the job,' he said. 'Clients who *don't* need their solicitor won't pay many bills.'

This was not a stupid boy. He looked up from the desk, his eyes both surprised and wary. 'How do you know he's a solicitor?'

'Didn't you tell me?' would be the easy way out, for someone who didn't mind bending the truth. 'My friend – the one I work for – knows him. She was married to a solicitor.'

Noah's brown eyes flared with concern. 'Were you talking about me?'

'No,' Daniel said immediately. 'We saw you in the café. Brodie said she knew your father, slightly. I said I'd taught you in a class once. That's all.'

Noah believed him. The habit of honesty hung about him like the smell of old books, worthy if a little fusty. 'OK.'

Daniel had brought some books with him, piled them on the desk. 'What does your mother do?'

'She makes money.' When Daniel laughed the boy looked taken aback. For a bright child he hadn't much sense of humour. 'No, really. For a charity. African Sunrise. It's her job to raise lots of money for them so that they can give it out where it's needed. She's very good at it. Her bosses say she saves a million lives every year. Imagine that. Doctors save a patient and everyone's impressed. Firemen save a family and they're heroes. But my mum saves a million lives every year, by raising money.'

'You must be very proud of her,' said Daniel.

'Oh yes,' said Noah enthusiastically. Then his face fell. 'Only…'

Daniel waited a moment before prompting him. 'Only?'

'I wish she was home more. I know what she does is important. I know people would die if she stopped doing it. But it takes a lot of time, and when she gets home she's tired. I wish…' He let the sentence peter out as if embarrassed to finish it.

Daniel said quietly, 'What do you wish, Noah?'

There was a lot of guilt and a note of defiance in the boy's voice. 'I wish she'd save half a million people a year and spend more time with me!'

Daniel's heart gave a little twist within him. He nodded sympathetically. 'I bet you do. Noah, it's all right to feel like that. She's your mum: of course you want her here. And I'd bet every penny I own – which, admittedly, wouldn't take you much further than Bognor – that she'd rather be here than working. That if it came to a straight choice between those million people and you, a lot of people would be in an awful lot of trouble.

'But we all end up making compromises. A million people in Africa with not enough to eat *do* matter, and people like your mum give them the hope of a better future. She doesn't want to let them down. So she tries to do both – to be an effective fundraiser *and* an ace mum. I don't suppose she manages to do both all the time. Which of us could?'

Noah cast him a grateful look. It wasn't that he was being told anything he hadn't heard before. It was that Daniel understood. Understood and didn't judge: neither him nor his mother.

'At least your dad works in Dimmock,' said Daniel casually. 'Maybe you see more of him than some kids do.'

'Mm,' said Noah pensively.

'Or does he work late a lot and come home tired too?'

'It works both ways,' the boy said honestly. 'Sometimes he's home when other fathers are working. If my mother's up in town he tries to work from home.'

'That's nice,' said Daniel. 'Isn't it?'

'He can be pretty grumpy when he's working,' admitted Noah.

Daniel nodded and kept his tone light. They were getting close to the heart of the problem and he didn't want to scare the boy off by pouncing. 'Lots of people are. They don't mean to be. They get tired and frustrated, then they snap at the person closest to them. In an office that's a colleague, at home it's their family.'

'I don't mind,' said Noah stoutly. 'He does lots for me too.'

'I'm sure he does. What do you like doing together?'

But Noah couldn't think of anything. 'Whatever he wants to, really.'

Daniel felt he'd pushed far enough. He opened a book. 'Well, today you get to choose what we do. But what I'm really *good* at – and I may have mentioned this – is anything to do with space.'

* * *

Brodie tried Daniel's number but there was no reply. She gritted her teeth. Whatever his personal inclination, now he was working for her he was going to have to carry a mobile phone. She waited for the tone to leave a message but then couldn't think what to say. So she rang off.

She might have called Deacon then. After all, it was more his business than Daniel's. But she didn't want an interrogation and she didn't want an argument, and he'd already made it pretty clear that this scrap of life within her provoked about as much paternal feeling in him as a house-brick.

So when Paddy was settled for the night – at least ostensibly settled, in fact reading a book about monster trucks – she went upstairs and tapped on Marta's door. 'Fancy coming down for a coffee?'

She struck lucky. In spite of being a tall and bony Polish piano teacher in her mid-fifties with a hit-and-miss approach to the English language, Marta Szarabeijka could not be counted on to be at home on a Saturday night. She had a long-term, casual, undemanding but mutually satisfying relationship with a jazz trumpeter and corner-shop keeper called Duncan in Littlehampton, and together they made music that – if not always sweet – was reliably loud.

Tonight Duncan must have had other plans, because Marta answered the door in her dressing-gown, her hair turbaned in a towel and nothing on her feet. Five minutes later she was folded into Brodie's armchair like a stork sitting on a nest, drying her long grey hair.

'So what's the problem?' she asked, the accent thick in her mouth warring for *Lebensraum* with Brodie's gingerbread.

Brodie shook her head decisively. 'Nothing.'

'Yeah, right,' said Marta, with the air of someone who'd been here before. 'You just couldn't do without my company a minute longer.'

Brodie smiled slowly. 'Something like that.'

'Come on.' The older woman helped herself to more gingerbread. 'Tell your Aunty Marta.'

They'd known one another for three years, since Brodie bought the flat under Marta's in the big Victorian house on Chiffney Road. It was not, on the face of it, a friendship made in heaven. They were of different generations, different backgrounds. One had a young child, the other had never wanted children. One needed her home as a quiet retreat, the other gave lessons to some of England's least talented pianists. Neither woman was particularly good at making friends, and for the same reason: neither had any reserves of tolerance.

Yet, unpredictably, they'd clicked. As a good-looking woman Brodie had always had more male admirers than women friends: for her it was a new and invigorating experience. And Marta found she enjoyed being a substitute granny to Paddy. She didn't mind children as long as she could give them back when she'd had enough of them.

There are things women say to their women friends that they couldn't say even to close family. Brodie said quietly, 'I think there's something wrong.'

Fertile, sterile, empty-nester or cover-girl for the contraceptives industry, it doesn't matter. Some things are built in at a genetic level. When a woman with a bump out front says that, any other woman knows instantly what's on her mind. Marta put her cup down and held Brodie's eyes with her own. 'With the baby?'

'Yes.'

'Why?'

Brodie shook her head. 'No reason. Just a feeling.'

'They said something at the hospital?'

'Not a thing. All the tests came back fine.'

'So...what? You think the tests were wrong? You think something's gone wrong since?'

'I suppose not.' But her eyes were clouded, her voice doubtful. 'Does everything show up on the tests?'

Marta raised an angular eyebrow. 'You're asking me? What I know about babies is they're noisy at one end and messy at the other. But maybe there wouldn't be much point doing all those tests if they missed things like the baby has two heads!'

A shade uneasily, Brodie chuckled. 'I think even I'd have seen two heads on the ultra-sound.'

She was making a joke of it but Marta knew it wasn't funny. Not to Brodie, not right now. 'But something has you worried. You think maybe it's just a phase of the pregnancy, like morning sickness? That it's hormones?'

'Could be,' allowed Brodie. 'But I didn't feel...'

'...This way with Paddy,' finished Marta, her voice a mocking sing-song as she picked up her coffee again. 'Brodie, how many times you got to be told? You're older now, and you're on your own. You got no one to share the responsibility with. Naturally you worry more.'

Brodie was regarding her with a mixture of irony and affection. 'No, don't spare my feelings,' she murmured, 'tell it like it is.'

Marta snorted a laugh into her cup. 'You're waiting for me to feel sorry for you, you gonna wait a while. You could have had Jack – you could have married him if you'd wanted. You could have had someone else. You're doing this alone because this is what you chose.'

'I didn't choose to split with Jack,' objected Brodie.

'You chose your independence, which comes to the same thing. You could have him back tomorrow. You know that. You go to him and say, "I'm scared about the future, I need help raising this child, will you marry me?" and you and me both know he would. Are you going to?'

'No,' said Brodie in a low voice.

'Of course no,' nodded Marta. 'Nobody thought yes. Not me, not Jack. But there's a price to pay for independence: it's called Loneliness. I don't think there's anything wrong with your baby. I think you're just feeling lonely.'

Brodie would have walked barefoot over hot coals rather than admit it. 'I don't think so!'

Marta nodded, complacently spraying crumbs. 'Of course lonely. Everyone feels lonely sometimes. The only difference between single people and married people is single people got the time to think how they feel. All you need, girl, is a good night out.'

'Oh sure,' growled Brodie. 'Let's fix a date. About six months from now, when I can get back into any dress I'd be seen dead in.'

'You look fine. And you don't need to get rendered to have a good night out.' She meant plastered. 'You and me've had some damn good nights when neither of us could *afford* to get rendered. What about it? Ask Daniel to babysit one night and you and me'll go paint the town.'

It was a tempting offer. And maybe Marta was right.

Maybe she was doing too much navel-gazing. 'Red,' she added absently.

'What?'

'We could paint the town red.'

Marta looked puzzled. 'Why would we do that? I don't *really* mean we should paint anything. I mean, we should hang out in bars and flutter our eyelashes a lot.'

Brodie laughed. She really *had* had some good nights out with Marta, mainly because the woman was incapable of being embarrassed. And there was this to be said for it. However unlikely it was that a pregnant woman in a little black sack was going to pull, at least she wouldn't suffer the indignity of having all the talent in the place cluster around her friend. Probably not, anyway.

She grinned. 'You could try your luck as a Pole dancer.'

CHAPTER TEN

On Monday morning Charlie Voss was at the office before eight. He still found Detective Inspector Hyde waiting for him. It wasn't an entirely new experience: when there was a push on Deacon often looked as if he'd slept at his desk. At least Alix Hyde looked as though she'd been home for a shower.

'Has something happened, ma'am?'

She lowered a well-shaped eyebrow at him. 'Don't call me Ma'am, Charlie – I'm not the Queen and I don't teach in a two-room schoolhouse. I'm comfortable with Alix; if you're feeling formal you can call me Boss. And the answer to your question is, yes and no. Nothing's happened. But I've had an idea. About Susan Weekes.'

She saw Voss trying not to blink and chuckled. 'Don't worry, Charlie, I'm not stupid. I know Susan's evidence is never going to nail Walsh. That doesn't necessarily mean she's lying. Maybe she was his mistress, maybe she wasn't, but we do know she worked at the casino. She could still be right about The Dragon Luck – that Walsh uses it to meet people he doesn't want coming to his office to talk about things he doesn't want overheard.'

Even a habitual liar doesn't lie about everything.

Somewhere in all the dross could be a nugget of gold. The difficulty would be finding it. 'But who's going to tell us about it? None of the people Walsh does that kind of business with. And if Caroline Walsh owns a slice of it, no one at the casino either. Susan was a fluke – she had even more to lose by keeping quiet than by talking.'

Hyde shrugged. 'If a week is a long time in politics, it's an eternity in our business. Allegiances change. Some of the people who worked for Walsh in the past may have moved on to other things. Some of them may have seen enough to know what he was up to and know they wanted no part of it. If we found someone like that – someone with a reputation to protect, someone who got out and wants to stay out – and applied just enough of the right kind of pressure, we might get something back.'

Voss was thinking about Al Capone again. 'I suppose, like any businessman, he'll have had professional advisers. He'd need accountants, if only for the bulk paper side. I can find out who. But even if they had suspicions about a set of books they weren't being shown, I can't see them wanting to talk about it.'

'There are limits to client privilege. Especially where money laundering is involved.'

Voss wasn't convinced. 'This is Terry Walsh we're talking about, boss. Love him or loathe him, you've got to admit he's smart. He'll *know* that. I can't see him leaving himself vulnerable. He'll have made sure of the loyalty of anyone in a position to hurt him.'

'I'm sure that was his intention,' agreed Hyde. 'However, the best-laid plans... Somewhere out there is someone who knows about Terry Walsh's business – his *other* business – and who might be persuaded to talk to us. I don't know if we can find him, but I do know we won't find him without looking. So let's give it a shot. Track down and talk to everyone who left his employment within, say, the last two years. See if you can find someone who left because he didn't like the way Terry works. Who knows he should have done something about it at the time, and didn't, and could be encouraged to do it now in his own best interests.'

Voss was pretty sure he knew what she meant. But some things you want in words of one syllable. 'You want me to cut him a deal?'

Detective Inspector Hyde gave an aloof smile. 'We don't do deals, Charlie, you know that. But we do have limits to work within – limits of time, money and manpower. Frying big fish is a better use of limited resources than frying little ones. Tell him that.'

Though they weren't all one-syllable words, it was clear enough. 'I'll get on to it then.'

Hyde nodded. 'You do that, Charlie Voss.'

The Vestigial Virgins' night out was planned for Wednesday evening. Marta coined the term. Brodie wasn't sure if she was being witty or just playing fast and loose with the English language, and also didn't care. She was in the mood to have as much fun as you can on a glass of fizzy orange and a packet of salt-reduced crisps.

Daniel was going home with her to babysit, so neither of them had any intention of working late. Brodie had been in Worthing, searching through church records for evidence that the wealthy but childless Colesworths of Maine were fruit of the same family tree as the impecunious but relentlessly fertile Cogglesworths of Dimmock's Woodgreen Estate. She got back soon after four and at half five they were ready to shut up shop. Brodie was reaching for her car keys when there was a knock at the door.

She glanced at it in irritation. 'I'll see who it is. If it's going to take long I'll get them to come back tomorrow.'

It was a large man in an expensive overcoat, and he seemed to fill not only Brodie's doorstep but half of Shack Lane. 'Mrs Farrell.'

'Mr Selkirk,' she said, surprised. 'How are you? I don't believe we've spoken since the Civic Ball three – no, four – years ago. Are you still dancing?'

A large frame, a florid face and an expansive manner all conspired to add years to Adam Selkirk. Brodie knew he was a contemporary of John's – he might have been forty by now, he wouldn't have been older. But the body language suggested a man in his fifties. He had an ICBM of a voice pitched to echo around courtrooms, but just now it was low, his chins on his chest, his eyes reproachful. 'I did apologise for that at the time.'

'Of course you did,' said Brodie generously. 'And I grew a new toenail. And the shoes were the most glamorous thing in Oxfam for weeks.' Seeing his discomfiture she relented and held the door open. 'Are you coming in? I have to go soon, but I can always find five minutes for a man with more left feet than a centipede.'

Sometimes she meant to be rude, sometimes it happened naturally. Sometimes what she thought of as a pleasantry was perceived by others as rudeness. She got away with it mainly because people who are offended by rudeness worry that it might be rude to say so.

Adam Selkirk said nothing because his mind was on other things. He was peering round the tiny lobby as if what he'd come here looking for might be lurking behind the hat-stand. 'I'm looking for someone,' he said gruffly.

'Ah,' said Brodie. 'Well, that might be a problem. You see, we're called Looking for Some*thing*? If you've lost some*body*, perhaps the Salvation Army could help.'

'Hood,' said Selkirk tersely. He spotted the door to the inner office and reached for it without pretending to seek permission. 'I'm looking for a man called Hood.'

It was too late to stop him, even if she'd thought it necessary. 'What a coincidence,' she said. 'I have one right here.'

At the sound of his name Daniel left off filing and moved towards the lobby. It was a very small office, three good strides took you from end to end, so they met in the doorway, the big man looking down, the small one looking up. 'I'm Daniel Hood. Can I help you?'

'Do you know who I am?'

Daniel regarded him calmly. 'Yes. But it would probably be polite to introduce yourself anyway.'

'Polite?' echoed Adam Selkirk. There was a timbre in his voice that reminded Brodie of Deacon. Specifically, of Deacon too angry to shout. 'We'll talk about polite in a minute. We'll talk about the etiquette of worming your way into someone's home and coming between the members of a family. We'll talk about using a child as a jemmy to force doors that wouldn't otherwise be open to you. But first, let's get our facts straight. Are you responsible for this?'

He struck Daniel on the chest with a fist containing a crumpled sheet of paper. Daniel took it.

It was a letter. It was a brief and to-the-point letter, because its author was conscious of the importance of other people's time. It was written in his best handwriting, and must have been copied out because there were no mistakes. It was signed with exquisite formality, 'Your loving son.'

Daniel felt the tears pricking at his eyes. He went on holding the letter as if it were something precious. 'Oh, I do hope so,' he murmured.

It wasn't the response Selkirk had been expecting. For just a moment he didn't know what to say. Then: 'What's the *meaning* of it?'

Daniel looked up at him. 'Mr Selkirk, isn't it pretty *clear* what he means? He's saying your behaviour is making him unhappy. He's asking you to reconsider your priorities to make more time for him. He knows both you and Mrs Selkirk have important jobs, he knows you can't organise your entire lives around him, but right now the only thing he feels to be getting his fair share of is stress. I think that about covers it.' He glanced at the letter, then up again, looking Selkirk full in the eyes. 'Oh yes. And, he loves you.'

All Brodie knew of this was what she'd been able to glean in the last two minutes. She guessed, now, that there'd been a reason for Daniel's interest in the Selkirk family that day in The Singing Kettle, and she'd have given odds it had something to do with Daniel being a sucker for a hard-luck story.

What she knew for sure was that when large men of florid complexion actually turn purple, a stroke is an imminent possibility. She touched his shoulder. 'Adam, why don't you sit down while we talk about this?'

He brushed her off like swatting a mosquito. 'I don't *need* to sit down because we're not *going* to talk about this. I came to tell *him*' – his eyes stabbed at Daniel – 'that I don't want him in my house again. Stay away from my wife, stay away from my son. I promise you, there is nothing – *nothing* – you can tell me about my family that I don't already know. If I find you've been bothering either of them again, I'll have the police round here.' He spared a glance for Brodie. 'You know I can do it. You know I *will* do it.'

Her attempt to play the peace-maker had been rebuffed. It wasn't a natural role for her, nothing in her better nature prompted her to try again. Instead she felt her own temper rising. 'The police are welcome to come here any time they like. If it's any help, I have Detective Superintendent Deacon's number on speed-dial.

'But I think you've already made one mistake and you're about to make a bigger one. Whatever you think Daniel's done, I'm pretty sure it's nothing to be ashamed of. And if you go to the police and accuse him of an unprovoked act of kindness, we'll be able to hear the laughter from here.'

'Besides which,' said Daniel, very softly, 'you aren't going anywhere near the police, are you?'

Brodie might not have known what he meant but Selkirk did. Sheer fury contorted his face. His fists balled at his sides. His voice was a kind of whispered shout. 'I don't know what you think you know about me, little man,' he snarled, 'but either it isn't right or it isn't enough. You don't want to take me on. You'd lose, and it would hurt. Much better to admit you got it wrong, and go peddle your do-gooding somewhere else.'

Daniel was nodding slowly. 'Well, maybe I would lose,' he agreed. 'I usually do. And maybe it would hurt. It usually does. But what you're forgetting, Mr Selkirk, is that – little or not – I'm a grown man. You may find it harder than you're expecting, imposing your will on someone who doesn't owe you anything, who doesn't depend on you for anything, and who doesn't give a shit whether you're annoyed.'

Brodie looked at him in astonishment. Daniel's idea of bad language was shaped by the 1950s sensibilities of the grandparents who raised him. It was a rare day she heard anything cross his lips that would be unseemly in a little girl. But it wasn't just the S-word: it was the sudden venom in his voice that startled her. Daniel didn't go in for hatred. In his time he'd managed not to hate a lot of people he'd been entitled to, including her. But that sudden edge on his voice, and the sudden diamond hardness in his weak grey eyes, could hardly have come from anywhere else.

'So I'll stay out of your house if that's what you want. But I won't stay away from your son, and if you make it impossible for me to know whether he's safe and well I'll take my concerns to the authorities. I don't care how important you are, Mr Selkirk. I don't care what you do or who you know, you're not entitled to take out your frustrations on a twelve-year-old boy. Machinery exists to make sure you don't. It's easier to start that machinery than to stop it, so now would be a good time to start treating your son with the respect he's due. He's a child, not a punch-bag.'

So that was it. Immediately Brodie thought she should have guessed. She could hardly think of any other crime the man could have committed that would have provoked her friend to such wrath. She said quietly, 'Is this true, Adam?'

He shrugged with his whole big body. 'Of course it's not true,' he said roughly. 'I love my son. He loves me.'

'Bizarrely enough,' said Daniel, his mouth twisting as if on a bad taste, 'despite the bruises that are there for the whole town to see, I know he does. Children can forgive anything. That doesn't mean they should be asked to. I'm absolutely serious about this, Mr Selkirk. You sort this out, or I'll sort it for you.'

Selkirk loomed over him like an act of God. 'Is that meant to be a *threat*?'

The traditional answer, of course, is, 'No, it's a promise.' 'No, it's a warning,' is also a time-honoured riposte. But Daniel didn't watch a lot of popular television. He watched programmes from the Open University. He said simply, 'Yes'.

Solicitors deal with a lot of different people; a lot of different sorts of people. But Selkirk had never come across anyone quite like Daniel before. He wasn't sure what his next move was. He barked a savage little laugh, mainly to cover his confusion. 'I've said what I came here to say. Leave me and my family alone. I won't tell you again.'

Daniel considered. 'I've said pretty much what I've been wanting to say as well. Noah is your son, but he doesn't belong to you. Other people care what happens to him. I'm one of them. The next time – the *very* next time – I see the print of your fist on his face, your chance to resolve this problem discreetly is over. Then I guess we'll both find out how influential a lawyer is after the law's had to step in to stop him beating his child.'

When Adam Selkirk had stalked off, while the burgundy front door was still vibrating on its hinges, Brodie turned to Daniel with arched eyebrows. 'Stay away from my wife?' she echoed.

Daniel shrugged uncomfortably. 'I think he got that wrong.'

'You *think* he got that wrong?'

Terry Walsh's accountants were the London firm of Findhorn & Carraway. Voss made an appointment to see the senior partner and travelled up to town in the late afternoon, as everyone else was coming the other way.

Mr Findhorn greeted him with polite wariness and set about walking the tightrope between client confidence and public obligation. 'What you must understand, Sergeant, is that I am not at liberty to discuss client affairs except where expressly required to do so by legal authority.'

'I do understand that,' Voss assured him. 'What you have to understand is that these are not trivial matters. I'm not interested in whether he claimed his wife's car against his income tax or wrote off his daughter's pony as a business expense. I'm investigating matters specifically designated as serious organised crime.'

Findhorn should have been shocked at the very suggestion. Perhaps he was just good at hiding his feelings, but Voss thought it wasn't the first time he'd heard it.

He could have declined to answer any questions until Voss produced lawful authority. The fact that he didn't suggested

Findhorn wasn't going to hold the pass for Terry Walsh. Soon it became clear why. 'I'll be as helpful as I can. If there are some questions I can't answer, it's not because I want to obstruct your inquiry. But we owe all our clients' – the words *even Terry Walsh* didn't actually cross his lips but that was what he meant – 'a duty of confidentiality that doesn't end when we cease to act for them.'

Voss pricked an ear at that. 'Mr Walsh has changed his accountants? When?'

'He closed his account with us last July.'

'Why?'

Mr Findhorn's smile was wintry. 'He felt it was in his interests to set up an in-house accountancy department.'

'After you'd done his books for – how long?'

'Some twelve years,' said Findhorn.

'What made him want a change?'

'There was...a little unpleasantness,' admitted the accountant.

It was after nine when Voss got back to Battle Alley. But Detective Inspector Hyde was still at her desk so he told her what he'd found out. 'Findhorn's firm were Walsh's accountants but it wasn't Findhorn handling the account, or even Carraway, but a guy called Leslie Vernon. He lives in Worthing so it made sense.'

'You said "was",' said Hyde. Voss had her full attention.

'Yes. Three things happened. Vernon stopped being Terry Walsh's accountant. He left Findhorn's firm. And Walsh set up his own accounts department. In July – seven months ago.'

Hyde was frowning, trying to piece it together. 'What

changed? Walsh has been in the paper business for fifteen years – if using chartered accountants was good enough for the first fourteen, what changed in June?'

'Findhorn described it as a bit of unpleasantness. He claimed not to know the details but Walsh and Vernon stopped seeing eye to eye. Findhorn blamed Vernon and let him go. Maybe he thought Walsh would reconsider if he offered Vernon's head as reparations. But Terry had already made other arrangements.'

Hyde was watching the rerun on the inward cinema screen that was her mind's eye. 'So after years of a mutually satisfactory business relationship, suddenly Walsh and his accountant were at odds. In an effort to keep his business, Vernon's employers sided with the client, but Walsh had had enough of sharing his secrets with outsiders. What do you suppose they fell out about?'

'That'll be my first question,' said Voss, 'when I see Mr Vernon tomorrow.'

If it had been Deacon, he'd have asked, 'Why not tonight?' But Alix Hyde used a little less stick, a little more carrot. 'Nice work, Charlie. I have a good feeling about this.'

Voss was worried about disappointing her. 'We shouldn't count our chickens yet, boss. They may not have fallen out over Walsh's activities. Maybe Vernon just isn't a very good accountant.'

Hyde shook her head decisively. 'If Vernon was no good Findhorn wouldn't have put him in charge of Terry's account. No – Vernon saw something or heard something he didn't like. He challenged Terry on it and Terry pulled the rug out from under his feet.' She let her gaze wander off round the room as she thought about it. 'A man would naturally feel aggrieved about that, Charlie. Losing his job because of a crook. I bet, given a bit of encouragement, he'll tell you all about it.'

She picked up her coat and headed for the door. 'You earned your pay today, Charlie Voss,' she said appreciatively. 'Earn it again tomorrow.'

CHAPTER ELEVEN

In the event, the girls' night out wasn't quite the riot that had been planned. Brodie explained what had happened before she closed the office up, and Marta plumbed her vocabulary for epithets appropriate to violent men, to men in general and to lawyers in particular. Which cleared the air nicely but didn't restore the necessary mood. So they had a meal, and Marta fluttered her eyelashes gamely at a couple of puzzled commercial travellers, and they went home about eleven.

Brodie found Daniel at the computer in the corner of her living room. One glance at the screen told her what he'd been doing. He'd also printed out a number of articles relating to child abuse.

'You're going on with this then,' she said quietly.

He sat back, nodding. He wasn't angry any more. His pale round face was calm and determined, and Brodie knew that when he looked like that you could bounce bricks off his obstinacy.

'I have to,' he said simply. 'He's a child, Brodie. He's twelve years old. And he's being struck by a man who could lift *me* in one hand, never mind Noah. And I don't know this but I suspect he's hitting his wife as well. Well, she's an intelligent adult, she has the right to decide whether to put up with it or not. But a child can't make those kind of choices. He needs help, and I'm the one he came to. I'm not going to shrug it off and say I tried, and hear next week that he's in Dimmock General with a fractured skull.'

Brodie pulled up a spare chair and sat facing him. 'Everything you say is true. But this is not an easy situation to deal with. Not as easy as pointing the finger and waiting for the law to take its course. If it was, there would be no child abuse.'

'The evidence is there,' said Daniel. 'Printed on that boy's face.'

'Bruises on a child mean nothing,' said Brodie. 'You know that, Daniel. How often have you seen Paddy black and blue the day after her riding lesson? Falling off things and running into things is a normal part of childhood. You can always explain away a few bruises. Hell, I could be hitting Paddy and only *telling* you she fell off a pony. You wouldn't know.'

'I know *you*.'

'And there'll be plenty of people who think they know Adam Selkirk better than to suppose he's hitting his son. Realistically, with a twelve-year-old boy, it'll come down to whether he wants to protect his father. If he does, all your efforts will achieve nothing except making the man even angrier. You could be making things worse for Noah. You've told Adam you know what's happening. Possibly, the best thing you can do now is back away and give the pair of them space to sort it out.'

'I'd love to see them sort it out,' nodded Daniel. Brodie believed him. 'But what if they don't? What if next time I see Noah he's sporting new bruises? What if he has his wrist in plaster or a tooth missing? How long do I keep backing away?'

It was an impossible question. There were a lot more ways of getting this wrong than getting it right, and any decision he took now could precipitate disaster. But Brodie didn't agonise long over her answer, for the simple reason that she knew his course was already chosen. There was no point honing her arguments when she knew this was one of those occasions when nothing she said would deflect him by so much as a degree. He was on a moral crusade, and blind to the fact that all crusades leave casualties in their wake.

She gave a graceful shrug. 'You must do what you think is best. But if this degenerates into a battle of wills between you and Adam Selkirk, the one who'll suffer most is Noah.'

Leslie Vernon worked for himself these days. But Voss had seen Findhorn's office, and seeing Vernon's in a slightly faded residential street in Worthing it was hard to see it as a career move. He was a man of about forty with a fractionally down-at-heel air. He didn't have a receptionist but answered the door himself, looking quickly both ways up the street as if worried his visitor might have been recognised. A detective at the door brings out the worst in most people, the innocent as well as the guilty. Voss was accustomed to causing little ripples of anxiety.

Once they were inside Vernon relaxed a bit; and relaxed more when Voss explained the reason for his call. As if there were dealings in his portfolio that were more problematic than his relationship with Terry Walsh. Or perhaps it was just that it would be easier to discuss an ex-client – this one at least – than a current one. 'So what do you want to know?'

'How long did you act for Terry Walsh?'

'About six years. I can get you the dates if you need them.'

'And how long before that were you with Mr Findhorn?'

'Four years.'

'Then, after ten years, you parted company with both of them.'

Vernon nodded, his lips a thin line. 'It wasn't my idea. At least, leaving Findhorn's wasn't.'

'What happened?'

He didn't answer immediately. Voss thought he wanted to, was weighing the likely cost. 'Listen,' he said in a low voice, 'I don't want any trouble. Not with you, and not with Terry Walsh.'

Voss did ingenuous well. It was something to do with the ginger hair and freckles. 'Why should there be any trouble? I'm not asking you to divulge professional secrets. All I want to know is if there was something shady going on – if that's why you felt you couldn't act for him any more. I have the right to ask that. You have the duty to answer.'

Vernon thought a minute longer. For eight months he'd been putting distance between himself and a hard place: now he'd bumped into a rock. He was going to have to say something. Policemen don't go away just because you ask them to. The best he could hope for was to make clear his own absolute non-involvement in anything not covered by the accountants' code of practice.

'I didn't know what kind of a man he was,' he insisted. 'Right up to the moment that I found out – and then it was all

I could do to get far enough away to feel safe. I don't want Terry Walsh turning up on my doorstep after midnight.'

'I don't know how you think these things work,' said Voss mildly. 'But what we don't do is pick up the phone and say, *Leslie Vernon is saying these things about you, Terry, what's your response?* If you feel threatened by Terry Walsh, the best thing you can do is help me. He won't do you much harm from inside Parkhurst.'

'You're serious this time? You're serious about putting him away?'

'This is a Serious Organised Crime Agency investigation. What do you think?'

Leslie Vernon had been a promising young accountant (so he claimed) when he went to work for Findhorn & Carraway. He was smart, competent and imaginative – which Voss wouldn't have considered a virtue in an accountant except for the pride with which Vernon said it – and he was developing a solid client list. When he was offered paper magnate and East-Ender-made-good Terry Walsh, he grabbed with both hands.

'So what went wrong?'

'Nothing,' said Vernon. 'At first. He's an amiable sort of guy, he was good to work for. And he was on the up. Maybe he sailed a bit close to the wind sometimes, but that was who he was – a bit of an operator. I swear to you, I had no reason to think his business was anything other than what it appeared to be.'

'Until?'

Vernon exhaled a long, edgy sigh. 'It's complicated. Does the name Achille Bellow mean anything to you?'

Some names are more intrinsically memorable than others. Monitoring the crime scene of the Balkans was not, thank God, any part of Charlie Voss's remit, but every police officer in Europe knew that Achille Bellow was a major player. Until his bullet-riddled corpse washed up on a French beach in the middle of the summer. 'The Greek godfather?'

'Is he? I was told he was from Serbia. Anyway, that's him – some kind of Euro-thug. I didn't know him from Adam until I happened to overhear Terry Walsh talking about him. Talking in the past tense, Mr Voss.' He cast the detective a hunted look. 'I was too stunned to take it all in, I can't quote him verbatim, but what he was saying – the gist of what he was saying – was that he took Achille Bellow out on his yacht, shot him and threw him over the side.'

Voss had come here looking for evidence of criminality on Walsh's part. But that was like turning over a stone and finding an elephant. He stared at the man in barely disguised disbelief. 'He said that? In front of you? Out of the blue, he told his accountant that he'd murdered someone.'

Vernon shook his head. 'It wasn't like that. He thought I'd left. He was on the phone to someone. I heard him laughing. And then he said—

'Look,' he said then. 'Let me tell you what happened. Everything that I can remember. Then, if you don't believe me...well, Norman Findhorn didn't believe me either.'

They had a meeting at Walsh's house on the Firestone Cliffs at the beginning of July. Nothing out of the ordinary – routine business between a client and his accountant. They completed it, had coffee, then Vernon took his leave and headed out to his car. But he wasn't out of the drive before he realised he needed another signature, on a share certificate. He went back the way he'd come.

Walsh was still in his office. Vernon could hear his voice through the closed door. He was laughing. Vernon realised he was on the phone and waited for him to finish. 'I wasn't listening,' he insisted. 'I was just waiting for him to put the phone down so I could knock and get him to sign for the shares. If he'd kept his voice down I wouldn't have heard what he said. But he was enjoying himself. Boasting. And what he said was, essentially, *Don't worry about Achille Bellow, he isn't a problem any more, he came out on* The Salamander *and tried to walk home.*

'And the guy at the other end of the line must have thought he was kidding because Walsh said, *No, really – I tried to talk to him but he wasn't prepared to be reasonable. So we shot him and tipped him over the side.*'

At which point, continued Vernon, Caroline Walsh had happened through the hall, and gave a puzzled smile at the white-faced accountant standing by the office door. So he felt to have no choice but knock, and enter when he was told to.

'Terry was putting down the phone. He looked surprised to see me. I waved the form and stammered an explanation. He signed it, we said goodbye again and I left. But he was wondering even then. I could tell. Wondering how long I'd been there, how much I'd heard. He knew what he'd been saying on the phone, Mrs Walsh knew I'd been standing outside the door, but neither of them was sure if I could have heard anything through three inches of oak.

'They must have decided I couldn't, or I doubt I'd be here telling you about it. At the same time, it underlined the risk of having people around him who weren't on his own payroll. That was when he decided to swap me for a tame accountant whose discretion could be counted on in any circumstances.'

Voss felt as if someone had slapped him round the ear with a sock full of gold-dust. He had to make himself concentrate long enough to finish the interview. 'But that isn't what he told Mr Findhorn.'

Vernon gave a little snort. 'Of course it isn't. He accused me of being indiscreet – he said information about his business was reaching his competitors, information that could only have come from me. It wasn't true so of course I denied it. And I tried to tell the old man that Walsh wasn't the kind of business he wanted, but he thought I was trying to wriggle off the hook. I should have told him what I'd heard, but frankly I was scared what Walsh would do if he found out. So Findhorn decided that in fact Walsh was exactly the kind of business he wanted – the profitable kind – but I was the kind of accountant he could do without.'

Nothing Voss knew about the man suggested Terry Walsh would deal with professional competition by shooting his competitors and dumping them in the English Channel. But then, nothing Voss knew had been enough to put Walsh in the prison cell where he richly deserved to be. There was another side to him, darker than the one he showed the world. Darker than the one that involved tricking gullible punters. Dark enough, possibly, to include murder. Voss thought and thought, and didn't know. But he knew someone who might.

All the way back to Dimmock he was weighing the

alternatives. Or perhaps it's more accurate to say he was juggling them.

There were three. To say nothing to Deacon – because this wasn't his case but also because there was now at the back of Voss's mind that nagging unease about Deacon's loyalties and he didn't want his suspicions confirmed. After Alix Hyde went home, with or without Terry Walsh's head in her briefcase, Voss would be Deacon's sergeant again. He hadn't always liked the man but he'd always respected him. He wanted to be able to think it had been a misunderstanding, that Deacon hadn't deliberately let him make a fool of himself over Susan Weekes.

Or he could tell Detective Inspector Hyde what Vernon had said and let her discuss it with Deacon. That got him out of the firing-line, but other than short term it altered nothing. And it introduced an additional complication, in that Deacon and Hyde didn't like one another. The Superintendent was more likely to help Voss than the high-flier from SOCA.

Or he could go direct to Deacon, without saying anything to Hyde first, and say what he'd been told and ask Deacon's opinion. In which case either he'd help or he wouldn't. If he didn't, Voss would never know for sure if this was because he knew nothing helpful or because he didn't want to help. But at least he wouldn't be hearing Deacon's response filtered through Hyde's mistrust. He drew a deep breath, and went and knocked on Deacon's door.

'Achille Bellow,' said Deacon, deadpan.

Voss nodded.

'Achille Bellow, trafficker in drugs, girls for the sex trade and babies for illicit adoptions, whose career came to a dramatic if fitting end on a Normandy beach this summer. That Achille Bellow?'

Charlie Voss hung onto his patience. 'That's the one, yes.'

'And your question is: Did he have a branch office in Dimmock?'

Put like that, it didn't seem terribly likely. But Dimmock was only a dowager duchess on the outside: at heart she was a bit of a floozy. 'It's not that improbable,' insisted Voss. 'The removal of internal European barriers was always going to lead to a kind of Common Market in crime. Hell, we've been arguing for years that we'd need extra funds to combat the spread of Mafia-type operations out of eastern Europe. Operations run by people exactly like Achille Bellow.

'We know the guy expanded as far as Marseilles. That's only one country removed from here. And England, like France, is the kind of prosperous middle-class state where traffickers want to traffic *to*. They wouldn't make much money smuggling into Romania, would they?'

'But – Achille Bellow?' objected Deacon. 'Achille Bellow setting up shop in Dimmock would be like the Pope turning up as parish priest at St Simeon's, Edgehill.'

'I expect that's what the chief of detectives in Marseilles said when people first reported seeing Bellow on his manor. He had an operation in France, England was his natural next move. And if he wanted a base in England, why not Dimmock? We're on the south coast, handy to some big ports but probably just off the Interpol radar. I can think of worse places to work from.'

'I'd have heard about it,' said Deacon with certainty. 'Achille Bellow setting up shop in Dimmock? Every villain from Bournemouth to Dover would have been bleating about it!'

That was a valid point. Every pond has little fish and big fish; but introduce a barracuda and they all get in a flap. 'So maybe he was doing it the smart way. Working through someone who was already established in the area. A partnership – Bellow's money and contacts, the local guy's set-up. We wouldn't necessarily hear about that. At least, not for a while.'

'The smart way wasn't smart enough to stop him getting killed,' Deacon pointed out.

'Well – if he was trying to move into this area, however discreetly, the local thuggery would know about it before we did. They were going to feel it in their pockets. If Bellow was bringing in cut-price working girls, the guys behind our resident toms – Joe Loomis on the one hand and Terry Walsh on the other – were going to notice a drop in profits. They weren't going to be pleased. They might have been displeased enough to do something about it.'

'Like kill him?'

'Like kill him,' agreed Voss. 'According to my witness, Walsh took Bellow out on his yacht, shot him and dumped him in the sea.'

'I don't buy it,' rumbled Deacon. 'Why Terry? If someone was going to kill someone, Joe's the one with the record of violence. Hell's teeth, we both know that! Terry's a crook – Joe's the thug.'

'You mean, he's the one we've caught at it.'

Deacon conceded that. 'Your witness.' He'd noticed that Voss had avoided giving him a name and made a point of not asking for one. 'Does he say he was there when Terry shot Bellow – that he saw it happen?'

'No. He overheard him boasting about it a few days later.'

Deacon's eyebrows rocketed. 'Oh come on, Charlie! Terry's certainly a criminal. He just might be a murderer. But a guy who boasts about it in front of people he doesn't know he can trust? He's smarter than that. You *know* he's smarter than that.'

Voss felt the sting of criticism. 'Maybe smart enough to guess that would be your reaction?' He saw astonishment in Deacon's eyes and hurried on. 'Look, I'm asking you because I don't know whether it's plausible or not. You've known Walsh a lot longer than I have. We both know he's a crook – the question is, what kind of a crook? How far would he go?'

'Not that far,' insisted Deacon. 'Not unless he was cornered and fighting for his own survival.'

'Achille Bellow wasn't a pillar of anyone's community,' Voss pointed out. 'He was a nasty and deeply dangerous man. Maybe Walsh thought he *was* fighting for survival.'

Deacon gave an elaborate shrug. 'I suppose it's possible. Almost anything *can* happen. Most things that could happen don't happen, but some things happen that you wouldn't expect. The Prince Regent's supposed to have slept off a blinder in my house when it was the town jail. I don't know if that's true but I could believe it. I'm not sure I believe that a conflict of interests led Terry Walsh to shoot Achille Bellow and sling him off his boat. And I definitely don't believe that Terry was overheard boasting about it by someone who was then prepared to talk to you. This witness. Is he credible? How much do you know about him? Can you trust what he says? You're playing with the big boys here, you can't afford to harness your reputation to a flawed witness. Can you put him close enough to Terry to overhear what he says he overheard?'

Voss was circumspect. Just in case...well, just in case. 'He's a professional man. He was advising Walsh until just after Bellow died, then he was sacked. We have independent confirmation of that.' Findhorn had furnished him with the date on which Leslie Vernon was paid off.

'Could that be a motive? Terry fired the guy and he saw a chance to get his own back?'

'It's a possibility,' admitted Voss. 'Another is that Terry realised he'd had a close call and got rid of him before he overheard something that could be proved.'

'So it's just one man's story? There's no corroboration?'

'Not yet. But then, I haven't started looking. If Terry took Bellow out on his boat, someone may have seen them. If I can come up with a good enough reason I can get *The Salamander* checked for fingerprints and DNA.'

'After eight months?' Deacon knew it was possible. He also knew it was harder than the cop-shows make it look. If Walsh was the man they all suspected, he knew how to clean up after himself. 'I wouldn't count on it.'

'Because Walsh wouldn't kill Bellow? Or because he wouldn't leave any evidence that he'd killed Bellow?'

Deacon was getting exasperated. 'Charlie, I don't know. If you were asking about an innocent bystander or the proprietor of a corner shop, I'd be pretty sure Terry hadn't killed them. Achille Bellow? – maybe. If he was ever here at all, and if he was muscling in on Terry's territory – maybe. We know Bellow washed up on a beach across the Channel from here, and we know Terry has a boat. But…' Deacon's eyes narrowed.

'I'll tell you what the problem is, Charlie Voss. There's nothing clever about it. You grab your competitor, shoot him and dump him in the sea – yes, sure, pretty effective, but anyone could do it. From Terry I'd have expected something…more elegant.'

Now Voss's eyebrows climbed. 'Elegant?'

'Elegant,' insisted Deacon.

Voss pursed his lips. 'You've known Terry Walsh since you were boys. Maybe, deep down, you still think of him as a street-urchin with an eye to the main chance. But you grew up, and so did he. Maybe he's been playing rougher than you know for a while. Hell, we never managed to prove *anything* – why would we get lucky with murder? That doesn't mean he hasn't gone that far. This may not even be the first time.'

There was a steely edge to Deacon's voice. 'You think, because I underestimated him, he's been getting away with murder?'

'That wasn't what I said!' But actually, it wasn't far from what he meant. 'Chief, I don't know any more than you do. I've been given a lead and I have to follow it up. Before I started, I wanted to know if it sounded feasible to you or not.'

'And I've told you,' growled Deacon. 'No, it doesn't. Not really.'

'OK then,' said Voss.

'OK.'

CHAPTER TWELVE

When Voss got back from Worthing he checked what Vernon had told him with the one source he could think of that might be able to confirm it. And came up trumps. There was a glow in his eyes and a kind of suppressed excitement in his voice when he hurried round to DI Hyde's office.

'I called the marina. Apparently, people file the equivalent of a flight-plan when they're going to be out overnight. It's a safety measure – it means someone would be missed if he didn't turn up where he said he was going to be around the time he said he was going to be there. Terry Walsh filed a sailing-plan for *The Salamander* for the weekend June 24th to 26th. He said he was heading over to Le Havre.'

'Which is a distance of…?'

'Less than a hundred miles,' said Voss. '*Salamander* would do it under power in a day. Breakfast in Dimmock, supper in Normandy.'

'Is there a record of who was on the boat?' asked Alix Hyde, watching him closely.

'Not a list of names, no.' He hadn't finished: she kept watching. He referred back to his notebook. 'They have it down as *Mr Walsh and guest, crew of three.*'

'Guest,' echoed Alix Hyde.

'That's what it says, yes.'

'And Achille Bellow was found dead on June 26th.'

'Yes.'

'Where, exactly?'

'Midway between Le Havre and Dieppe.'

'And is that feasible?'

The marina was run by experts, people with vast experience of boats and tides and weather conditions. Voss had quizzed them until he was sure of his facts. 'If Achille Bellow was on *The Salamander* when she left Dimmock at eight-fifteen a.m. on June 24th, he could have been well on his way to Spain by the 26th. She's a serious sea-going yacht: she regularly makes passages between here and the Mediterranean. Terry could have taken Bellow back to the Balkans if he'd wanted to. He could sure as hell have taken him halfway to France.'

Detective Inspector Hyde looked like a woman who was trying not to get too excited. 'So we have Walsh and a guest sailing for northern France two days before Bellow's found dead on a beach in northern France. It doesn't prove Vernon heard what he says he heard, but it certainly suggests he may have done.'

'Grounds to do a search on *Salamander*?'

Hyde gave it some thought. 'I don't know. I'd almost like to hold that in reserve. If we search her and find nothing, we've rather shot our bolt. If we can put Walsh and Bellow together on the deck of *The Salamander* on the last weekend in June, and we can't find anyone who saw Bellow alive after that, then we have a case with or without forensics.'

'I thought I'd take a picture of Bellow to the marina, talk to people who'd have been out and about at that time. And see who else was off the coast of Normandy that weekend. Maybe someone can put *Salamander* even closer to where Bellow was found.'

By now Hyde had given up trying to contain her pleasure. A little smile lifted the corners of her mouth. 'You're pretty good at this, Charlie. At seeing both the big picture and all the little pieces that make it up. Not everyone can do that.'

'I had a good teacher,' said Voss.

'Yes,' said Hyde levelly. 'Still, the time must be coming you'll be wanting to spread your wings. There's a limit to just how far you can go in a small seaside town.'

Voss forbore to comment. There was something unseemly about insisting that, on the contrary, Dimmock was a hotbed of crime, vice and psychosis, and a detective could get all the experience he wanted just by waking up here every morning.

'You know, if you did want a change,' continued Hyde, 'I'd be happy to help.'

Nobody resents a compliment. 'Thanks. I haven't given it much thought.'

'Perhaps you should.'

None of which was helping to get Terry Walsh out of circulation. 'In the meantime,' said Hyde, 'what have we got? We've got an accountant who overheard Walsh claiming to have killed Achille Bellow and slung him in the sea. We've got Walsh's yacht in the Channel off Normandy a couple of days before Bellow's body was found. We've got documentation of an unidentified guest on board. If we just had independent…'

Her voice petered out and her eyes went distant. 'And

actually,' she said softly after a minute, 'we have. We have someone who was still close to Walsh in the period leading up to this and who's already expressed an interest in talking to us. If there was bad blood between Walsh and Bellow, it didn't start on June 23rd. It had probably been coming for weeks. Bellow muscling in on Walsh's territory, Walsh warning him off, Bellow surrounding himself with Eastern European weight-lifters. Someone who was part of that circle would have heard the raised voices and stamped feet.'

'Who...?' But before the word was out of his mouth, Voss knew. He tried and failed to keep the whistle out of his voice. '*Susan Weekes*?'

'Susan Weekes,' agreed Hyde. 'She knew Walsh – that's incontestable, everybody agrees that she knew him. Even on the Walshes' account she had a crush on him, hung around him any time he was in The Dragon Luck. She was still working at the casino when Bellow was killed. There's every chance she heard Walsh threatening what he'd do if Achille Bellow didn't back off. She may even have heard him boasting after the event, the way Vernon did.'

Voss thought about it. 'It's possible. But even if she did, who'd believe her?'

'If she was all we had,' Hyde conceded, 'no one. But if she's confirming things that we've got other witnesses to, everyone will believe her.'

It was true. Weekes on her own was clearly a flawed witness. But she could still add weight to the case against Terry Walsh, and they knew she was willing to do it. It remained to be seen if she had anything useful to say. 'Do you want to see her again?'

Hyde's smile broadened. 'No. Charlie, I think you should do it. I want your name on this. I want you to get the credit you're due. Find out where she is now. Go and see her.'

Susan had had a rough month. Not agonising or terrifying so much as grindingly unpleasant. She'd considered the possible consequences, good and bad, of a career in drug smuggling and had thought herself prepared even for the worst. But no one is ever prepared for the mind-numbing, soul-sapping drudgery of prison life, and one of the hardest things to deal with is the company.

On the whole, they're not nice people that you meet in a remand wing. Yes, legally they're all innocent until they're proven guilty, but most of them will be proven guilty and most of the others will get off on a technicality. Even in the remand wing of a women's prison, you meet hardly anyone you'd want to take to the office party. You meet stupid women, and greedy women, and sly and vicious women, and women who never look you in the eye. You meet women so degraded by their lives that prison seems a step up, and others so enraged by their circumstances that a careless word can lead to mayhem. It's a fallacy, that *There but for the Grace of God* thing, dreamt up by the terminally empathic. Lots of people have bad luck in their lives. Most people don't respond to it with the sort of actions that get you sent to prison.

Susan was sharing a room – and it was called a room, not a cell, and it had gingham curtains at the high windows and what almost amounted to an *en suite* – with a woman who'd got away with passing dud cheques, right up to the moment that she found something wrong with a pair of designer boots and demanded a refund. She was called Tracie, and had six children by four different men, and spent all day and most of every night recounting their deeply unedifying activities. Susan didn't find her frightening so much as a crashing bore.

So she greeted Charlie Voss like an old friend and was happy to talk to him, about The Dragon Luck and Terry Walsh and his business, for as long as Voss would listen. He bought her cups of tea. If he hadn't, she'd have bought him some to prolong the interview and delay the moment when she'd have to go back and find out what happened to Tracie's daughter Simone in Lanzarote.

'You told us you were Terry Walsh's mistress,' said Voss, gently reproving.

'So?'

'That's not how Terry remembers it. Or Mrs Walsh, come to that.'

'And you believed them?' The woman tried for indignation but hadn't the spirit left to carry it off. 'Of course you believed them. They've got money.'

'We didn't just take their word for it. Mr Deacon investigated. He found no evidence that it was true.'

Susan sniffed. 'So what are you doing back here? Don't you think if I could prove it I would have done?'

'You talked about Terry doing business behind the scenes at The Dragon Luck. Not bulk paper business – the other kind.'

'So?' she said again.

'You heard him talking enough to know where most of his money was coming from?'

'Sure.'

'And who his competitors were? Rivals – men who were fighting for a slice of his cake?'

'I suppose.' For the first time she sounded a little doubtful.

'Do you remember any names?'

She got one almost without thinking. But then, Mrs Puddy who ran the knitting-wool shop in Baker's Lane could have done as well. 'Joe Loomis.'

'We know about Loomis,' agreed Voss. 'Anyone else? Anyone new – maybe in the last year or so?'

Susan gave it some more thought. 'Yes. But I can't remember their names. Terry didn't like me to look as if I was listening.'

Voss nodded. 'What about a man called Achille Bellow?'

Susan's brows drew together in a little frown of concentration. Then it cleared. 'Yes. Terry said he was taking too much of his business and he was going to have to do something about him.'

'Like, report him to Immigration?' hazarded Voss. 'Or drop him in the Channel in a concrete life-vest?'

'The Channel,' said Susan Weekes firmly. 'Definitely the Channel.'

Dimmock's marina wasn't on the scale of, for instance, Brighton's. Until ten years earlier it had been Duffy's Boatyard, a couple of sheds, an area of hard standing and a slipway into a dredged area of the Barley estuary. It did a steady trade rather than a roaring one, building two or three wooden sailing-boats a year, refitting a few others, doing winter haul-outs and scrub-downs for more again.

It was the third generation of Duffys who spotted the magic

word *grant* and recognised that a marina is only a boatyard in its Sunday best. They built a mole out into the estuary, installed pontoons, decorated the office and soon filled every berth. It wasn't the grandest marina on the south coast, but cognoscenti considered it had charms all its own. She was called Becky, she ran the office, and defied the experience of lifetimes by being both decorative and efficient.

She looked at the photograph Voss showed her and listened carefully to what he wanted to know. Then, herself unable to help, she took him outside and introduced him to two old salts in guernseys and sailcloth caps. They were sitting on the weather-bleached deck of a gaff cutter even older than they were, apparently knitting rope. 'They're always here,' murmured Becky. 'They live on board. They don't sail any more, they just sit there watching the boats come and go. If anyone saw the man in your photo, they did.'

And they did. 'Foreign gent,' grunted the slightly older and more grizzled of the Hawkins brothers. 'Talked with an accent.'

Voss's heart hammered against the inside of his ribs. He nodded. 'And he was with Mr Walsh?'

'Walsh?' queried the other brother.

Becky translated. '*Salamander*'s owner.'

'Oh – him. The townie. That's right, he went on *The Salamander*. Nice boat that. Roller reefing. Sail a boat like that through an 'urricane, you could.'

'Did you see them come back?' asked Voss.

'Saw *The Salamander* come back. Didn't see who come off her. It was late.'

'They turn in about nine,' explained Becky.

'Any way of saying when this was?'

'Last summer,' said the elder Hawkins.

'June,' said the younger.

'Late June,' said the elder judiciously. 'After Regatta Week.'

Before Voss could skip and whistle his way back to Battle Alley, though, Becky had another joy to add to his pile. She checked through the log – this, Voss discovered, was nautical-speak for diary – and found three other boats that had been sailing in the same area as *The Salamander* the last weekend in June. She made a few phone calls and found him someone who'd raised Walsh's yacht five miles off the Normandy coast, a scant ten miles from where Achille Bellow's body was found.

'Raised it?' queried Voss, puzzled. 'It sank?'

Becky grinned. 'It means they saw and identified her.'

Voss took the phone so quickly you'd have to say he snatched. 'And when was that, sir?'

The skipper turned out to be a Miss Lawson who didn't appreciate being addressed as *sir*. Huffily, she consulted her own log. 'We left Dimmock on the Friday evening – June 23rd. This must have been the Sunday afternoon, about four.'

'And it was definitely *The Salamander*?' An affirmative grunt. 'Was it anchored?'

'Five miles off shore?' said the woman dryly. 'Not a sailing man, are you, sonny? No, she was pottering along under the jib.'

'The little sail at the front,' whispered Becky.

'So they weren't in any hurry. How close did you pass her?'

'Within about half a mile.'

'Did you see who was on board?'

'I could see there *were* people on board. I couldn't tell you who.'

It didn't matter. The Hawkins brothers had told him that. Terry Walsh, and his guest – the foreign gent in the photograph. It was more than he needed to search *The Salamander*. It was enough to reserve Walsh a suite at the Parkhurst penthouse.

'We've got him.' The excitement was like a guitar-string thrumming in Voss's voice.

'Walsh?' As if he might mean someone else. But Hyde wanted it clear and unambiguous. '*What* have you got?'

He went through it, building the case a piece at a time. 'I spoke to French criminal intelligence – their last positive sighting of Achille Bellow alive was in Marseilles on June 20th. I don't know how or when he got into England – he'd have been stopped if Immigration had spotted him – but obviously he had a way in. He may not have been fronting the operation here, but he must have been around enough for Terry to realise it was Bellow who was giving him problems and to figure out how to deal with him.

'On June 24th Walsh took a guest aboard *The Salamander* and told the marina office that he was heading for the north Brittany coast. Later that day he was seen – *raised*,' he amended, with a little smile Hyde didn't understand, 'ten miles from the spot where Bellow's body turned up the following day. The Hawkins brothers identified a photograph of Achille Bellow as Terry Walsh's guest. A couple of weeks earlier Susan Weekes heard him complaining in The Dragon Luck that Bellow was costing him money and would have to be dealt with, and early in July Leslie Vernon overheard him boasting about killing Bellow on the phone.' He spread his hands, unable to contain his triumph. 'Boss – what more do we need?'

Hyde was watching him with a light like wine in her eyes. The exhilaration of the chase was passing between them like a current. 'Not a damn thing, Charlie. You're right. We've got him. *You* got him.'

Voss actually blushed. He wasn't used to having his contribution acknowledged. Deacon tapped his thought processes endlessly, and hadn't even the grace to buy the drinks while he did it, but Voss was resigned to the fact that his input went largely unrecognised. Until now it hadn't occurred to him that there was anything wrong with that. Junior officers did the legwork, senior officers made the decisions, and if there was any recognition going the best he could hope for was along the lines of, 'Congratulations to Detective Superintendent Deacon *and his team*'. Which was fair enough, since criticism was mostly directed the same way. Only, since he and Deacon made a good team, there were more bouquets than brickbats and it would have been nice occasionally to smell the roses.

But leading an inquiry was a whole new experience. He'd have had doubts about his ability, except that Detective Inspector Hyde of the Serious Organised Crime Agency thought he was ready. She believed his grasp of the situation was sure and his judgement good, and clearly she was delighted with the outcome. It was impossible for even a famously level-headed detective sergeant not to feel flattered.

'So what do we do?' he asked. 'Go and see him again? Invite him to come and see us? Send a Black Maria?'

'I'm an old-fashioned girl at heart, Charlie,' beamed Alix Hyde. 'Let's do it the old-fashioned way. Go to his house and arrest him on suspicion. If you can find a black car you can take it.'

Terry Walsh was a self-made man. All he inherited from his father – or at least, the man his mother said was his father – was brown eyes and the kind of dense, curly hair that never falls out and may not even go grey. Even his name came from the distaff side. He started with nothing but a quick wit and a flexible approach to the law, and now in his fiftieth year was a very wealthy man. It would be nice to be able to report that his ill-gotten gains hadn't made him happy, but in fact they had.

And like self-made men the world over, he had the security of knowing that what he'd done once he could do again. If he lost it all, he wouldn't stay broke for long. This is the difference between self-made men – and women – and their children. It's not, as is commonly supposed, that brains skip a generation. It's that being born with a silver spoon in your mouth leaves little incentive to fight for what you want. Hunger is the best motivation in the world.

In consequence, Terry Walsh was not going to be easy to intimidate. He knew, and Hyde knew, that even if she succeeded beyond her wildest dreams, the worst she could do to him was not enough to destroy him. He could do prison time if he had to. He could lose everything he'd acquired. Some time, and probably sooner than anyone expected, he'd be back.

So there was no fear in his eyes, even deep in his eyes where anyone other than a police officer would have been too polite to look, as he and Hyde regarded one another across the formica table-top in Interview Room 1 at Battle Alley Police Station. There was anger. Not rage, because his control was absolute, because now more than ever it was important to think clearly and see the situation undistorted by the lightning flashes of fury and the red fog of hate. But anger nonetheless. In another man you might almost have described it as righteous anger: that aura of quiet outrage surrounding him like the God-light in a medieval painting. He wasn't here to help the police with their inquiries. He was here to put them straight.

Alix Hyde was enjoying herself. She was an experienced detective and a realist: she hadn't got Walsh's head on her wall yet but she had got some of her buckshot into his backside. Right here and now, he was stinging and she was holding the smoking gun, and it felt good.

She gave him a friendly smile. 'He must be a popular man, this brief of yours. You're sure you don't want to start without him?'

Walsh's eyes were frosty. 'He *is* popular. Because he's good at what he does. He was in court when he got the message.' Now he smiled, coldly. 'Knocking holes in what some detective inspector fondly believed was a watertight case.'

Hyde chuckled. 'It happens. Once or twice. More than that, given a top-class brief. It doesn't upset me as much as it used to. I just wait. Sooner or later the water stays in the bucket.'

There were footsteps in the corridor and Charlie Voss opened the door. 'Mr Walsh's solicitor, ma'am.'

They hadn't met. Voss performed introductions. 'Detective

Inspector Hyde of the Serious Organised Crime Agency: Mr Adam Selkirk.'

Hyde waved the big man to the seat beside his client. 'Good day in court?' she asked pleasantly.

He shrugged negligently. 'Some you win, some you lose.'

Hyde looked at Walsh and her smile was positively sunny. 'A good day for justice, then.'

He was taking possession of the table in front of him by the simple expedient of unpacking his briefcase onto it. He looked up briefly. 'Indeed, Inspector. Today I won.'

Hyde turned the tape on, told it who was present and what they were doing there, and began the interview.

She and Voss had discussed strategy before they went for Walsh. There was, they agreed, no point laying carefully crafted snares in the hope that he'd stumble into one. He wouldn't be tricked into saying the wrong thing, and he wouldn't be panicked. There was nothing to be lost and valuable time to be gained by laying their cards on the table and letting Walsh worry how to respond.

As expected, the immediate response was a blanket denial. Mr Walsh had never met Achille Bellow. Yes, he was vaguely aware who he was. Yes, he remembered the media coverage at the time of his murder. But Mr Walsh was not then, nor at any time prior to that, either a business associate or a personal acquaintance of Mr Bellow. He had never visited Mr Bellow at his home in Marseilles, nor had Mr Bellow ever joined him for a jolly weekend in Dimmock.

'So if someone said they'd seen you together, they'd be lying?'

'Probably not,' said Walsh calmly. 'Probably, they'd just be mistaken.'

Hyde considered that. 'It wouldn't be an easy mistake to make. You're a familiar face in this part of the world. And while Achille Bellow wasn't exactly a household name in Dimmock, in his own way he was famous too. Particularly after he died. You still reckon it would be a case of mistaken identity if someone thought they'd seen you together?'

Walsh remained untroubled. 'You know better than I do, Inspector, eyewitness testimony is about the least reliable evidence you deal with. Honest upright citizens with no axe to grind make mistakes like that every day – say they've seen someone or something that they haven't. The mere fact that Beulah's face was all over the news…'

'Bellow,' Hyde corrected him quietly. 'Achille Bellow.' She knew it wasn't a slip of the tongue.

'Bellow,' agreed Walsh. 'The notorious Turkish trafficker, who met a richly deserved end on a French beach and whose face was immediately beamed into every household in Europe in celebration. Every news bulletin, every newspaper. You could just about guarantee that, after that, some local rube was going to think he'd seen him. Ask Interpol. I bet they had reported sightings of him all over the continent.'

She already had, and they had. But the last one that stood up was that one in the south of France on June 20th. She nodded a rueful acknowledgement. 'Of course that happens. People think they're telling you what they saw, but with the best will in the world they can be wrong. Always we look for corroboration. Some kind of physical evidence. Or a second witness. Or – hey, we can hope! – a third. Or fourth, or fifth.'

For just about as long as a hiatus can be made to stretch, the little room was silent. Voss counted the slow seconds crawling by. He watched Terry Walsh, waiting for the careful blankness in his eyes to turn to comprehension. To an understanding that Hyde wasn't bluffing. That he'd finally rolled the dice and lost.

Then the two men across the table turned to one another and continued the conversation as if they were alone.

'Well, there can't be any physical evidence,' said Walsh with certainty. 'You can't have physical evidence of something that never happened.'

'So they've got another witness,' said Selkirk.

'Sounds a bit like it,' said Walsh. 'Oh, hang on... They're not counting Susan again, are they?'

For a moment both men looked at Hyde. Then they resumed their private discussion. 'No,' said Selkirk. 'Not after everything that's happened. Nobody's *that* dim.'

'I don't know,' said Walsh, grimacing. 'People get an idea in their heads, and nothing'll do but they try to prove it right however much the evidence is against them. *I* know you can't trust a word Susan says, and you know that, but Detective Inspector Hyde's new in these parts. Maybe she fell for it.'

'She must have checked the file.'

Walsh shrugged. 'Maybe she didn't.'

They pivoted again. Adam Selkirk said, as if explaining to a child, 'Susan Weekes's allegations against my client have been thoroughly investigated and discredited. I hope you have something more serious than that to put to Mr Walsh.'

Hyde was too experienced an officer to let the pantomime unsettle her. 'Yes, I know about the history between Ms Weekes and Mr Walsh. Mr Walsh himself was kind enough to fill me in. So naturally I'm treating anything she tells me with caution. Looking for corroboration. From the sort of witness who *would* stand up in court.'

'And did you find one?'

'No,' she admitted ruefully. Then she smiled. 'I found four.'

Selkirk gave her the satisfaction of a startled blink. Whatever he'd been expecting, it wasn't that. Fielding four witnesses is a bit like turning up at Balaclava with a Trident missile: a touch of overkill. 'Very well, Inspector. You'd better tell us what it is you think you can prove so we can show you that you're wrong.'

Voss kept watching Walsh as Hyde spelt it out. The man's expression didn't flicker. Not by so much as a twitching eyelid did he indicate either that he feared himself cornered or that he had an answer to the charge. He waited patiently, giving nothing away, until she finished.

Then he turned to Selkirk again. 'Why's that date ringing a bell with me?'

'June 24th?'

'Yes. It means something to me.'

'Good,' said Selkirk. 'I hope it means you were in another part of the country, and twenty total strangers can vouch for the fact.'

Walsh's eyes were merry. 'No, I was definitely on the boat that weekend. And I definitely had a guest aboard. But it wasn't some Balkan brigand. You *know* who it was.'

Selkirk's eyes widened. 'Was that…?'

'Yes,' beamed Terry Walsh. 'Let's by all means check the diaries, but I'm pretty sure. I had to re-arrange a meeting.'

A slow smile was spreading across Selkirk's heavy features. 'Well, this is a little awkward. This isn't really why I came.'

Hyde was running out of patience. Her gaze, flicking between the two men opposite, was developing an edge. 'Any time you're ready you can tell me about the watertight alibi you've got for the last weekend in June.'

Now Selkirk was actually chuckling, a low rumble in the base of his throat. 'I don't know about watertight. I seem to remember getting quite damp on a number of occasions. Mr Walsh did indeed have a guest aboard his yacht that weekend, Detective Inspector Hyde. But it wasn't Achille Bellow. It was me.'

CHAPTER THIRTEEN

'There's a reason they call that man the Teflon Cockney,' said Voss tiredly, when they had the interview room to themselves. 'Nothing sticks to him. I don't get it. What went wrong? All those people couldn't have been lying!'

'Of course they weren't lying,' said Alix Hyde savagely. 'Walsh was lying, and his pet brief was lying. Everyone else was telling the truth.'

Voss shrugged. 'Not according to Selkirk's diary.' The solicitor's secretary had brought it down to Battle Alley inside fifteen minutes. Fifteen minutes that Terry Walsh had spent regarding the detectives with unbearable smugness. 'It looked genuine. There were no obvious alterations. The same sort of pen was used to make contemporaneous entries.' If he'd said that to Deacon the Superintendent would have hit him for being clever.

'Jesus, Charlie,' said Hyde disgustedly, 'get it into your head – these people aren't amateurs. Terry Walsh is making a lot of money. He no doubt pays a lot of money to Selkirk to keep him out of places with barred windows. And no doubt Selkirk pays his secretary a fair bit of money to back up everything he says and produce persuasive paperwork. It *all* comes down to money. That's the problem you've had nailing this bastard before. You kept thinking of him as a jumped-up blagger. We need to think of him as an international businessman.'

'They forged the diary?' said Voss doubtfully. *Sailing with Terry*, it had said for Saturday June 24rd to Monday the 26th. *Waterproofs, sea-sickness pills, Archbold.* 'But – how would they know what to write? What dates we'd be interested in? I don't think the secretary could have forged it and brought it here in fifteen minutes.'

Hyde shook her head. 'She didn't have to. She did it at the time, using the same pen that she used for everything else. Maybe she didn't know it was a lie. Selkirk told her to put it in the diary and she put it in the diary. And the reason Selkirk wanted it there,' she went on, anticipating his next question, 'is that Walsh needed to know he had an alibi if anyone ever asked who was on his boat that weekend. See? Businesslike. It might never have been a problem. But an entry in Selkirk's diary made sure it would never be a problem.'

Voss was still coming to terms with the implications. 'You're saying Selkirk's bent.'

'*Yes*, Charlie,' said Hyde in exasperation. 'That's exactly what I'm saying. That Terry Walsh bought himself a bent brief. Don't look so shocked. You know these things happen. You just didn't think they happened in Dimmock. But anywhere Walsh is, that's a crime nexus. You people have got to up your game. You've been training for Accrington Stanley. But you're playing Chelsea.'

'So that's it? His solicitor lies for him and Walsh walks? In spite of everything we've got on him?'

'For now he walks,' said Hyde, tight-lipped. 'But only for now. That's a bent alibi and we know it. And we'll break it.'

* * *

When Daniel asked to see him first thing on Friday morning, Des Chalmers thought that his new job hadn't worked out and he was ready to return to teaching. The Principal was delighted. The newest recruit to the maths department wore Batman socks and told jokes where the punchline was a formula.

'The answer's yes,' he said before Daniel had even got in through his door.

'Oh. Good,' said Daniel, taken aback. 'What was the question?'

Chalmers squinted at him. 'You are here to ask for your job back, aren't you?'

'No. Sorry, Des,' he said, and meant it. 'You know I'd rather work here. But right now…' He gave an apologetic little shrug.

'Yeah. I know,' said Chalmers. 'Just wishful thinking. So what can I do for you?'

'It's a bit delicate,' admitted Daniel. 'And I'd ask you to treat it in confidence except that a moment may come when you couldn't and I wouldn't want you to.'

'OK,' said Chalmers carefully, 'then let's say I'll use my discretion. What's happened?'

Daniel told him everything. About Noah Selkirk visiting his office, and their chance meeting at *Ye Olde Junk Shoppe*; about the bruises; about the father's attempt to scare him off.

'I suppose I'm just giving you the head's up,' said Daniel. 'You're Noah's head teacher, I thought you ought to know.'

Chalmers nodded sombrely. 'Did he tell you his father was hitting him?'

'No. But I've seen the bruises. And he did tell me both his

parents worked so hard they were tired and life at home was difficult because of it.'

'But Selkirk denied it.'

'Of course he did,' said Daniel. 'What else was he going to say? "That's right, when I've had a rough day in court I come home and give my twelve-year-old a couple of back-handers."'

'Have you spoken to Mrs Selkirk?'

'Not about this. I think Selkirk's violent with her too. Noah's worried about her – that's why he came to see me. And things Selkirk said to me suggested it too. "Stay away from my wife" – something like that.'

Chalmers was thinking. It wasn't the first time he'd confronted the issue of parental violence to a pupil. There was a carefully thought-out mechanism for dealing with it, set in concrete because a lot of people – the pupil, his teachers, the innocent parent, even the accused parent if the suspicion turned out to be unfounded – could be damaged if it wasn't followed to the letter. They could even if it was, but following the guidelines gave a measure of protection.

'Have you spoken to the police? Or Social Services?'

'Not yet. I will if it doesn't stop. What I'm hoping is that now Selkirk knows it isn't a secret any longer he'll keep his hands in his pockets. If he can, I doubt we'd be doing Noah any favours by broadcasting this. He doesn't want to see his father in court. I'm hoping this will have been a wake-up call and Selkirk will get himself under control. But if I'm wrong, you'll see the proof before I do. Don't believe it if Noah says he fell off his bicycle again.'

The Principal was wrestling with his conscience. 'Maybe *I*

should be talking to Social Services and the police.'

Daniel spread an appellant hand. 'I don't want you to do anything you can't defend to the Governors. But if you could see your way to holding off for a while...'

'All right,' decided Chalmers, 'this is what I'll do. Right now I only have your word for this – and though I believe you, you're not a teacher at this school, you're not a member of the family or a neighbour or a person of any authority so it could just be gossip. I'll watch the boy. The next time I see a mark on him, he's in here and I'm on the phone. All right?'

Daniel nodded. 'Yes. Thanks.'

'I'm glad you brought this to me,' said Chalmers. 'However we deal with it, one way or another we'll sort it out now.' He scowled at the window, troubled. 'Maybe we should have realised ourselves. Half a dozen of us see him five days a week – you wouldn't think we'd need telling he was having too many accidents.'

Daniel was quick with reassurance. 'It was a fluke, Des. I wouldn't have known either, except that he had the wit to come looking for help. In all honesty I'm not sure how much help I've been, but one thing I can do is make sure the beatings stop now. Quietly if I can, the other way if I have to. I appreciate your help.'

'Any time, Daniel,' said the Principal, adding hopefully, 'And if that job of yours doesn't work out...'

Daniel smiled. 'You'll be the first to know.'

The thing about walking everywhere – Looking For Something? ran one car and usually Brodie had it – is that you meet a lot of people. People walking the same way naturally fall into step and start talking to you. And people who know you even slightly stop their cars to offer you a lift.

Daniel Hood and Charlie Voss were of a similar age, and events had conspired to draw them into one another's orbits so that after two years they enjoyed an undemanding friendship. Voss gave Daniel lifts when he saw him, Daniel gave Voss coffee when he was passing. The conversation was always the same: Brodie and Deacon.

Daniel was walking back into town from Dimmock High when Voss drove past. Unless he had the hood up on his parka you couldn't miss Daniel. Voss braked and pulled in. 'Where are you heading?'

'Shack Lane,' said Daniel. 'Are you going to Battle Alley?'

'Hop in.' When they were on their way Voss added thoughtfully, 'Actually, can I come in with you? I want a word with your boss.'

'Brodie?' Daniel's eyes were alarmed. 'What's she done now?'

Voss chuckled. 'Nothing. At least, nothing I know about. But her ex is a solicitor, isn't he? I'm looking for a bit of legal gossip.'

'Ask her by all means. She should be back by now. I don't know how much help she'll be, though. It's getting to be a while since she moved in those circles.'

They left Voss's car on the derelict plot behind Shack Lane. Brodie's was there already, so she was back from her morning excursion. Daniel knocked politely in case she had someone with her, and she let them in.

'Hello, Charlie,' she said with every sign of pleasure. 'I haven't seen you for a bit.'

Voss hadn't seen Brodie for a bit either. There was a lot more of her now. He tried not to stare. 'You know what it's like when there's a push on. Only now more than ever, 'cause there's two of them pushing me. We've got a specialist down from Serious And Organised.'

Brodie rolled her eyes sympathetically. But actually she wasn't too interested in Voss's problems. 'How's Jack?'

'Fine, I think,' he said. 'I haven't seen much of him recently. We're working on different things.'

'Ah.' Voss wondered if she knew she could convey disappointment in a single syllable.

'I want to pick your brains,' he said apologetically. 'Do you know Adam Selkirk?'

He was expecting a reaction: he wasn't expecting Brodie to lean as far forward across her desk as her bump would allow and Daniel, who was making coffee, to shoot out of the tiny kitchen like the man in the Bavarian weather-house at the first sign of rain.

'Now why would you ask that?' Brodie wondered softly.

Voss was clearly startled. 'Because you've lived in this town longer than I have. You worked as a solicitor's researcher and then you married him. I thought you probably knew the town's other solicitors. Maybe I'm wrong. It's not important.'

It was, though. Voss was feeling much as a dinghy might when someone on the big yacht cuts the painter: adrift, bobbing around, directionless. He was used to having Deacon tell him what he wanted and then finding a way of doing it. Hyde was allowing him more freedom but also giving him less guidance. And with the pair of them at one another's throats it was hard to ask either for advice.

Plus, for a policeman, Voss had a touching faith in human nature. He was finding it hard to believe what both Deacon and Hyde would have accepted without a murmur, that a lawyer with a reputation to protect would lie outright to help a crooked client. It wasn't that he thought Brodie could tell him that. He hoped she could give him background on the man that would help him with his own judgement.

'No, you're not wrong,' Brodie said slowly. 'John knew Adam Selkirk so we met socially from time to time. He's a rubbish dancer, I can tell you that much. What else do you want to know?'

Charlie Voss may have been a touch naïve sometimes but he was nobody's fool. 'The first thing I'd like to know is why you both reacted as if I'd sat on a whoopee cushion when I mentioned his name.'

They traded a glance, unsure what – if anything – they should say. Daniel had been prepared to go to the police but only as a last resort. But did this count as going to the police? Voss had come to them and asked Brodie's help. She had to either give or withhold it – there was no third way.

Still picking her words carefully she said, 'We were approached by a client for advice on a situation in which Adam Selkirk is also involved. I can't go into much detail, but if we got the story right he doesn't come out of it well. Later Selkirk came here to warn us off. We showed him the door, but not before threats and insults were issued. There was a moment when I thought he was going to thump Daniel, but it passed.'

'Mm. Business as usual then,' said Voss thoughtfully, and Brodie grinned.

'So what's your interest in Adam Selkirk?' asked Daniel.

Voss gave an apologetic shrug. 'I can't go into much detail either. I suppose what I'm trying to establish is whether the guy's to be trusted.' Their faces froze, telling him nothing.

'We get a pretty jaded view of solicitors sometimes,' Voss went on. 'We see them across the formica table and they're always making life difficult for us. Well, that's all right, that's what they're paid for – to represent their clients and protect their interests. It's nothing we have any right to object to, even if our job would be easier without them.

'But if they're just doing their job, there's no reason to tar them with the same brush as their clients. Every accused person is entitled to a proper defence and someone has to provide it. When he's not representing thugs and criminals, Adam Selkirk may very well be a decent upright citizen.' He looked at Brodie. 'You know him. You've probably heard people talk about him. I don't need you to break any confidences. Only, on the balance of probabilities, when this man tells me something as a fact – not repeating a client's instructions but claiming personal knowledge of something – should I believe him or not?'

Brodie wasn't sure how to answer. She'd known Adam Selkirk, both professionally and socially, not well but over a period of years. She was aware of his reputation for toughness, as someone who positively enjoyed swimming with sharks, who was as easy to intimidate as a pit-bull terrier. Until this week she had never heard anything to his detriment as a man.

While she was still considering her response, Daniel came

to his own conclusion. 'I don't know what he's told you so I have no idea whether it's the truth or not. But he was certainly lying when he told me he wasn't hitting his twelve-year-old son.'

The philosopher says, *All men are liars.* Therefore the philosopher is a liar. Therefore all men are *not* liars. Therefore perhaps the philosopher is not a liar. Therefore…

Start from the known and work towards the unknown. Fact 1: Terry Walsh is a crook. People with no reason to lie saw him take a rival crook out on his boat, and two days later the guy's bullet-riddled body was found close to where Walsh was sailing.

But Walsh has an alibi. No less a person than his solicitor says that he, not the bullet-riddled rival, was on Walsh's boat that weekend. The only people who positively identified the rival are a couple of Ancient Mariners who couldn't be relied on to spot a battleship in time to avoid it. But a woman who may have been Walsh's mistress says she heard him threaten Achille Bellow and the man who used to be his accountant says he heard him boast of killing him. Either of them could be lying. But why, and how, would they be lying in concert?

In normal circumstances Adam Selkirk would be the perfect alibi. Solicitors have to deal with criminals but must themselves remain above reproach. Selkirk's testimony should be beyond question. But if a man lies about beating his twelve-year-old son, can you trust anything he says?

If a man beats his twelve-year-old son, of *course* he lies about it. Does that necessarily mean he'd give a criminal a false alibi? Even if the criminal is both a client and a personal friend? The philosopher says, *All men are liars…*

Helen Choi had had a hard shift in Intensive Care on Friday night and stumbled home in the early hours with nothing more ambitious in mind than a shower, a bite of supper and a good sleep. Now it was four in the morning and her fiancé was lying immobile beside her, thinking hard enough to fill the darkened room with electricity.

'Charlie,' she mumbled plaintively, 'you're keeping me awake.'

'I'm not doing anything,' he said, surprised.

'*That's* what's keeping me awake. It's like trying to sleep next to a corpse!'

'Well – what do you want me to do?'

'Go to sleep.'

'I can't sleep. Don't mind me, I'll just lie here quietly and think…'

'*Charlie…!*'

When the Chinese nurse shouted, rugby-playing housemen and substantial porters jumped to obey her. Most of the time she didn't have to shout at Voss to get her own way – nobody bats her eyelashes like an Oriental girl. But this time he was incapable of doing as she asked. He did his best – he shuffled a bit from time to time, even feigned the odd snore – but remained unrelentingly awake until his alarm went at seven.

But the night had not been wasted. By then he knew what to do.

Alix Hyde liked it. She liked it a lot.

'So what he thought was his ace in the hole turns out to be his…' She wasn't a poker player, couldn't finish the analogy.

Neither was Charlie Voss. 'Toad in the hole?' he suggested hopefully.

The Inspector gave an appreciative chuckle. 'Near enough, Charlie. Walsh thought his bent brief would get him off the hook. What he doesn't know is that Selkirk is himself facing investigation – the kind of investigation where even if the charge doesn't stick the mud will.

'I don't doubt that if we quietly let Selkirk know what we know he'll take another look at his diary and discover that – goodness gracious! – that entry was actually made for the wrong month. But if he's stubborn enough to stick to his story, we can cast enough doubt on him as a husband and father to fatally undermine his value as a witness. We've got him, Charlie, and that means we've got Walsh too. Thanks to you.'

Voss just wished he felt a bit happier. 'We can't really use it to blackmail him,' he pointed out uneasily. 'We can't leave a child to be abused by his father, however keen the man is to cooperate in another case.'

'Of course we can't,' agreed Hyde. 'But we can proceed one way rather than another. With discretion rather than blues-and-twos. Of coursc we'll make sure the kid's OK. But we can do it off the record. Let's face it, Charlie, this could ruin Selkirk's career. When he knows we're onto him, he'll mend his ways. We can protect the kid and still nail Walsh. It's like I always say.'

They hadn't known one another long. 'What do you always say, boss?'

Alix Hyde smiled serenely. 'When you have them by the balls, their hearts and minds will follow.'

He'd expected she'd want to take over at this point. He was wrong. 'Your idea, Charlie. Your local knowledge, your contacts. You bring it home. As long as I get Walsh I'm a happy bunny.'

He gave a little thought to where he should start. He didn't want Selkirk thinking his son had betrayed him. On Monday morning he took Jill Meadows and went to Dimmock High School, and they took the area car because he wanted to be noticed. He wanted Selkirk to think that one of Noah's teachers had become concerned about him. After all, if they hadn't noticed his bruises they should have done.

It wasn't the first time Chalmers had had detectives in his office. He'd learnt to be courteous and patient and wait for them to declare the reason for their visit. 'So what can I do for you, Sergeant Voss?'

Voss chose his words with care, not because he was uncertain of his ground but because that was the kind of policeman he was. 'I'm here about a pupil of yours. Noah Selkirk.'

'Oh yes?' The tone of his voice, and the audible question mark, told Voss a couple of things. That Chalmers knew the boy, and that he wasn't as surprised as he should have been to have policemen making enquiries about him. This was a nicely brought-up child from a good family; his head teacher should have been astonished to be asked about him in this way. But he wasn't, which raised the possibility that he had some idea what was coming.

'Have you seen him today?'

'As a matter of fact I have,' said Chalmers.

'Did he seem all right?'

'Yes, he did.'

'You seem quite sure of that, sir.'

'I made sure of it, Sergeant.'

Voss nodded slowly. They could pussy-foot around for a while longer, but it was becoming obvious the Principal knew what he was talking about. So he put it on the table. 'Only we've been alerted to the possibility that Noah's father is hitting him. I don't mean the odd shove – enough to leave bruises. Mr Chalmers, is that why you're keeping a close eye on him too?'

Des Chalmers pursed his lips while he thought. But silence wasn't an option and he certainly wasn't going to lie. 'I can't vouch personally for the truth of the allegation. I noticed he had a black eye but I don't know how he got it. Noah hasn't confided in me or any of his teachers. Someone else raised his concerns with me.'

'Who?'

'Someone who asked me to be discreet, for fear of giving the boy even more problems. Someone who wouldn't lie to me, and would fully appreciate the seriousness of what he was suggesting.'

'Someone you know.'

'Yes.'

'A usually reliable source.'

'Yes.'

Charlie Voss nodded. 'You're talking about Daniel Hood.'

'Ah.' Chalmers didn't like secrets, was glad it was out. 'He's spoken to you too? When we talked he was thinking of the police as a last resort.'

Voss sniffed in a manner he'd picked up from Deacon. 'People always do. No one ever thinks, *We've got a little problem here – let's get the police in before it turns into a disaster.*'

Chalmers grinned. 'I thought your days of seeing little old dogs across busy roads were gone.'

'Dogs, yes,' said Voss. 'Children, no. We still go to a fair bit of trouble to keep them safe.'

Chalmers nodded. 'So what is it you want me to do?'

Nothing wrong-foots a detective like someone genuinely trying to help. For a moment Voss couldn't think of a thing. All he'd wanted to achieve by coming here was to be seen coming here.

Meadows stepped in to fill the gap. 'Actually, sir, you've already done it,' she said smoothly. 'We wanted to know if you were aware there could be a problem, and we wanted to ask you to keep an eye on the boy. And to call us if you've any reason to be concerned.'

'Of course I will. To be honest,' said the Principal, 'I'm glad to have this made official. As I told Daniel, the moment I saw something definite I was going to take it up with our designated person for child protection. But that carries the tiny risk that the first thing you see is an obituary. Keeping children safe is a minefield. You can get it wrong both ways – keep a watching brief for too long, or start a train of events that'll leave the kid worse off than before you knew. You're very welcome to the hot potato.'

'Thanks,' said Charlie Voss sourly.

CHAPTER FOURTEEN

Voss gave careful thought to where he should confront Adam Selkirk. But the more he considered, the clearer it was to him that actually there was no decision to make. It couldn't be anywhere public, because not making a song and dance about it was what he had to offer Selkirk in return for the truth about his little sailing trip – i.e., that it was a week earlier or later than claimed, or perhaps never took place at all. If everyone whose opinion mattered to Adam Selkirk already knew that he'd been beating his twelve-year-old son, the incentive to cooperate would be gone.

There were good reasons, too, why he shouldn't take this to the man's home. Voss didn't propose to arrest Selkirk and lead him away in handcuffs, which meant that after he'd told Selkirk what he knew and intimated what it was going to cost him, he was going to leave the house in River Drive and Adam Selkirk would be alone with his wife and son. Afraid, perhaps, but also very, very angry. The least Voss could do was ensure he had some time to think, to calm down and work out the least painful option before he went home to his family.

So it was the offices of Selkirk & Fine, Solicitors at Law, in Butterfield Square. Dimmock didn't really have a smart area, but if it had this would have been it: three ranks of Georgian stucco houses in the middle of town, ranged around one end of the park. For a hundred years it had been a residential area. But even before the First World War these tall, many-roomed buildings were proving difficult to run without staff, and some were divided into large comfortable flats and some were adapted to commercial use. Adam Selkirk and his partner Miriam Fine had the whole of one four-storey house in the middle of the western terrace, looking down the park to the monument. It was gracious accommodation for successful professionals.

Successful professionals who could afford the best help. The receptionist didn't ask the detectives if they had an appointment: she knew who they were. She called Selkirk's office and he came downstairs and showed them to a conference room that had nothing in common with the interview rooms at Battle Alley.

Selkirk saw them seated before settling himself at the head of the walnut table. 'To coin a phrase,' he said, his low voice musical with good humour, 'should I call my client?'

Meadows smiled dutifully, Voss not at all. 'We're not here to discuss Mr Walsh, sir,' he said, face and tone void of expression. 'It's possible you may wish to have your own solicitor present. Though I'm guessing not.'

The expansiveness of Selkirk's welcome had frozen on him like wet clothes on a winter washing-line. Only the mental activity behind his eyes continued unabated. Voss could almost see the cogs whirring, the belts running, the machinery of the brain processing information and churning out thoughts and conclusions and plans of action. The man was still because the brain was racing.

Finally he said, 'I think you'd better tell me what this is about, Sergeant.'

Voss nodded. 'We've just come from Dimmock High School. Are you aware that your son's head teacher is concerned about him?'

Selkirk managed to look surprised. 'No. As far as I know he's doing well at school. Except' – the machinery behind his eyes changed gear – 'that's not what you mean, is it? However good or bad, a twelve-year-old's marks in design and technology are never going to attract the attention of CID. So what's happened? What's the little sod been up to?'

Charlie Voss didn't often feel the urge to thump someone. But he felt it now.

Meadows stepped in quickly enough that she must have guessed. 'What makes you think it's something Noah's done? Most parents finding a policeman on the doorstep need reassuring that their child is safe. But you immediately jumped to the conclusion that Noah was in trouble. Why is that, sir? Does he have a history of getting into trouble?'

Selkirk was regarding her with basilisk eyes. 'I'm not most parents, Constable,' he said, his tone barely the right side of objectionable. 'I deal with police officers every day of my working life. And I'm perfectly well aware that if some harm had come to Noah you'd be handling this interview in a quite different way. So somebody's in trouble. I haven't murdered anyone this week, so I'm guessing it's Noah. So I'll ask you again: what's the little sod done?'

'Absolutely nothing,' said Voss firmly. 'I haven't seen him. It's not his behaviour I want to talk to you about.'

That was the moment that Adam Selkirk knew why they

were here. In his eyes Voss saw all the whirring machinery stop dead, as if a girder had been thrust among the cogs. The weight of understanding dragged down the corners of his mouth. But he said nothing, just watched Voss with still eyes and waited for the sky to fall.

'Good,' said the detective softly. 'Now, how do you want to do this? Do you want to tell me all the ways a twelve-year-old boy can collect bruises? Or shall we talk about what happens in the leafy fastness of River Drive when you come in at the end of a hard day and the housekeeper goes home?'

'I don't hit my son,' Adam Selkirk said, as precisely as if he was chiselling the words in marble.

Voss sighed, disappointed. 'All right. So tell me about the time he fell off his bike, and the time he walked into the patio door, and that time you played American football in the park and didn't make enough allowance for the fact that you're bigger than he is, and...'

'You're not listening to me, Sergeant,' said Selkirk, with the kind of quiet force that Deacon employed when he was too angry to shout. 'I don't hit my son. I love my son.'

'The little sod must be glad to know it,' said Voss stonily.

Surprise made Meadows look away from Selkirk and quickly at the Sergeant. She'd never heard him speak like that to anyone, including thugs and drug dealers. He was famously even-tempered, polite even in the face of provocation. He didn't work at it: it happened naturally, it was who he was. Now all at once he was starting to sound like...

She hesitated, and edited the thought in the privacy of her own head. No, it wasn't Detective Superintendent Deacon he was starting to sound like. It was Detective Inspector Hyde.

Again she pushed the verbal equivalent of a shoulder between the two men. 'Sometimes, though, it isn't a question of love. People do hit children they love dearly. And wives and lovers. Some people find it difficult to control their anger. Everybody shouts at their family sometimes, and feels guilty about it afterwards. Some people find it difficult to stop at just shouting.'

Selkirk looked down at her in such a way that even Meadows, a fit and well-trained young policewoman who believed she could probably take him if she had to, felt the pressure of intimidation. For his wife and his son, trapped with the big angry man in their charming, desirable, above all private home, the pressure must have been crushing. Waiting for him to explode. Never being quite certain what would set him off this time.

'Constable,' he said, and his tone was so low it rumbled like the voice of an elephant, 'I spend half my life in courtrooms. I know at least as much about domestic violence as you do. In fact, I know more. I know you're accusing me of something I haven't done. Ever. I have never laid a violent hand on my son. Who told you that?'

It wasn't a question the detectives wanted to answer just yet. 'I'll tell you who it wasn't,' volunteered Voss. 'It wasn't Noah. And it wasn't his mother.'

'I know *that*,' Selkirk said with towering disdain. 'Neither of them would say anything so absurd. You say you've been to Noah's school? But I don't think this came from the school. I know where this came from. That meddling little...maths teacher.' He managed to invest the words with a venom more usually associated with terms like *paedophile* and *vivisector*.

'I'm not prepared to disclose the source of our information at this stage,' said Voss stiffly. 'Someone who was concerned for Noah's well-being drew our attention to what was happening, and we're taking it from there.'

Whatever else Adam Selkirk was, he was an intelligent man. Even this angry he was capable of quality thinking. Now he was thinking beyond the accusation that had been made, beyond even who had made it, to why it was being investigated at precisely this time in precisely this manner. The low stridency in his voice softened. 'Yes, you are, aren't you?' he said. 'Not Social Services, not Child Protection – you. The Criminal Investigation Department.'

'Child abuse is a criminal offence,' Meadows pointed out.

'Of course it is,' he agreed. 'But it's not – how shall I put this? – the most rewarding kind of investigation. The kind that leads to plaudits and promotions and the prospect of a division of one's own some day. Unlike, for instance, Serious Organised Crime. Now there's a way to make your name – taking down criminal masterminds when other policemen, good policemen, have failed. There's a way of getting noticed. Don't you think so, Sergeant Voss?'

So he knew what they were doing. So much the better, thought Voss, who hadn't looked forward to explaining it. 'We do our best to deal with all the crimes that come to our attention,' he answered, deadpan.

'I just bet you do,' sneered Selkirk. 'So what's the deal here? I suddenly remember I wasn't on *Salamander* the last weekend in June and you let me get on with thumping my kid?'

If he'd thumped Meadows she could hardly have been more astonished. It was an extraordinary thing for anyone under investigation to say, let alone a man whose career depended on verbal aplomb. He couldn't *really* think there was a deal like that on offer – or that, if there had been, it wouldn't have been dressed up an awful lot more carefully, since one party couldn't be seen offering such a trade and the other couldn't be seen needing it.

Which meant that Adam Selkirk wasn't in the market for a deal even had one been available. He thought they had nothing on him. He thought they were bluffing and he could afford to call them.

Voss said evenly, 'Am I to take that as an admission, sir?'

Selkirk smiled coldly. 'You can take it any way you like, Sergeant. You and I both know this conversation is never going to be reported in court. That's not why you're here.'

'Why do you suppose we're here?'

'To put me on notice, Sergeant Voss. To make me aware that I can look after Terry Walsh's best interests or I can look after my own but I can't do both. To tell me what you know, or think you know, about things that might be happening within my family. To give me to understand that if I mend my ways now – *all* my ways – this need go no further, but if you feel the need to talk to me again it won't be in the privacy of my offices. And finally, to put it on record that I've been the subject of a police investigation and should therefore be considered a flawed witness in any future prosecution.' His head lifted, the broad jaw jutting. 'Have I missed anything?'

'No, sir,' said Voss, considering, 'I don't believe you have. I'll just underline the salient points again, should I? Tomorrow, and every day next week, and every day if needs be until he turns eighteen, someone will make it their business to check that Noah's in school, that he's all right and that he hasn't had any more of those unfortunate little accidents. And if he isn't, he isn't or he has, I'll know about it within ten minutes. That's when we stop trying to help you find alternative methods of stress management and charge you with child abuse.

'And if I can arrange to do it on the courthouse steps on a Wednesday morning, with half the town's legal profession and maybe a television camera looking on, that's exactly what I shall do. Now,' he said, holding Selkirk's eye with his own, 'is there anything *I* missed out?'

It was a cloudy night. Daniel did a bit of housework, failed to find anything riveting on the TV and went to bed early. For an hour, though, he lay sleepless, thinking, turning over in his mind the situation he found himself embroiled in.

No, that wasn't entirely true – and Daniel put a lot of value on the entirety of truth. To a large degree he'd embroiled himself. Noah Selkirk had come to him for a little advice, not to hire a dragon-slayer. He didn't want the dragon slain. The boy didn't want to hurt his father, he just wanted Selkirk to stop hurting *him*. And he only wanted that if it could be achieved without destroying his family. If it came to a straight choice between a black eye every weekend and seeing Selkirk taken away in a police car, Daniel had no doubt Noah would exhaust every excuse in the book and then start back with the patio doors again.

In which case, had Daniel the right to force help on him? Perhaps he had both the right and the duty. A twelve-year-old boy can't be expected to take rational decisions on matters of such immediate personal importance. Daniel believed fervently that nothing Adam Selkirk had to offer in return – not expensive holidays, not top-of-the-range toys and computers, not even the good days when he wasn't too stressed to remember that he loved his son – was worth the reddened print of a hand on the child's face. But Noah Selkirk was an intelligent boy. If it was worth it to him, was it possible Daniel was wrong?

Because if he was, this whole thing was in danger of spiralling out of control. With nothing but the child's best interests at heart, he'd spoken to his school and he'd spoken to the police, and the genie wasn't going back in *that* bottle without a fight. If this ended in tears – if the Selkirk family broke up over it – it wouldn't be his father that Noah blamed.

Well, Daniel had broad shoulders – philosophically if not physically – he could carry the responsibility if he was sure he'd done the right thing. But the blame game wouldn't stop there. Noah would be painfully aware, and would carry the burden for the rest of his childhood, that Daniel didn't come from nowhere in a puff of red smoke, like the demon king in a pantomime – that it was Noah's own actions which brought him in contact with the Selkirk family. In the fullness of time he would come to understand that both he and Daniel had done what was required of them. But before that coming of maturity lay a childhood of self-loathing Daniel would have spent blood to save him from.

So had there been another way? Was there still some other choice to be made that safeguarded Noah without threatening his family? And of course there was, but it wasn't for Daniel to make. If Adam Selkirk could control himself long enough to see that he was being given a chance for a better relationship with his son, to break the cycle of anger and abuse and move forward, this could still be a win-win situation. But what if he couldn't, or didn't? Armies were on the move now, significant forces with their own rules of engagement, and the one thing every commander knows is that it's easier to start a war than to end one.

So Daniel lay awake until after midnight, anxieties like the gallopers on a carousel chasing one another round and round and getting nowhere. Some time after that he slept.

The phone kicked him awake at ten to one. He lifted it with his left hand, scrabbling for his glasses with his right. 'Wha'? Who…?' He tried again as some of his scattered wits returned. 'Hello?'

'This is your fault,' cried the piping little voice, high with panic and accusation. 'You shouldn't have interfered. Nobody asked you to. Now they're angry and they're fighting again, and it's all your fault!'

Daniel was wide awake now, didn't need to ask who he was talking to. He kept the alarm he felt out of his voice, went for low and authoritative. 'Noah. Are you safe where you are?'

'What?'

'Go to the bathroom and lock the door. Don't open it till I get there. I'm on my way. Do you understand? Don't open that door however much he shouts. Give him time to calm down.'

'My mother…'

'I know,' said Daniel briefly, the heart twisting within him. 'But if you're safe she only has herself to think about. Do as I say. I'll be there in ten minutes.'

He knew as soon as he'd put the phone down he couldn't keep that promise. An athlete might have run from the shore to River Drive in ten minutes, but Daniel was no athlete. Which wouldn't have mattered if he'd had a car. He tried the numbers of the local taxi firms but got only recorded messages. With most of his ten minutes already gone, he did what he always did when disaster loomed. He called Brodie.

And she did what she always did in a real emergency. As a matter of habit she might be caustic, she might want for patience, she might take rather more pleasure than necessary in having her own way and the means by which she got it, but in a crisis all that went by the board. She would stint nothing to get matters under control, and he wouldn't hear a word of criticism until the dust had settled and there was time for an inquest.

At which the verdict would be – he knew as if it had already sat – that he'd been stupid and she'd saved his sorry ass; but he could forgive all that because when he phoned her at one in the morning and said he needed her car, she didn't even ask why. Seeing a light still on upstairs she explained briefly to her long-suffering neighbour and was on her way while Marta was still settling herself on Brodie's sofa with a mug of hot chocolate and a lurid paperback.

Daniel was waiting on the Promenade. But though the matter was clearly urgent – and Brodie still didn't know what was going on – he wanted to take her home before dealing with it.

'Don't be ridiculous,' she said dismissively.

'It's already got nasty,' he said, trying to explain without whetting her appetite, 'it's already got violent. It's no place for you. Not now.'

'And it is for you?' She stayed where she was in the driver's seat. She was always hard to shift once her mind was made up, and right now she was being stubborn for two.

'I'm not pregnant. I can take the odd knock if I have to.'

She eyed him sternly. 'Daniel, I can take you in a fair fight any day of the week. Even now. Even now *with one hand tied behind my back*. So get in the damn car and tell me where to drive.'

This wasn't what he wanted. She seemed to leave him no choice. And time was pressing. He got in. 'River Drive. You'll stay in the car?'

'River Drive? As in, where Adam Selkirk lives?' Her voice inflected upwards like a raised eyebrow.

'Yes.' His voice low, Daniel explained while Brodie drove.

'Do you think he was hurt?' asked Brodie when he finished.

'I don't know. I don't think he was terribly hurt. He was more worried about his mother. But I don't know whether he did what I told him to, and locked himself where Selkirk couldn't get at him. He may have thought helping Marianne mattered more.'

She drove fast, keeping her eyes on the road. 'You don't think we should call the police?'

'We may have to,' agreed Daniel. 'But...'

She'd heard that *But* before. It packed more import than most three-letter words – more than many sentences. It said he was thinking several moves ahead, more concerned with the end-game than the attrition. For a moment she tried to think the way Daniel thought. 'Ah...'

'What?' he asked, looking at her, suddenly defensive.

'You think if you roll up in the middle of a family spat

Adam Selkirk's going to deck you. *Then* you call the police, and from then on it's you that's the complainant, not Noah.'

He didn't deny it. 'That kid's got problems enough without being the one who puts his father in jail. And I'm not sure,' he added tersely, 'that it's helpful to think of it as a family spat.'

'Of course not,' acknowledged Brodie, contrite. 'Not if people are getting hurt.'

'He's got a black eye, a grazed wrist and something wrong with his left arm that'll never heal if he doesn't stop scratching it. That's what I know about. What I don't know about is what's hidden by his clothes.'

'Then of course we have to do something.'

Brodie had a number of strengths and a good few weaknesses, and people who knew her as well as Daniel recognised that sometimes they were the same. One was her habit of muscling in on the action. Nature never designed her to sing in the chorus: she had to be at the front of the stage, and if at all possible conducting. It was certainly a fault, intensely infuriating to those whose rights and authority she trampled in the process. But sometimes, having her adjust the natural grammar of a sentence from second person singular to first person plural like that was like hearing the bugles of the Seventh Cavalry topping the rise.

There were lots of reasons, big and little, why he loved her, but one was that he never felt now that it was him against the rest of the world. He always had an ally. To be sure, she complained more than Tonto, and had a longer memory than Lassie, but when push came to shove – even literally – he was not alone, and he knew he never would be. He felt the tears prick and had to avoid speaking for a moment.

Oblivious, Brodie grumbled, 'Only, if you get a bloody nose, keep it away from me. This bell-tent has to do me till the baby's born.'

River Drive was probably the best address in Dimmock. There were more expensive properties on top of the Firestone Cliffs, beloved of those who liked their consumption to be conspicuous. But the River Drive houses were substantial in a different way: not understated but not boastful either, just thoroughly good houses on large wooded plots with good cars in the driveways and staff flats over the double garages.

There was an elegant Arts & Crafts feel about the whole street, not hindered by the use of converted gas-lamps for street lighting. Brodie pulled up under the one nearest to the Selkirks' house. 'What do we do? Knock on the door?'

'*I* knock on the door,' said Daniel firmly. 'You stay here, ready for a fast getaway.'

'You don't really think Adam Selkirk's going to chase you down the drive with a golf club?'

'I don't know what to expect,' Daniel said honestly. 'But I believe in being prepared.'

He took a couple of steps towards the big house, then stopped and turned back. 'And just for the record, it isn't a bell-tent. You look beautiful.' He squared his narrow shoulders and headed for the front door.

CHAPTER FIFTEEN

He wasn't exaggerating: Daniel had no idea what would happen when he rang the bell. There were lights on both upstairs and downstairs so he wasn't concerned that the drama was over and he was rousing people from their beds. On the other hand, he could hear nothing. Not an argument, not an altercation, not even a disagreement. Perhaps that was how domestic violence was done in places like River Drive – quietly. But there'd been sound and fury enough to terrify Noah only twenty minutes ago, and Daniel doubted there'd been time for a lasting peace to break out. Perhaps it was a lull in the hostilities.

Or perhaps one of the parties had stormed out. There was only one car on the drive – Marianne's midnight-blue Porsche. Of course, Selkirk might have parked in the garage. Daniel wasn't going to know until someone answered the door. If it was Selkirk, the pregnant hush was unlikely to last much longer.

But Adam Selkirk didn't fling wide the door and come out fists first. No one came. Daniel stood on the mat for three or four minutes during which time the house remained lit but entirely silent. He rang again. He turned back to Brodie, watching from the pavement, and shrugged helplessly.

'Try round the back,' she called in a low *It's half-one in the morning in River Drive* sort of voice.

He nodded and was backing away from the door when he heard movement inside. The lock turned and the door opened. 'Daniel.'

It was Marianne Selkirk as he'd never seen her. If this hadn't been her house he mightn't have recognised her. The ash-blonde hair, released from its elegant restraint, fell about her shoulders in a profusion of sweaty curls, and perspiration made huge damp patches on her T-shirt. It was an old T-shirt, for slopping around at home or even sleeping in, but someone had printed it specially for her. It said: *Fundraisers do it again and again because the need never ends.*

Daniel had seen her in the power suits that went with the Porsche, and in the designer jeans that are the off-duty uniform of powerful women. He had not seen her in a sweaty T-shirt and leggings before, he had not seen her barefoot, and he'd never seen her with blood on her face from a split lip and bubbling nostril, and the redness that precedes bruising on her forehead, her feet and both wrists. The sight took his voice, and momentarily his breath, away. She didn't look old enough to be the mother of a twelve-year-old son. She *did* look old enough to be the mother of a country.

When he found his voice he said, 'Where's Noah?'

Marianne smiled ruefully. 'In the bathroom. He won't let me in.'

Daniel gave a little chuckle, half sympathetic, half apology. 'Is he all right?'

'I think so. Come in and ask him yourself.'

Daniel did as he was bid. 'Where's your husband?'

She didn't look at him as she led the way upstairs. 'He went for a drive.'

Daniel didn't like to quiz her but it was important to know. 'Will he be long?'

'An hour or so. It's what he does when he needs to calm down – he goes for a drive in the country.'

Daniel reached for her wrist. The bruises stopped him just in time, but the thought went all the way. Marianne paused on the landing and looked round at him.

'You shouldn't be here when he gets back,' Daniel said simply.

She didn't answer. She tapped on the bathroom door. 'Daniel's here now, darling. You can open the door.'

After a moment they heard the catch and the door opened, and Noah Selkirk stood there in abject despair and his Chelsea pyjamas.

Daniel crouched in front of him, studying the tear-streaked little face and then, lifting the blue shirt, the child's abdomen. There were new bruises, but nothing that seemed to require medical attention. This time his mother appeared to have fielded the worst of the violence.

'Are you all right?' Daniel asked quietly.

Noah nodded.

'Honestly? You're not dizzy? Your tummy doesn't hurt?'

The boy shook his head.

'OK.' Daniel stood up. 'You did absolutely the right thing calling me. Now go and get dressed, and put some things in a bag. Clothes for a couple of days and anything else you're going to want. You're coming to stay with me till things calm down a bit.' He looked round. 'Both of you. I've only one spare bed, but we can make Noah comfortable on the sofa.'

Marianne Selkirk dabbed the blood away from her nose. 'That's kind of you, Daniel. But there's no need. We'll be all right. Won't we, Noah?'

The boy said nothing.

'All right?' Daniel's voice soared incredulously. 'Have you looked in a mirror? Marianne, you've had the crap beaten out of you! I'm not leaving you here. If you won't come with me I'll stay, and then he'll beat the crap out of me. Is that what you want?'

The woman shook her head, not knowing whether to laugh or cry.

'Me neither,' said Daniel. 'So get some things together and come down to my house. At least for tonight. We can talk about what you do next in the morning.'

'What's Adam going to think? When he gets home?'

'Leave him a note. Don't tell him where you are. Just say you're both safe and you'll call him tomorrow.'

'What if he calls the police?'

'Oh yes,' said Daniel, '*that's* going to happen! Marianne, don't let him make you feel this is your fault. You and Noah have the right to feel safe. If you aren't safe with him here, we'll find you somewhere else. Rent you a cottage somewhere. Once you're safe there'll be time to talk about how you work this out. But putting distance between you is the first priority.'

'I suppose...'

Daniel thought she'd never actually considered it before. That the violence had become part of their way of life so insidiously she thought of it rather as she thought of cleaning the cooker: not the most pleasant of chores but what are you going to do? If you want the meals you've got to clean the cooker. She couldn't see that these were not inseparable elements – that she could be safe, that her son could be safe, that they could go on living here, but they didn't have to pay for that with weekly eruptions of violence. That if Selkirk couldn't control himself he could be controlled. If they weren't safe living with him he could live somewhere else.

'Then pack some things.'

Still she didn't move. 'Maybe you should just take Noah. I'll talk to Adam when he gets back. We'll both be calmer then, and at least Noah will be getting some sleep.'

The boy was hovering on the brink of tears. 'I don't want to…'

'Come on, darling,' she said briskly. 'Daniel will look after you. And Daddy and I can talk without worrying that we're upsetting you.'

'You don't talk,' he whined. 'You shout.'

'Well – sometimes,' she conceded.

'Actually,' interjected Daniel, 'I don't think it's a great idea either. When he comes back and he finds I've taken Noah, he'll be incandescent. If you're still here, you're going to take the brunt of that. Please, Marianne. Please come with us. Just for tonight. Give the dust a chance to settle. Then we'll come back here and talk to him together tomorrow. Please?'

It was in her eyes that, even knowing he was right, she was about to decline. He couldn't believe what she was prepared to take from this man. 'What are you waiting for?' he demanded impatiently. 'For him to put one of you in hospital? For the neighbours to call the police? For me to?'

The glance she flicked at him was surprised and – for the first time – afraid. 'We don't need the police.'

Daniel shook his head, bemused. The approval of her neighbours mattered more to her than the violence of her husband. Whatever, he thought: if that's what works, that's what we'll go with. 'But it won't be your call,' he pressed. 'If they get a complaint they will act on it. They've been told to move domestic violence right up the agenda. These days they don't even ask the injured party if she wants to bring charges. They see the evidence and they take it from there.'

She glanced uncertainly at the stairs, at the front door. The way he left; the way he'd come back. 'I suppose, if it's just for tonight…'

'Get some things together.'

He went out to explain to Brodie. 'They're coming home with me for a couple of days.'

Brodie looked surprised. 'All three of them?'

Daniel smiled. 'Selkirk's not here. Apparently, after beating his wife bloody he feels the need of a little drive to clear his head.'

Brodie pursed her lips. 'When he comes back and finds them gone, he'll have a good idea where to look for them.'

'Fine,' said Daniel. 'He tries beating my door in, I have no problem calling the police. But he won't. Men who hit their wives and children mostly do it because they're not brave enough to take on anybody bigger.'

Brodie was remembering the scene in the little lobby in Shack Lane. She sounded doubtful. 'I don't know, Daniel. Last time I saw him he *looked* brave enough to take a swing at you.'

'That's fine too,' said Daniel shortly. 'He'll only make it easier for everyone.'

'Except you.'

'He's a lot bigger than me.'

'Exactly.'

'No. I mean, he's a *lot* bigger than me. If he hits me I'm going down; if I go down I'm staying down. Unless he wants to continue the assault on his hands and knees, that'll be the end of it. Don't worry about me, Brodie. I'm not tough enough to get hurt in a stand-up fight.'

The town hall clock struck twice as Marianne Selkirk's Porsche purred through the centre of Dimmock towards the Promenade. 'Quarter past two,' murmured Daniel.

Marianne glanced at him, ready to correct him, but then didn't. She considered for a moment instead. 'You're very much at home here, aren't you?' she said quietly.

He didn't understand. 'What do you mean?'

'Here – in this town. You know how it works. You know the town hall clock is always fifteen minutes slow. It makes sense to you.'

Daniel was still puzzled. 'The clock?'

She shook her head. 'The town. Small town living. You aren't from here. You haven't lived here as long as I have. But you fit in here in a way I never have and never will. Things like the damn clock drive me mad. You just make the necessary adjustment in your head. I envy you that.'

Daniel wasn't sure it was a compliment. 'Being provincial?'

Marianne laughed softly. Noah was asleep on the back seat, exhausted by fear and emotion, wrapped in his mother's coat. As they left the house, Daniel carrying Marianne's bag, the boy faltered; and Marianne threw her coat around her unhappy son and swept him up into her arms. Noah wasn't a big twelve-year-old, but plainly Marianne wasn't as fragile as she looked either.

'Being adaptable,' she said. 'If something doesn't suit me I go to a lot of time, trouble and usually expense to change it. I think, if something doesn't suit you, you amend your expectations.'

It was partly true and partly not. The bit that was accurate was perceptive for someone he knew very little. The bit that was wide of the mark indicated how little she knew him. Daniel said, 'Which is why you're a high-powered executive with a Porsche and an office in London, and I'm not.'

'And perhaps also why you're happy and I'm not.'

They'd reached the netting-shed. Marianne stopped the car and they looked at one another in the backwash of the street-lights. The night, and the fact that most of the town was sleeping around them, encouraged both honesty and intimacy.

They weren't friends in the way that Daniel and Brodie were friends; and they hadn't known one another long enough for that other sort of friendship to develop – less intense but still worth having – that comes of simply moving in the same orbit till familiarity breeds a kind of mutual amiability way-marked by the sharing of newspapers and holiday snaps and updates on the dog's boil. In other circumstances it might have been a sexual attraction, but neither of them was looking for an affair, Daniel because all his hopes were vested in Brodie, Marianne because she already had more than enough on her plate.

What was left was two intelligent people recognising in each other a kind of kinship. They were both natural outsiders. Daniel's odd little netting-shed and Marianne's gracious home with its own grounds and top-notch address were both ivory towers, different to the way most people lived. Even the fact that Marianne drove a Porsche and Daniel didn't have a car at all underlined their apartness. Both were in the community but not really of it. Outside the window looking in.

Daniel had said something like that to Paddy once. She'd thought for a moment then nodded. 'Like Father Christmas,' she'd said, filling his heart.

'Come inside,' he said. 'Put Noah to bed and get yourself cleaned up, and I'll make some cocoa.'

'*Cocoa*?' If he'd offered her a lightly grilled earthworm she could hardly have sounded more appalled.

Daniel gave an apologetic shrug. 'After the night you've had, coffee'll keep you awake. Cocoa will help you sleep.'

'You think I'm going to sleep? I'll take the coffee and the consequences.'

With Noah settled – not in fact on the sofa but in Daniel's bed next door, Daniel wryly resigned to sleeping on the couch himself, reminding himself that this was one of the few up-sides to being short – Marianne headed for the bathroom to make repairs. She hadn't brought make-up, made do with soap and the contents of the first aid box, and emerged looking fresher and less battered than he expected. She'd changed her T-shirt for one of his, without the sweat-stains and spots of blood.

'Feeling better?'

'Much.' She came and sat on the sofa. 'Daniel, this is good of you.'

He put the tray on the low table in front of her. 'I had to do something. It was at least partly my fault.'

That surprised her as much as the cocoa. 'How is it *your* fault?'

He didn't think he was breaking a confidence. 'Noah asked for my advice. I thought I was helping. I didn't expect... Well. I didn't expect things to turn violent.'

'Noah came to you?'

'He was unhappy, he needed to talk to someone. But he didn't tell me how bad things had got. He said he was worried about you, but I thought he meant the long hours and the fact that you're away from home so much. I didn't realise he was worried *for* you.'

'We've shocked you, haven't we?' she said in a low voice.

He saw no point denying it. 'A little. It's one of those stereotypes, isn't it? You think of the drunken navvy staggering home at closing time, belting the kids and giving his wife a shiner. You don't think it happens at the better end of town. However much the experts insist it has little to do with either class or income, that domestic violence is just easier to hide in genteel leafy suburbs, it's not what you expect.'

'And what *do* you expect of us, Daniel?' There was something faintly amused, faintly provocative, in her tone and in her eyes. He wasn't fooled. She didn't think it was funny. She just wasn't prepared to be embarrassed.

'I don't know. Not this. I mean, from where I'm sitting – from where I was sitting a week ago, anyway – you seem to have the perfect life. Two intelligent, high-achieving people, both in demand for their skills, with the kind of home most of us can't even afford to look at. On top of that you have a charming son who obviously thinks the world of both of you. He's proud of you and he loves you and he wants to make you happy. He thinks it's his fault he isn't succeeding.'

That made her eyes fill. 'He said that?' she whispered.

'Pretty much. Didn't you read his letter?'

Marianne shook her head, bemused. 'What letter?'

So it never reached her. His father read it first and hit the roof. 'It was my idea,' Daniel confessed. 'I didn't realise then how volatile things were. I thought if he could tell you exactly how he felt – that it isn't easy being the son of two important people – you'd find a way to make more time, more space, for him. I'm sorry, that sounds impertinent. But he asked for my help, I couldn't turn him away. I thought you just needed a wake-up call, the pair of you…'

'Oh yes,' she said softly. 'That's just what we needed.'

Daniel said nothing more until he saw the coffee doing its job, putting the strength back into her body and her resolve. Then he said, 'How long has it been like this?'

He didn't have to elaborate: she knew what he meant. She sighed. 'Oh – a year, maybe more. But it's been coming for longer. We were too successful for our own good. If either of us had been a little less accustomed to getting our own way we'd have made a better job of marriage. We're not good at compromising. At work, if Adam compromises his clients can lose whole chunks of their lives. If I do, the people I think of as my clients can lose their entire lives.

'When you're used to playing for stakes that high, it's hard to scale down your ideas when you go home. To adjust to the fact that what you do there is utterly insignificant in the grand scheme of things and yet still important to someone. Do we go to his parents for Christmas or have my mother to us? Who cares? There'll be food on the table, presents under the tree and arguments over the mince-pies whatever we do – and all the time we're doing it, every three seconds someone somewhere in the world is dying because there's nothing on their table at all, and there hasn't been for months. It just makes me feel so helpless. And so angry.'

'You save lives every day, Marianne,' Daniel said quietly. 'You know that. You're one of comparatively few people in the world who do actually make a difference. Noah knows that too. He's intensely proud of what you do. It's why he didn't want to add to your concerns. Why he tried to pretend it didn't matter that he doesn't see enough of either of his parents, and the time he spends with his father is marred by anxiety – wondering what'll set him off this time, whether it'll be just shouting or fists. But it does matter. It matters terribly. Noah's desperate. He came to me because he couldn't think of anyone else. He needs to be protected, whatever that takes.'

'You think I should leave Adam.'

Daniel thought for a moment. 'I think you have to put an end to this situation. If the only way you can be sure your husband will never raise his hand to either of you again is to leave him, I think that's a choice that makes itself.'

'Everyone blames the man…' she said lamely.

'Stop right there,' said Daniel sharply. 'Don't tell me you ask for it. Don't tell me you provoke him, and Noah provokes him, and he's tired at the end of a busy week and he strikes out without thinking, and you're sure he loves you really. Don't you dare tell me that, Marianne. A family brings comforts but it also brings responsibilities. The first one, the *very* first one, is that nobody gets hurt. If he can't promise you that and stick to it, then you have to get out. You have to protect yourself and your son. You have to start doing it right now.'

'I know,' she mumbled, 'I know. It's just…it's more complicated than you think. It happens, I'm not saying it doesn't happen, but it happens in a minute. All the rest of the time – all the other minutes that make up our lives – we're good.'

'No,' said Daniel. 'You're not.'

'Really,' she insisted. 'Most of the time we have a good marriage, a good family life. Noah has a good home.'

'No,' Daniel said again, forcefully, 'he hasn't. If he isn't safe from physical assault, nothing else he has is worth a damn. If you aren't safe, all those other minutes when everything seems to be fine are a sham. You're falling for the oldest con in the book – you're letting him get away with doing things no man should even *want* to do just because, when he's finished, he says sorry.

'I don't know what your husband's problem is. I don't know if he's a decent man with an ungovernable temper, or a vicious man that you and Noah are good at tiptoeing round. But I know what *your* problem is: it's him. You have to put some distance between you – mentally, emotionally and actually – so that when you're ready to talk to him you can do it from a position of strength.'

'You're talking about moving out,' she said. 'Not just staying here tonight. Finding somewhere else to live.'

'I think you have to. At least for now. If you go back, nothing will change.'

'No,' said Marianne Selkirk pensively. 'Whereas if I walk out...?'

'Don't think of it as walking out. Think of it as taking control. Take yourself and Noah, and go somewhere the violence can't reach you. Take the time to reassess your priorities. Work out a plan of campaign. Convince yourself that nothing any man can offer you is worth what you've been paying for it.

'Take some time off work, too. I know it's difficult, but you can't be fighting battles on different fronts. You're good at what you do, Marianne, everyone knows it – no one wants to see you burn out trying to be all things to all people. Just for the moment, forget everyone else and their needs – concentrate on yours and Noah's. Make the time to get to know yourself again, to work out what matters to you and how to get it. Let your friends help you. Get out of that house and you'll realise you don't have to deal with this alone.'

'You paint an attractive picture, Daniel,' she whispered.

'Compared with what you've been putting up with, *anything* would look attractive. Which also means that any improvement to your situation will bring real benefits. Try it. Try living without the tension – without the fear that any argument, any little disagreement, is going to spiral away down to rage and violence. Try it for a week. You won't be prepared to live with that risk ever again.'

'Live where?'

Daniel shrugged. 'Anywhere. Rent a place – somewhere quiet where you and Noah can just enjoy one another's company in safety. I know an estate agent. We'll pay him a visit in the morning.'

CHAPTER SIXTEEN

They wouldn't all fit in the Porsche so Mr Turnbull drove them in his people-carrier. It was navy blue. Edwin Turnbull had always hankered after a red open-topped sports car, but Doreen said a people-carrier was more practical for a man of his age and occupation, and navy blue was a respectable colour. She was right on both counts, but in any event Mr Turnbull tended not to argue with his wife. It was too much like getting amorous – Mr Turnbull was also careful about his language – with a porcupine: the odds were unfavourable.

'It's only a short-term let,' he said, checking his records. 'Six months, with the possibility of another six months after that. The owners are working abroad. Would six months be enough for you?'

'Plenty,' nodded Marianne. 'In fact, I don't want it for six months. I'll take it for two months, and if I want an extension I'll let you know.'

Mr Turnbull wasn't sure. 'My clients were rather hoping to have it occupied until they were ready to return.'

'I dare say they were,' said Marianne with a smile. 'Unfortunately, people don't always get what they want. It's standing empty now, and the winter isn't over yet. Surely it would be better to have it occupied until the weather warms up than to leave it empty. But it's up to you, Mr Turnbull. There'll be other cottages to rent on the Three Downs.'

Of course, this was what Marianne Selkirk did every day – what she was world class at doing: negotiating with people who didn't really want to give her what she wanted, and coming out ahead, *and making them feel good about it*. That was the clever part. They didn't have to give her anything. They ended up not only giving her what she wanted but feeling sufficiently positive about the experience that they'd probably give her some more next time she asked.

If Marianne Selkirk was born to be a fundraiser, Edwin Turnbull was born to be an estate agent. He knew two things in the depths of his soul: that anyone who walked through his door was a potential customer, and that letting a potential customer walk through somebody *else's* door was professional suicide. 'Let me call the owners, Mrs Selkirk. That's a very good point about the weather. And it's not like you're going to trash the place and move on when it needs cleaning.'

Marianne beamed. 'No, Mr Turnbull, my student days are long gone.'

So were Daniel's, and they hadn't been like that at the time. He coughed politely. 'There's another point Mrs Selkirk needs you to be clear on, Mr Turnbull.'

'That's right,' said Marianne, almost as if she'd forgotten. 'I don't want to go into detail, it doesn't affect the tenancy, but I'm looking for a bit of peace and quiet. I don't want to broadcast my whereabouts. If someone asks if I've rented a property from you, would you feel comfortable declining to give out this address?'

'Perfectly comfortable, Mrs Selkirk,' said Mr Turnbull stoutly. 'I'd say it's a matter of policy. If you don't want your address giving out, nobody's going to get it from me. Oh.' He looked at Daniel then, suddenly wary. There was history between them: he knew that events concerning Mr Hood were not always straightforward. 'Unless it's the police.'

Marianne gave a high, spritish chuckle. Daniel shook his head. 'It won't be the police. Can I be frank?' He glanced to Marianne for permission, received it with a dip of her head. 'Mrs Selkirk has family problems that she needs a little respite from. She may not get that if her family know where she's staying.'

'I understand,' said Mr Turnbull soberly. She was wearing long sleeves but there'd been no easy way of disguising her bruised forehead. He'd assumed she really had walked into a patio door – or fallen off a horse, or had a prang in the car, or suffered any of half a dozen little misfortunes that can befall a respectable woman. It had not until now occurred to him that there might be anything sinister about it.

'Thank you, Mr Turnbull,' Marianne said with a smile. 'That's all the reassurance I need.'

And Edwin Turnbull, who was a fool for an attractive woman, blushed until his bald pate shone.

With the paperwork done, Marianne drove Daniel home and collected her belongings and Noah's. 'I'll go home when Adam's in court and get the rest of what we'll need.'

Daniel nodded. 'I'll come with you, if you like.'

'There's no need. I can pick a time when I know he won't be there. Daniel,' she said, and she took his hand in hers. 'I'm very grateful for what you've done for us. I'm sure it's been embarrassing, and maybe worse than that. I don't think Adam knows how intimidating he can be sometimes. Most people would have made disapproving noises and walked away.'

'That was never an option,' said Daniel honestly. 'I'm a teacher. I have an obligation to kids – all kids. From the moment Noah asked for help I was involved, whether or not I wanted to be, whether or not you wanted me to be.'

'He's a pretty smart boy, isn't he?' said Marianne, with a pride she didn't even attempt to disguise. 'A town of sixty thousand souls, and he found the one man who felt like that.'

Daniel shrugged awkwardly. 'I don't suppose I *am* the only one who feels like that. Other people would have helped him too.'

'Well, maybe. But then we'd have ended up dealing with policemen and social workers, and any chance we might still have of finding our way through this would have been scuppered. I know you don't think much of my marriage, Daniel, but I do. I think it's worth fighting for. I'm not ready to give up on it. And I don't want to see it smothered by the well-meaning attention of a bunch of heavy-handed professionals. I think you were our only chance of having something worth salvaging at the end. I'm not sure how things'll work out, but I'll always be grateful for your support.'

It was half past eleven before Daniel turned up to work. Brodie had steam coming out of her ears. 'Where the hell have you *been*? Why weren't you answering your phone?'

'Sorry – I wasn't at home.' He'd have explained further if she'd given him the chance.

'Your *mobile* phone?'

He'd forgotten about it, had to hunt through his pockets. 'It's turned off.'

'I *know* it's turned off,' snapped Brodie. 'If you'd take the trouble to learn how to use the thing you'd know it *says* when it's turned off. But Daniel, it's not *supposed* to be turned off. I provided it for you at great expense' – this was an exaggeration – 'so I can find you when I need you. So I'm not stuck behind this desk on my own for two hours wondering where the hell you are and what's happened to you.'

'Sorry,' he said again. 'I was with Marianne. Mr Turnbull found her a cottage to rent.'

'She couldn't find the estate agent's on her own?'

He didn't understand her hostility. 'You know what the situation is. She needs a bit of looking after.'

'So does this business,' said Brodie forcefully. 'Daniel, you don't work for yourself any more. Personal matters get dealt with outside office hours. And if it really can't wait, the least you can do is phone me. I thought Adam Selkirk had got you up a dark alley.'

In a way she was right, although most employers don't talk that way to staff who *aren't* also close personal friends. 'All right,' he said quietly. 'I'm sorry you were worried. I should have called. Was it a problem? Have I missed something?'

She shook her head, the dark curls shading her eyes. 'No. It's just...' The annoyance had evaporated with his apology, leaving something in her voice he couldn't remember hearing before. She sounded forlorn.

Daniel lowered himself onto the sofa on the other side of her desk. His pale astute eyes sought hers. 'Brodie, what's the matter? This isn't because I'm late for work. What is it about?'

She blew out her cheeks in a dispirited sigh. 'I don't even know, Daniel. I just wanted you here. I needed you.' She ran distracted fingers through her hair. 'I think I'm falling apart. Three months ago I ran this business entirely on my own. Anything that came up, I dealt with. It never occurred to me I needed help.' She looked down fiercely at her now quite impressive bump. 'I don't like what this pregnancy's doing to me, Daniel! I don't *like* feeling this pathetic.'

Everything Daniel knew about having babies came from books. But then, everything he knew about astro-physics did too. He smiled gently. 'You're not pathetic. You *are* a bit vulnerable. It's a vulnerable time. Nature needs expectant mothers to be careful. It's how the species survives. You won't go on feeling like this. When the baby comes you'll get back to normal.'

'Yeah, right,' she growled. 'Midnight feeds. Nappies. Paddy jealous of all the time a new baby takes up. Post-natal depression...'

'And a baby,' said Daniel.

'And Jack's no help,' she grumbled. 'All right, I didn't expect much, he didn't want this any more than I did, but I thought he might make a bit of an effort. I thought, when he got used to the idea, he might even be *pleased.* Oh no. It's just something else coming between him and his work. As far as he knows this is the only child he's ever fathered, and his idea of doing right by it is signing some cheques.'

'I'm sure that's not what he said,' murmured Daniel.

'It's what he meant,' insisted Brodie. 'And that's four months ago. He hasn't exactly been keeping an eagle-eye on its progress ever since. I swear to God, he'd have been better pleased if I'd asked him to pay for a termination.'

'*I* don't think that,' said Daniel quietly. 'I don't think you do either.'

But she was getting a kind of wounded satisfaction from her sense of grievance, wasn't about to give it up. 'Damn right I do. I could see him doing the sums. Which would be cheaper – getting rid of a baby or raising it? No comparison, is it? Eighteen bloody years you're responsible for them – and that's if you're lucky and they leave school and get a job. If they go on to university you can still be feeding them when they're twenty-five! By which time Jack'll be in his seventies. I'll be pushing sixty!' The realisation appalled her. 'Maybe he was right. Maybe I should have got rid of it while I had the chance.'

'I *know* you don't mean that,' Daniel said with certainty.

Her voice was shadowed with fear. 'I don't know, Daniel. Maybe I do. I'm too old, and too single, to be doing this. It's hard graft. You need to be fit, and you need to be young.'

'You're only thirty-three,' he reminded her.

'All the evidence shows you should do this in your twenties.'

He didn't know whether she most needed a slap or a hug. 'Never mind the statistics, just think about the women you know. Women who've had first babies in their thirties, never mind second ones. It's very common and most of the time it's very successful. Most people have a lot more money in their thirties than in their twenties, and more money means less worry. As for being on your own…' He let the sentence fade away.

'What?'

'You're not really, you know. You're surrounded by people who care about you and this baby. People you can call on for help. You've got Marta living upstairs, and she'll be cooing and clucking over it like an old hen gone broody. Whatever you say, Jack won't see you lack for anything. I don't doubt John and Julia will be happy to lend a hand if you ask them – Julia thinks the world of Paddy, she won't make much distinction between her and her brother or sister. And then there's me.'

Brodie gave him a wry smile. 'My emergency service.'

'If you like.'

'My fall-back position. My' – if she'd seen the words coming she'd have stopped them – 'last resort.'

Daniel flushed. 'If you say so. I'd rather be your last resort than no resort at all.'

She knew she'd managed to hurt him again – unintentionally but carelessly, thoughtlessly. She swept the dark hair from her face and leant over the desk, her eyes grabbing his. 'Daniel, that's not what I meant. Of *course* it's not what I meant. You must know how much you mean to me. Dear God, it's these pregnancy hormones – I can't even talk straight any more!

'You're my rock. You're the strength that keeps me going when my own strength is gone. You're my best friend, my dearest companion, the better part of my soul. And yes, you're my last resort. You're the place I come to when I can't even go home. The place where, whatever tempests rage outside, I know I can lay down my head and rest and be safe. Without you, it wouldn't matter what riches or lovers the world might offer – I'd be lost, forever.' Her eyes were luminous, not with tears but with truth. Every word of it came straight from her heart.

'I love you, Daniel Hood,' she went on intently. 'Well, you know that. And I know that the way I love you and the way you love me aren't exactly the same any more. I wish they were. I wish with every fibre of my being that I could do what you want – take what you're offering with a clear conscience, knowing I could return it and never short-change you. There's no one on this earth I'd rather spend the rest of my days with, and grow old and deaf and crotchety with.

'And I'd do it in an instant,' she said, and he knew she meant it, 'except for one thing. Only a little thing, except to you and me. It would be a lie. I might wish with all my heart I could feel that way about you, but I don't. I'd end up hurting you – hurting you more – and I honest to God think I'd rather die than do that.'

He tried to interject, to say maybe that was his call, not hers, but she wouldn't let him – ploughed on determinedly, hunched urgently over the desk so that the long dark curls framed her pale, intense face. 'Don't ever think that what I feel for you is less than what you feel for me. It isn't. It's just different. But it's still, apart from my child – my children,' she amended ruefully, 'the most important thing in my life. Jack used to say that and I denied it, but he was right. I wasn't fair to him. How could I be? I was fond of him, in lots of ways, but I didn't care for him the way I care for you. If the three of us had been on the *Titanic* and I'd had two life-jackets, Jack would have had to swim to Nova Scotia.'

That wrung a little chuckle out of Daniel. Nothing she was saying was much of a surprise to him. What stunned him speechless was that she'd come right out and say it. That she would admit it to herself.

'Oh Daniel,' she murmured brokenly, 'I'm making such a mess of my life! I've had the choice of two good men to love and be with – and even that's not enough for me, I want that bit of this one and this bit of that one, and I've already driven one of them away, and if I lost you too through being so bloody stupid I'd *deserve* to be alone. *Can* you forgive me? Can you believe that this isn't how I want to be, it's just how I am? And if it was something I could change I would, tomorrow, but I don't think it is. I think it's something I have to live with. I do so hope it's something you can live with too.'

He got up from the sofa. For a heart-stopping moment she was afraid he was going to leave the way Deacon had left, driven away by the contrariness of her passions. Instead he moved round the desk and put his arms around her. His slight body contrived to enfold her bulky one, his cheek resting on top of her head so that his words came to her through the bones of her skull.

He said simply, 'Don't you dare change a thing. We're all right. We'll *be* all right.'

CHAPTER SEVENTEEN

That night wasn't the first Daniel never made it to his bed. More than once he'd set up the telescope on his balcony to take advantage of those particularly clear conditions that can occur when there's the tin taste of frost in the air, and spent an hour or so looking for comets and another half hour admiring a planetary conjunction, and been surprised when his evening's observation was curtailed by the milky bleaching of the sky that heralds the sun.

But this night was cloudy. Even had it been crystal clear, he had too much on his mind for star-gazing. A drinking man would have opened a bottle of Scotch: Daniel made himself a pot of coffee at eleven o'clock, and another some time after two, and sat alone in his calm grey living room, sipping and thinking.

The same man who would have opened the bottle of whisky would have been mulling how he could turn the situation to his advantage. That would not have made him a bad man. He would probably have believed that what he wanted was the best for both parties and the woman would thank him later; and who's to say he'd have been wrong? Sometimes there is no perfect outcome to be sought: no Holy Grail, no glass slipper. What's best is what those involved believe is best, and sometimes the act of believing strongly enough is sufficient to make it so. The man with the bottle might have got his heart's desire *and* made the woman happy.

But Daniel was not that man, and even if he'd thought of exploiting Brodie's vulnerability in that way he couldn't have done it. For an intelligent and self-sufficient man he had remarkably little confidence in his own worth. The mere fact that it was what he wanted above all else would have persuaded him it was not in Brodie's best interests. Not now; probably not at all.

So he sat all night alone on the beach, and heard the tide come in and then heard it go out again, and everything that passed through his mind – and was considered and dismissed, but instead of disappearing from the scene merely slinked away and joined the back of the queue again – was not his own needs but those of his friend.

By the time the false dawn was painting the sky with oyster-coloured streaks he knew what to do.

Wednesday was when the magistrates sat in Dimmock. They dealt with speeding motorists, with the sort of crime that Alix Hyde had no interest in, and with remands. It wasn't usually necessary for Deacon to attend remand hearings – often he sent Charlie Voss, sometimes it was enough to have a DC utter the well-worn formula. *We believe we can connect the defendant with the offence and ask for a remand in custody* (or on bail if Deacon was in a good mood) *to the court of...* Usually they got what they asked for. Occasionally the bench looked at the white-haired old lady in the dock and decided that, even if she did make a run for it, she wasn't going to get far with two walking-sticks and a pacemaker.

Today Voss was busy. *Playing with his new friend* was the expression that sprang unbidden to Deacon's mind. He knew it was childish. He'd offered Voss to Detective Inspector Hyde: it was perverse and, yes, childish now to resent the fact that they were working well together. Any one of his CID team could have represented him adequately at the magistrates' court. The only reason he went himself was to give Voss a twinge of conscience when he heard.

Now that he mostly went to court only to win important cases – or at least, to be so bad a loser that the bench would think twice about crossing him next time – he'd forgotten just how boring most of the work is. Careless drivers. Reckless drivers. Dangerous drivers. Drunk drivers. Driving without a licence. Driving without insurance. Driving without a Road Fund Licence. Unlawful possession of controlled substances. Unlawful possession of a fireman...

Deacon beckoned the clerk. 'I think there's a typo here.'

The man looked, looked again, hissed 'Oh shit!' and took the list back for amendment, leaving Deacon feeling his morning had not been entirely wasted. Duane Childers, five foot three in his bovver boots, could have proved beyond reasonable doubt his inability to even pick up a fireman – at least, not without first putting down his scatter-gun.

With Duane charged with the right offence, and bail sought but denied in view of the fact that said firearm had been discharged no fewer than four times when the Woodgreen Raiders beat the South City Stars at baseball, the defendant headed – disconsolate but not entirely surprised – for the prison van and Deacon headed for Battle Alley.

Daniel was waiting for him on the steps of the courthouse. 'Have you got a minute?'

Deacon eyed him suspiciously. 'I suppose.'

'Thanks.'

They took the scenic route, through the park. Daniel talked and Deacon listened. Every time Deacon opened his mouth to respond Daniel talked faster. At one point they sat on a bench, Deacon with his legs stretched out in front of him, staring up at the monument, Daniel still talking so earnestly it meant using his hands. Only when he'd exhausted every argument he'd rehearsed in the silent hours of the night did he stop.

Without looking at him Deacon said thickly, 'You're a very strange man, Daniel Hood.'

Daniel blinked. 'Possibly. But then, I'm not asking you to marry *me*.'

'But you *are* asking me to marry Brodie.'

'Yes.'

'Because she's carrying my child.'

Daniel shook his head. 'Not really. If she was carrying somebody else's child I'd still be asking you to marry her.'

'Tell me why again.' Deacon held up an admonitory finger. 'The short version.'

'Because she needs you. She needed you before – the difference the baby's made is that now she *knows* she needs you.'

'That's not what she told me.'

Daniel laughed. Deacon thought he'd never heard such a lonely sound. 'Did you expect her to? Jack, the one thing we both know about Brodie is that she hates to admit to weakness of any kind. Of course she said she could manage alone; of course she pretended not to care. She didn't want you to feel you owed her anything, and she didn't want to push you into a marriage that wasn't your first choice.

'That doesn't mean she's happy with how things are. She's worried and she's scared. And she misses you. And I don't know if there's any chance of repairing what the two of you once had, but I know that not long ago it gave you a lot of pleasure and it gave her a lot of pleasure, and I'm hoping you'll think it's worth a try…'

Finally Deacon looked at him. There was twenty years between them, and even that wasn't the biggest difference. They lived by different creeds, different ideologies. The only thing they had in common was Brodie, and being a woman rather than a football team she was the cause of more not less division between them. 'Daniel – if you think she'd welcome a proposal right now, why aren't you in there chancing your arm?'

'You know why,' said Daniel in a low voice.

'I know she cares more for you than she ever cared for me.'

'That's not true. But even if it was, me and her isn't an option. Don't think I haven't suggested it because I have. She looked at me as if I was proposing incest. Much as I might regret it, that's not the kind of relationship we have. That's the kind of relationship *you* have. Had. Could have again. She needs you, Jack. Not me – you. If you miss this chance there may not be another.'

'That's not the best argument I've ever heard for getting married,' growled Deacon. 'Grab her while she's low – when she's back on form she'll expect to do better.'

Daniel gave a slow grin. 'Perhaps we're all getting a little long in the tooth to hang on for ungovernable passion.'

'You're not,' Deacon pointed out. 'You're twenty-seven, for God's sake!'

'Twenty-eight,' Daniel corrected him. 'And Brodie's thirty-three, and she thinks she's too old to be having another child much less raising one alone.'

Deacon tilted his eyebrows. 'She said that?' Daniel nodded. Deacon drew a deep breath. 'All right. I'll talk to her. I'm *not* going to propose to her. I'm not even going to proposition her. But I will talk to her.'

'You won't regret it,' promised Daniel.

Deacon fixed him with a gaze like a pikestaff. 'Daniel – I'm regretting it already.'

They walked on through the park and crossed into Battle Alley, and parted at the steps to the police station as Deacon turned in and Daniel continued towards Shack Lane.

But he didn't get much further. Before Deacon had even gone inside a car squealed round the corner and ground to a halt, spitting dirt, a metre from the pavement. Adam Selkirk leapt out, leaving the door wide, a hazard to traffic. 'You little bastard!' he yelled. 'What have you done with them? Where are my wife and my son?'

You shout, 'What have you done with my wife, you bastard?' in front of a police station and people are going to come to the window. One of those who came to the window of the top-storey CID offices was Alix Hyde.

Deacon changed direction as smoothly as Ginger Rogers, so that anyone who hadn't seen him a second earlier would have sworn he was coming out of the building and heading down the steps. It wasn't so much that he felt the urge to protect

Daniel from a large and overwrought solicitor, more that he wanted to watch.

Daniel was fully conscious of where they were. He couldn't have chosen a better spot for the confrontation. He quelled his natural urge to run and waited for Selkirk to reach him.

If you're a lot bigger than most people, there are three ways you can go. You can compensate, choosing your every word and gesture to reassure people who might otherwise feel intimidated – the gentle giant approach. You can make the most of a natural advantage and do a lot of looming, and excuse yourself on the grounds that it's not bullying if you keep your hands in your pockets. Or you can do what Deacon did, at least most of the time – not make an issue of it unless someone else did, and then flatten them with a clear conscience.

Adam Selkirk was not a police officer. There were few occasions in his professional life when it was really useful to be built like a brick privy. Nor was it any great advantage at home – his son was a pre-pubescent twelve-year-old, his wife a slight woman: it didn't take a big man to physically dominate either of them. In consequence, Daniel thought he wasn't sure what to do about the fact that he was so much bigger than the object of his ire. Obviously he wanted to hit him – that was how he resolved all his personal frustrations. But this was not just a public street, it was a public street with a police station on it. However much trouble it gave him usually, restraint was undoubtedly the best policy today. So when he was close enough for Daniel to smell his aftershave he stopped, hands fisted by his sides, quaking with rage.

Daniel said quietly, 'Were you looking for me, Mr Selkirk?'

Deacon watched with interest. All he wanted for was popcorn.

'Where is she?' demanded Selkirk. For the moment he was going with the low-voice-full-of-menace option.

Saying *Who?* would be disingenuous to the point of dishonesty. Daniel said, 'She's safe. They both are.'

'Where?'

'I'm not telling you.'

'She's my wife!'

'Yes. Not your punchbag.'

There was no way of knowing if Daniel was the first to have noticed the bruises on Noah and his mother, only that he was the first to have done something about them. A man who'd been getting away with a little murder every week, possibly for years, must have been stunned to find suddenly there were consequences. Like, having it said out loud in the middle of the street. Discretion, like good manners, is one of those oils that help the world go round smoothly, and some things are not mentioned in polite society.

There are certain advantages to being an outsider, Daniel had found. One was, if you're not used to having society's approval you're not afraid of losing it.

'Did she tell you that?' demanded Selkirk. His voice was unsteady.

'No. Neither did Noah. It's hardly a secret, though, when they're walking round with the evidence printed on their faces.'

'You don't know what you're talking about,' sneered Selkirk. 'Now tell me where I can find my family.'

'No,' Daniel said again. 'Mr Selkirk, your wife knows your phone number. If she wanted to talk she'd call you. If she wanted you to fetch her, she'd call you. If she hasn't told you where she is, I'm not going to.'

Veins were thumping like jack-hammers in Adam Selkirk's temples. 'You can't do this. Noah is my son. I have a right to know where he is. He hasn't been in school since Monday. Why not? Where is he? Where has she taken him?'

'Your faith in the value of education is touching,' said Daniel ironically. 'But I don't think a few days off school will do him much harm. That's a bright boy, Mr Selkirk. I'm not worried about his academic prowess. I'm worried about him not sustaining brain damage in the next few months.'

'Then why the hell…?' Selkirk heard himself shouting – half Dimmock heard him shouting – and tried to get a grip. 'Listen, Hood, let's at least try to behave like civilised men. I'll pretend you really do have my son's best interests at heart, you're not just a meddling busy-body, and you can pretend I give a gnat's whisker what you think of me. Noah is in no danger from me. I don't hit him, I have never hit him. When he's with me, he's safe. Right now I don't know where he is or what's happening to him. But if he comes to any harm, I'll know exactly who to blame.'

Daniel favoured him with a cold smile. 'It's a good act,' he acknowledged. 'I bet most people fall for it. Of course, telling lies convincingly is what you're good at – what you're paid for. I'm sure you're worth every penny.

'But I don't believe you, Mr Selkirk. It's as simple as that. I've seen a little of your family. I saw your wife last night, after you left the house. I don't believe she got like that walking into a door. I don't think you could get like that walking into a revolving door.'

'I didn't hit my wife!' yelled the big man; and the fists bounced up and down at the end of his arms as if they simply couldn't wait to be pounding Daniel Hood's face to pulp. 'She…'

Daniel waited, eyes wide with curiosity, but Selkirk had choked on his anger and no more words came. 'What?' Daniel prompted after a moment. 'Took a ride in the tumble-drier? Head-butted the fridge?'

Deacon heard the door behind him open and Detective Inspector Hyde passed him on the steps. She joined the two men in the street, looking between them – up at Selkirk, down at Daniel. 'Is everything all right here? Mr Selkirk?'

Selkirk had to clench his teeth to get his voice under control. 'Not really, no,' he gritted.

'Do you want to talk about it inside?'

'Yes,' Daniel said immediately. After a second's pause Selkirk nodded.

They followed her back up the stone steps into the police station. As they passed him Deacon did an about-face and joined on the end.

When Alix Hyde realised he was there she hesitated. 'I think this is probably to do with my investigation, Superintendent,' she said pointedly.

'May well be,' nodded Deacon, never missing a step.

'So…where should we go for a bit of privacy?'

'You can bring them to my office,' said Deacon generously.

It was clear that Hyde was unhappy, but she was both out-ranked and out-flanked. This was Deacon's manor and Deacon's nick, and if she took him on she'd lose. One of the secrets of winning battles is knowing which ones to fight.

And having the right allies. As Charlie Voss came out of the CID room she captured him with one arm through his, swung him round and added him to the party bound for Deacon's office.

There weren't enough chairs. Deacon took the big comfortable one behind the desk and left the others to fend for themselves.

Everyone in that room was thinking hard – except for Daniel who knew exactly what he was doing. And what he wasn't.

Adam Selkirk was thinking that what had been a private difficulty a week ago was now in the public domain. There were too many people now privy to it for the secret to be kept. The question was no longer whether the lie would continue to serve but whether he could put a better spin on the truth.

Alix Hyde was thinking that sometimes mid-stream is the exact right spot to change horses. If Selkirk had been shouting in the street about his family problems it was probably too late to offer him discretion as a reward for his cooperation. It was time to hit him with the full force of the child protection legislation in order to permanently destroy his usefulness to Terry Walsh.

Charlie Voss was feeling as deeply uneasy in this gathering as if it was him who was suspected of child abuse, and he wasn't sure why. He didn't think he'd done anything wrong. He'd had two imperatives – to protect Noah Selkirk from his father and society from Terry Walsh – and he thought he'd been meeting both. His senior investigating officer seemed to think so too. Which suggested that what he was anxious about was how Detective Inspector Deacon would react. This came as a bit of a shock. Voss didn't like thinking he might have done something even Deacon would disapprove of.

And what Deacon was thinking was, This is where I listen lots and speak little. Because everything here is not as it seems to be. Well, there's nothing unusual about that, in my world virtually *nothing* is quite as it appears. But usually I can count on the other police officers, and today I'm not sure I can.

He said benevolently, 'So who's going to start?'

CHAPTER EIGHTEEN

Alix Hyde said, 'Charlie?'

Voss hesitated. He was used to being the Victorian child in these situations, seen and not heard. But Detective Inspector Hyde did things differently to Detective Superintendent Deacon, and Voss was in as good a position as anyone to set out the facts, and appreciated being given the chance.

He cleared his throat. 'It has been drawn to our attention that Mr Selkirk's twelve-year-old son has suffered a number of unexplained injuries. We've been trying to establish how he sustained them, to find out who was responsible and to prevent any recurrence.'

Behind his eyes, which remained impassive, Deacon was thinking: Well done, lad. Whether or not you know what she's doing – and I don't think you do – that was the right answer. He said aloud, 'Where's the boy now?'

'He's with his mother,' said Daniel.

'And you know where they are.'

'Yes.'

'But you don't want to say.'

'No.'

Deacon turned to Selkirk. 'And you want to know?'

'Of course I want to know,' said Selkirk, managing not to

shout though it played havoc with his blood pressure. 'Last time I saw them they were both upset. I need to know they're all right.'

'They're all right,' said Daniel. When he was angry his voice didn't soar, it developed this edge like honed steel.

'How do you know that?' demanded Selkirk. 'You're here and they're not. How do you *know* they're safe?'

'I saw them yesterday. They were fine. They were together and there was nobody else there. As long as nobody knows where they are, I think we can assume they're fine.'

'Oh do you?' snarled Selkirk. 'Can we quote you on that? Will you accept the responsibility if you're wrong?'

Daniel half-turned to look him full in the face. With both of them standing it wasn't a question of him looking the solicitor up and down so much as up and further up, but the message it conveyed was unmistakable. Daniel Hood despised Adam Selkirk and didn't care who knew it. 'Oh yes,' he said with conviction.

'I see,' said Deacon thoughtfully. 'But that clearly isn't enough for you, is it, Mr Selkirk? Do you want to explain why not?'

There was the briefest hesitation before he came back. 'You want me to explain why the word of last year's head prefect isn't enough to reassure me? He took them from my house in the middle of the night, and he won't say where they are, and we only have his word for it that they wanted to go. Do you *expect* me to find that acceptable?'

In fact Daniel never made head prefect. He wasn't good enough at sports. And if he had it would have been ten years ago. But it was meant as an insult and it felt like one, and

Daniel felt himself flush. 'My word is good. Ask anyone.'

'Your word *is* good,' agreed Deacon, nodding slowly. 'Your judgement, however, can be flawed. So tell me: how did you get involved in this?'

'He's a boy, Jack,' said Daniel, an odd mix of anger and entreaty in his voice. 'He's twelve years old. Not the kind of twelve-year-old you were – the kind I was. And every time I saw him he had a fresh crop of bruises. He's been hit – regularly, and hard. I didn't find *that* acceptable.'

'And I told you,' snarled Selkirk, 'I never laid a hand on him.'

'So you did,' acknowledged Daniel coldly. 'But then, you're a man who lies for a living.'

If he was attempting to provoke violence, this time he came close to succeeding. Selkirk's broad shoulders lifted in a way that said one of his ham-sized fists was close behind. Deacon continued watching with interest, Hyde with anticipation. But Charlie Voss stepped quickly between them, physically shouldering Daniel aside. Angry as he was, Selkirk was not ready to strike a police officer. He subsided.

'So you think he beats his twelve-year-old son,' summarised Deacon, 'and he denies it. Detective Inspector Hyde?'

Alix Hyde gave a tiny nod. 'That's the allegation that's been made to us. We've interviewed Mr Selkirk. He denied it on that occasion too. Our investigations are on-going.'

'Have you spoken to Noah's school?'

'I have, sir,' said Voss. 'They weren't aware there was a problem. At least...' Unsure how much to say in front of Selkirk he ground to a halt.

Unconcerned for himself, Daniel dispensed with discretion

and finished the sentence for him. 'Des Chalmers wasn't aware there was a problem until I told him. I asked him to keep an eye on Noah, to see how many more bits of furniture he was going to be careless enough to walk into.'

Adam Selkirk was already too flushed to redden further. But there was vitriol in his eyes.

'I see,' said Deacon. 'So what happened yesterday?'

'I got a phone call, after midnight. I went to their house and found Mrs Selkirk bleeding and Noah terrified. I took them home with me.'

Deacon looked at Selkirk. 'Where were you?'

Again the slight pause. 'I went for a drive.'

Deacon had been a detective for a lot of years: he'd heard just about every falsehood, every half-lie and every improbable truth it's possible to tell. But his eyebrows climbed as if he'd never heard the like of that. 'In the early hours of the morning? Leaving your wife bloody and your son in hysterics? *Why?*'

'We'd been arguing,' growled Selkirk. 'Marianne and I. We both needed the space to calm down. I drove up and down the coast for an hour. When I got back the house was empty.'

'What did you do then? Call us? Call the hospital?' Selkirk shook his head. 'Why not? You left your wife upset and bleeding, and when you got home she'd gone. Didn't it occur to you she might have gone to the hospital?'

'He knew she wouldn't have gone to the hospital,' said Daniel tersely. 'She never had before, she wouldn't this time. She left him a note to say she was spending the rest of the night with a friend and would be in touch shortly. Unless he's suggesting she wrote it at gun-point, there was never any question of her leaving the house unwillingly.'

Deacon was still nodding – slowly, hypnotically, like a plush bulldog on somebody's parcel-shelf. 'Who called you?'

Daniel didn't want to say. But Selkirk already knew. 'Noah.'

'Did you hear him make the call?' asked Deacon.

'No. But it wouldn't be Marianne, and arguments don't wake the neighbours in River Drive.'

'So there was a domestic going on, Noah called Daniel for help and Daniel went round and found Mrs Selkirk hurt and Noah terrified. He offered to put them up for the night and they accepted.' He stabbed Selkirk with a lancet eye. 'What the hell do you find so objectionable about that?'

The solicitor gave a sniff that curled his lip. 'About that, nothing. About the assumptions he's been making, plenty, but that's another issue. What's worrying me now is that I can't find either of them. Noah's not in school and Marianne's not at work. Both of them have mobile phones: both of them are switched off. They're not at his house' – he couldn't bring himself to say Daniel's name – 'I checked, and I couldn't see any of their things there either. And he knows where they are, and he won't tell me.'

Deacon swivelled. 'Daniel?'

'That's right,' Daniel said evenly. 'I won't help him find them and hurt them again.'

Deacon looked back at Selkirk. 'In the circumstances, it's a reasonable attitude.'

'You don't know the circumstances,' grated Adam Selkirk. 'I do. And I'm telling you my son is in danger right now.'

Daniel felt confident enough of his ground to call his bluff. His yellow head tilted back so he could look the solicitor in the eye. 'I really don't see how that could be, Mr Selkirk. He's with his mother and you don't know where they are. That's all that boy needs to be safe.'

'According to you.'

'According to me, and anyone else with an eyeball in his head,' said Daniel acidly.

Selkirk found himself squaring up to a man who barely came up to his chin and could have camped out in his jacket. 'You arrogant little bastard! What do you know of my family? What do you know of me, that you can say that about me? You're a failed teacher who tried to give him a bit of help with his maths. And maybe you mean well, and maybe you were worried about him, but you haven't the skill, the knowledge or the authority to rip my family apart in an effort to help him with anything else. Now you've hidden him and his mother away where not only I but no one else can check that they're OK.'

Adam Selkirk drew a deep breath before committing himself – before saying that which, once out, could never be private family business again. And then he said it.

'What if I tell you that you misread the situation from the start? That it isn't me who hits the child when the pressure of work builds up. It isn't me that gets so frustrated I lose all control and lay into whoever's nearest with anything that comes to hand. It's Marianne. It's his mother.'

For a moment the sheer effrontery of it stole Daniel's breath away. He was aware of gaping at the man like a stranded goldfish. Finally he managed, 'That is the most *outrageous* thing I ever… And you're supposed to be this high-priced lawyer with the gift of the gab? *I* can lie better than that!'

'It's the truth,' gritted Selkirk.

Deacon wouldn't have admitted it, but the fact that he left it at that, didn't try to embellish it with evidence for the defence, impressed him somewhat. The biggest mistake people make when they're lying is not knowing when to stop. They try to prove everything they say. Their alibi is never that they were having a bath: they were always in a busy pub with five friends.

Of course, anything Deacon knew about the criminal mentality, Selkirk knew too.

'I *saw* her!' cried Daniel. 'Her nose was bleeding. There were bruises on her forehead. There were bruises on her wrists.'

'I grabbed her by the wrists.' Selkirk's voice was low. 'She headbutted me.'

'Don't be ridiculous!' snorted Daniel.

'Why is it ridiculous?' demanded Selkirk. 'Because she's a woman? Because she's small and looks fragile? If you knew a thing about her, Hood – if you knew anything about any of us – you'd know Marianne's tough. Mentally and physically. She has to be to do her job. It doesn't just involve sitting at a desk making plaintive phone calls. Sometimes it involves trekking out to disaster areas and living in a tent on a bottle of water and a packet of biscuits a day. Sometimes it involves cornering dictators – war-lords, men with armies at their backs – and telling them to sell the second-best executive jet and feed their people on the proceeds. She risks her life on a regular basis, and millions of people survive because of it.

'But it takes its toll. Sometimes she gets back from one of these war zones and it's as much as she can do to walk from the taxi to the front door. I've carried her upstairs before now. I've undressed her and put her to bed. I've held her in the night when things she's seen come back to haunt her, and they don't even go away when she wakes up. My wife isn't fragile, but she is under the kind of stress that nobody here has ever experienced – can even imagine.'

Deacon cleared his throat. 'Actually…'

Daniel knew what he was going to say and broke in quickly. 'I don't doubt it. What I don't believe is that *that* makes her want to come back and beat the living daylights out of her son.'

'Of course she doesn't *want* to hurt him!' spat Selkirk. 'She loses control. That's what it does to her – all the suffering, and knowing that she can make a difference, and knowing that she can never do enough. It eats her up, and when she can't bear it any more she explodes. Sometimes it's just the crockery. Sometimes it's me. Well, that's all right, I'm a lot bigger than she is and I love her, and if I can absorb some of her pain that way I will. But sometimes it's Noah. And he's willing too, but he's a lot smaller than I am and sometimes she hurts him. He denies it, but I know she does. I try to keep them apart when she's in danger of losing it. Most of the time I succeed, but not always.'

Both his voice and his gaze hardened. 'And you've set them up in a cosy little home-from-home somewhere, and nobody knows where they are and nobody's going to disturb them. And next time the demons come there'll be nobody to know, and nobody to hold her wrists until the rage passes.'

The silence in Deacon's office was so profound that traffic noises came up from the street and the murmur of someone on the phone from the floor below. Almost, they were spellbound. None of them knew whether it was the truth. But it was a credit to Adam Selkirk's skills as counsel that they were all thinking about it. Thinking what it meant if he wasn't lying.

Daniel's voice was hollow. If this was the truth... He couldn't *afford* for it to be the truth. 'Then why did you leave them alone? On Monday night. Why did you go for a little drive and leave them alone?'

'Because that's what works,' said Selkirk, almost too tired now to continue hating him. 'That's what experience has taught us is the best thing to do. Her fury is like a fever: it mounts until it breaks. After that there's no question of anyone getting hurt, she just needs some time alone to pull herself together. And by then, so do I. I go for a drive. When I get back we don't speak of it again.'

Daniel had no answer. If Adam Selkirk was telling the truth, Marianne was lying – and he didn't know the difference.

Deacon said, 'Where did she headbutt you?'

Selkirk replied without thinking. 'In the kitchen.'

'I mean, where on your body? Your face?'

The solicitor shook his head. 'I'm a lot taller than Marianne, Superintendent. She got me in the chest.'

'Show me.'

He pulled down his tie, undid a few buttons. His sternum was stained every colour between yellow and black. *Every* colour. Some of the bruises were old.

Deacon considered for only a moment longer. Then he

nodded. 'I don't know if you're telling the truth, Mr Selkirk. Your wife could have done that attempting to defend herself. But I'm not willing to wager your son's safety on my guessing right. We need to find them, and then we'll sort out who did what to who. Daniel – where did you take them?'

Daniel felt every eye in the room coming round to him, felt the weight of their expectation, knew as a dull ache in the pit of his belly that he was about to draw to himself all the hostility that had been going Selkirk's way. It wouldn't be the first time and it didn't have to matter, there were higher priorities than making this easy for him, but he took a moment to recognise the irony. For a mild and unambitious man, it was remarkable how often he found himself being struck off people's Christmas lists.

'Jack – I'm sorry, but it's not good enough. I think he's lying. I think if he knows where to find them he'll hurt them again. Maybe this time he'll do worse than hurt them.'

Deacon frowned. 'You saw his chest. He's not Tarzan – that isn't a self-inflicted injury.'

'But what does it prove?' demanded Daniel. 'That he was involved in some kind of violence. He took blows to the chest. Look at him, Jack, look at the size of him! He's bigger than you. If he was beating his wife, who's my size, or his son, who's half my size, don't you think they'd try to defend themselves? Pick something up and swing it at him? A saucepan, maybe. He says this happened in the kitchen. If Marianne swung at him with the saucepan to keep him off Noah, and he grabbed her arms and hit her in the face, wouldn't the physical evidence be the same? And isn't it a damn sight more likely that it happened that way?'

Pursing his lips, Deacon looked again at Selkirk. Then at Daniel. Short of giving them pistols and standing them back to back, he couldn't think of a way of deciding who was right. And it mattered. If he guessed wrong, someone was going to suffer. If Daniel was right, he was about to take an abusive husband to Marianne Selkirk's last refuge. If Selkirk was telling the truth, he was leaving Noah with a violently unstable mother.

Alix Hyde had said nothing since the confrontation began. Her primary concern was still nailing Terry Walsh, and drawing together those strands of evidence that would help her do it. She had a vested interest in not believing Adam Selkirk. If he was telling the truth he was an honourable man doing his best in a difficult situation and she'd lost her hold on him. If Daniel Hood was right he was a vicious bully and it didn't matter if he gave Terry Walsh an alibi because no one would believe him.

It occurred to her that the best thing that could happen was if Selkirk put his wife in hospital. Nothing too serious – a broken nose, a broken wrist, something that would heal quickly. But something of which a record would remain.

She said quietly, 'If we don't know who to believe, we have to assume that Noah could be in danger right now. Mr Hood, you'll have to tell us where they are. If they need protecting, we'll protect them.'

'How?' cried Daniel. 'How will you protect them? Will you keep them under twenty-four-hour guard for the foreseeable future? Of course you won't, it'd cost a fortune. And all he needs is ten minutes alone with them. In ten minutes he could kill them both.'

'That's not your responsibility,' said DI Hyde firmly. 'Tell us where they are, and we'll take it from there.'

'Of course it's my responsibility – he won't find them without my help! I promised I wouldn't tell him where she is. I won't break that promise just because he spins a plausible yarn.'

'And if it isn't just a yarn?' asked Deacon, his voice low.

'Then…' It was no good – there was no safe default. The consequences of getting this wrong were equally serious whether Selkirk was lying or telling the truth. The only question for Daniel was whether he trusted someone else's judgement better than his own. 'I can't do it, Jack. I don't believe him, and I won't let him hurt them again. I said I'd keep them safe.' He sounded close to tears.

'But it isn't your call,' insisted Hyde. 'It may have escaped your notice but this is a police station. This is now a police matter. You have information we need to carry out our duties: failing to divulge it amounts to obstruction, which is an offence. You tell me what I want to know, Mr Hood, or you'll be the one facing charges.'

If she'd asked, Deacon could have told her that was not the best approach with Daniel. He might look as if a stiff breeze would bend him: in fact there was a vein of adamant running up his spine. The more he was pushed, the more he resisted. It was one of those nexus points where his virtues tipped over into vices. Brodie described it as moral courage: Deacon considered him an obstinate little shit. And both of them were right.

Daniel's gaze wandered off round the ceiling as if seeking divine guidance. 'Let me think about that. If I don't do what you want I could end up in front of the magistrates. If I do, Marianne Selkirk could end up in surgery. Gee,' he said, the irony thick enough by then that even those who didn't know him recognised it, 'talk about the horns of a dilemma!'

Alix Hyde had been a police officer for almost twenty years. She'd had every possible insult, and things worse than insults, flung at her, and learnt to dodge most of them and brush off those she couldn't. She took it as a kind of compliment when she'd managed to rattle someone enough to lose his cool. This was different. She hadn't frightened Daniel Hood, she hadn't even unsettled him. She'd threatened him with the full force of the law, and it was in his voice and in the mild grey eyes behind his bottle-bottom glasses that he found both her and her threat contemptible. She felt herself blushing as she never did.

Daniel didn't think she was bluffing, he just didn't care. Some principles are worth defending even if there's a price to be paid. He'd told Marianne Selkirk that he wouldn't reveal her whereabouts, and nothing Detective Inspector Hyde could do to him would make him break his word.

Deacon had known Daniel Hood for a couple of years now. He knew that once he got on his high horse, nothing short of dynamite would shift him. 'How about you tell me, and we don't tell Mr Selkirk until I've had a chance to talk to his wife?'

That was enough to make Daniel hesitate. But only for a moment. 'Jack, don't take this the wrong way. But you're a police officer. You're a professional in a professional organisation. You have superiors. If they tell you to do something, you have to do it. Whether or not you want to, whether or not you believe it's the right thing. If word comes from Division that you're to tell this man where his wife's hiding, either you'll do it or you'll lose your job.

'You're a powerful man, in lots of ways. But there's a couple of things that I can do that you can't. One is tell Division where to go. Sure they can charge me with obstruction, but how much damage will that do me? Even Hanging's-Too-Good-For-'Em Higgins isn't going to send me down for more than a fortnight, and it's worth that to me. To protect a woman and her son from a violent thug? Of course it is.'

'You don't know that,' growled Deacon. 'I know you think you're right, but you don't know that he's lying. And we need to know. Maybe there's only an outside chance that Noah's in danger from his mother, but we can't take that chance. We have to find out. If you won't let me go and see her, will you go yourself? Take Charlie Voss. He can wear a blindfold if it'll make you feel any happier.'

Daniel thought about that rather longer. But the same problem applied. Indeed, impatient higher-ups could do Detective Sergeant Voss more harm than they could do Detective Superintendent Deacon. 'I'll tell you what I will do. I'll go to see her on my own.'

But Deacon shook his head. 'If she is the violent one, just asking about it may be enough to set her off. If she goes ape, you won't be able to hold her till she calms down. She could hurt you, herself and Noah, and nobody would be able to help or even know about it. At the very least you need someone in the car to whistle up assistance if the situation gets out of control.'

They looked at one another, and neither of them liked to be the first to say it. But if Daniel wouldn't take a police officer, and Deacon wouldn't let him go alone, the options were limited.

Deacon blew out his cheeks in a graceless sigh, half exasperated, half resigned. He reached for the phone. 'I'll have her pick you up at the front door.'

CHAPTER NINETEEN

'It's a load of nonsense, of course,' said Daniel confidently as Brodie drove. 'We're only doing this so Jack can say he didn't dismiss Selkirk's claims out of hand. Twenty minutes there, five minutes to check they're OK, twenty minutes back.' He dared a sidelong glance at her. 'I'm sorry to involve you. You were the only one Jack and I both trusted.'

'Don't apologise,' she said, in a tone that suggested he probably shouldn't take her at her word. 'It's not like I had anything better to do. Anything profitable, for instance. Anything I could send in a bill for afterwards.'

'I'll pay you,' Daniel said shyly.

That made her laugh. He was uncomfortable enough to mean it. 'Don't be silly. There's nothing I'd rather do. A nice drive in the country *and* spitting in Adam Selkirk's eye? That's not work, that's pleasure. Besides which, Jack reckoned if I refused you were probably going to jail.'

'I think he was exaggerating.' Daniel gave a troubled little smile. 'I'm quite glad not to have to find out.'

She glanced at him then, shaking her head, returned her gaze to the road. 'You were prepared to, though, weren't you? Find out.'

'I suppose so.'

'Suppose be damned – we both know you were. If Jack hadn't come up with an alternative, you'd have held out against anything he threw at you – including charges, including court, including prison if need be. Wouldn't you?'

After a moment he nodded. 'Rather than betray a woman and child into the hands of their abuser? Yes, I would.'

'But you hardly know them!'

'I don't *need* to know them. It doesn't come down to who they are. *Nobody* should have to put up with that. And anyone who can put a stop to it should.'

Brodie tilted her eyebrows in a little facial shrug. 'You can't carry the whole world, Daniel. Hell, you've trouble carrying your own shopping. And I have to tell you, you wouldn't like prison.'

'I don't think anybody *does* like prison,' he pointed out reasonably. 'I think that's the idea. I'd have survived prison. The damage she's been taking, I'm not sure how much longer Marianne could keep bouncing back.'

Startled, Brodie flicked another glance at him. 'You really think he could have killed her?'

'I think he could have killed either or both of them at any time.'

She thought a little longer. 'Then you're right. You really didn't have much choice.'

'Let's hope the magistrates agree.'

They turned off the main road into the wilds of the Three Downs. Brodie had never been able to work out just where one stopped and the next began. The centre-point of Menner Down to the north-west was marked by the standing stone – the menhir – on its crown. Chain Down in the south-west was host to the twin villages of Cheyne Warren and Cheyne Treacey, and Frick Down held the eastern flank, distinguished by nothing but sheep. Perhaps there were little water-courses or ancient trackways that told the locals when they'd strayed off one onto another, but they never shared the information with outsiders. Those born and bred on the Three Downs were insular to the point of paranoia.

Daniel had a good sense of direction. It was as if he could always see the Pole Star in his head even when it was hidden by daylight. He confidently picked one lane that looked like all the others they'd passed, half a mile down it he selected another indistinguishable turning, and five minutes after that Brodie was parking the car outside a chalk-and-flint cottage built end-on to the road, its makeshift driveway occupied by a midnight-blue Porsche.

More cumbrous, less graceful than usual, she climbed out and looked around with the innate distrust of the city-dweller for real, non-manicured, non-picturesque countryside. 'If someone starts playing the banjo,' she said firmly, 'I'm off.'

Daniel wasn't a country-boy either: he grew up in a suburban semi in Nottingham. But in the same way that he never seemed entirely at home in any situation, nor did he ever seem entirely out of place. He was a like a snail, or a camper-vanner, carrying his own small world with him. 'I'll let them know it's us.'

'I'll stay with the car.'

That was what Deacon had wanted. To Daniel it seemed absurd. 'OK. I shan't be long.' He walked up the path and tapped on the front door. This wasn't rose country: there was ivy clustered round it.

For a minute no one came. Then he heard the key turning and Marianne Selkirk was there, her ash-blonde hair bundled in a scarf, smuts of dust on her face. She was cleaning.

'Bad time?' winced Daniel. 'I just wanted to see that you were all right.'

'Thanks to you,' said Marianne, with the smile that made dictators putty in her hands. 'Come in and I'll put the kettle on. Noah's about somewhere. In the fields, possibly. He's fascinated by all the space.'

'I mustn't be long. Someone gave me a lift and we have to get back.' But he followed her through the little house into the kitchen and sat where Marianne pointed, and watched while she filled the kettle. 'Actually,' he admitted, 'there's a bit more to it than just wanting to see you were OK.'

'Oh?' She sat across the table from him. 'What?'

'Your husband,' said Daniel. He gave her a brief digest of the encounter outside the police station.

Marianne's eyes flared in alarm. 'He didn't hit you?'

Daniel shook his head immediately. 'No. There were other people around, a lot of them policemen. That's not what I came to tell you.'

'No?' Under the scarf her brow was puzzled. 'Then what?'

'He's telling people... He told the police...' Daniel was finding this unexpectedly difficult. He bit it off and spat it out. 'The police hauled us inside and asked what the hell was going on, and he told them it was you who was beating Noah, not him.'

Her mouth opened wordlessly as her jaw dropped. Her eyes were enormous. 'The shit,' she breathed incredulously.

'That's pretty much what I said too,' agreed Daniel. 'I don't expect anyone believed him. The police had to give him a hearing but they're not stupid. They'll sort this out. They'll put Noah first and they won't let him come to any more harm.'

Marianne was shaking her head in disbelief. 'Adam and I have had our problems, but I'd never have believed he'd tell the police that. Him, who's so keen on keeping everything in the family!'

'Desperate people do desperate things,' said Daniel. 'Now it's in the open and he knows it's going to be dealt with, he's doing all he can think of to shift the blame. I'm sorry to dump this on you,' he added wryly. 'I felt you needed to know.'

Marianne nodded slowly. 'You're right, I did.' Suddenly her gaze sharpened. 'You didn't tell him where we are?'

'No,' Daniel said quickly. 'They wanted me to but I didn't. I said I'd come out and make sure you and Noah were both OK, and the police were happy with that.'

The woman still looked edgy. 'No one followed you?'

Daniel couldn't vouch for that because he hadn't thought to check. 'I really don't think so. Jack Deacon knows what the situation is – he wouldn't let your husband leave Battle Alley on our tail.' At least, he didn't think so.

Marianne nodded and tried to smile. But after a moment she got up from the table. 'I'm sorry, Daniel. Will you make the tea? I want to find Noah.' Her footsteps turned to running on the stone flags in the hall.

Brodie followed Deacon's instructions to the letter – something she never did when they were closer. It occurred to her, waiting by the car with her phone in her pocket, that before the baby was even born she was thinking of Deacon not as its father but as a policeman.

It. She still didn't know the sex of the imminent infant. She'd been offered the information but declined, mainly on grounds of superstition. The less she knew about it, the less emotional commitment she had invested in it, the less things were likely to go wrong. It hadn't had the best start in life – had been exposed to powerful drugs before she even knew it was on its way – and early on the chances had seemed high that the pregnancy would fail. Early on that wouldn't have seemed a disaster to her. The baby not only hadn't been planned, it could hardly have come at a worse time – when the relationship it sprang from was foundering and the demands on her time and energies were greater than ever.

But a baby isn't like a new three-piece suite, something you start saving for when the last one's getting shabby. They always come at inconvenient times – when their parents are too young, too inexperienced and too impoverished, or else too old and already stretching the seams of their house. It doesn't matter, because a new baby comes ready-equipped with that most valuable of personal assets, the ability to inspire love. However unpromising the circumstances of its conception, by the time it arrives its mother and most of its immediate family are ready to adore it and care for it and sacrifice their own needs for it. Which is probably just as well, or the only life in the universe would be plants and the odd amoeba.

By now, seven and a half months into the pregnancy, Brodie would have walked on coals to keep it safe.

She was aware of being observed before either sound or movement announced anyone's arrival. She looked around warily – back down the lane and across the surrounding fields

– but still she saw no one until the boy stepped clear of the tangle of ivy and shadows at the end of the little house. Brodie's brow cleared. 'Hello.'

'Hello,' he replied politely.

'You must be Noah.'

'Yes.' He waited a moment, then said, 'Can I help you?'

Already primed by the hormones of her pregnancy, Brodie's heart went out to him. She understood why Daniel had found it so difficult to distance himself from the child's plight. This was exactly the sort of boy Daniel had been: small, self-contained, polite to the point of old-fashioned. And from all she'd heard, a great deal stronger than anyone supposed.

'Daniel's inside with your mum,' she said. 'I'm his taxi-driver.'

Noah smiled solemnly at the joke. 'I'll go and find them. Would you like to come in?'

Brodie nodded. 'In a minute. I'm just enjoying the views. Do you like it here?'

He thought before answering. 'It's different to living in town.'

'I'll say. It's so peaceful.' Her gaze dropped from the panorama to his quiet, introspective little face. 'Or do you miss school and your friends?'

Noah shook his head. 'Not really. Anyway, I'll be back at school soon. They don't let you stay away too long.'

Brodie chuckled. 'No, they don't. Well, this isn't too far from Dimmock. Your mum can drive you in every morning and pick you up after school.'

'If we're still here,' said the boy. 'I'm not sure how long we're staying.'

'I don't suppose your mum knows yet, either. There are things she and your dad need to sort out. But you'll be fine here until they do.'

'Do you know my father?'

Brodie nodded. 'I've known him a while. He and my ex-husband are in the same business.'

'Please – does he know where we are?'

Brodie shook her head reassuringly. 'No. He knows you're safe, he knows we were coming here to see if there's anything you need, but he doesn't know where you are.'

'Oh,' said Noah, expressionless.

A light, rapid footstep on the stone path heralded Marianne Selkirk's arrival. Noah met his mother with quick reassurance. 'It's all right, Mum, she's Daniel's friend. I'm sorry,' he said then, crestfallen, unable to complete the introduction, 'I don't know your name.'

'Brodie Farrell,' said Brodie, coming forward with a handshake ready. 'Daniel was concerned about you, he asked me to drive him out here.'

Marianne took her hand as if it might be a trap. 'I see.'

'If you're wondering,' said Brodie, 'the answer's no: neither of us has told your husband that you're here. Neither of us will.'

The other woman's face cleared a little. 'Thank you. I see you understand the situation. I'm sorry you've been dragged into our little family drama.'

Brodie glanced down at her bump with a rueful shrug. 'Makes a nice change from my own.'

Marianne gave her spritish chuckle. 'Daniel's brewing up. You'll come in for a cup?'

'Love to,' said Brodie, and they headed inside.

Round the kitchen table the mood was amiable. Daniel asked if Noah was keeping on top of his maths, and Noah asked if Daniel had found a comet yet. Marianne asked when Brodie's baby was due, and Brodie said, 'Six weeks.'

Marianne looked expectantly at Daniel. 'And are you…?'

The flicker of pain that crossed his face told her it had been the wrong question. He answered it anyway. 'Mrs Farrell is my friend and my employer. I can't claim any closer kinship to her baby than that.'

Brodie smiled at him. 'Daniel is the world's best honorary uncle. Ask my daughter Paddy.'

Daniel changed the subject. He said to Noah: 'People have been a bit worried about you. Can I tell them you're all right now?'

'Oh yes,' said the boy with conviction. 'Everything's fine now. Isn't it, Mum?'

Marianne nodded. 'We're fine. Thank you.'

'It must be nice,' supposed Brodie, 'getting some time together. I don't need telling how hard it is, having young children *and* a grown-up job.'

'There aren't enough hours in the day,' agreed Marianne. 'I've felt guilty about that. Noah's been terrific, but I know I haven't given him as much of myself as I should have done.'

Brodie shrugged. 'We're all just doing the best we can. Paddy spends so much time with our neighbour she knows more Polish swear-words than English ones.'

Marianne chuckled. 'Anyway, we're making a fresh start, aren't we Noah? Less work, more fun.'

Noah nodded enthusiastically.

Brodie asked him: 'What do you like doing best?'

'I don't care,' he said expansively. 'Anything. Mum's good at lots of things. She can bake cakes. She took me out in a boat once. Or we play table-tennis. Or fly a kite. Or...'

'You just enjoy one another's company,' suggested Brodie, and the boy nodded again.

Brodie's smile developed an impish quality. 'Nobody's good at everything. What's she really *bad* at?'

He shook his head immediately. 'Nothing.'

Brodie raised an eyebrow. 'Really? She's a better mother than I am, then. For one thing, I'm *always* late. I never allow enough time to get things done so I'm always in a rush. And then I blame everyone else for holding me up. Ask Daniel: a lot of the time I blame him.'

Daniel opened his mouth to say something but changed his mind and shut it again.

'Not my mum,' said Noah loyally.

'And then, if I'm tired, I don't just *say* I'm tired so people can help. I come over all moody – and then I'm cross because they haven't *guessed* what the problem is!'

'My mum's never moody,' insisted the boy stoutly.

Marianne put an arm around him. 'I am sometimes,' she reminded him softly. 'Everyone is sometimes.'

But Noah Selkirk fixed Brodie with his firm bespectacled gaze. 'She's only saying that. She's a brilliant mum. The best. Honestly.'

The tea finished, the visitors rose to go. Noah saw them to the gate. Daniel helped Brodie into her car, then got in beside her. She said, 'We'd better tell Jack what we found out.'

'OK.'

She still had his number on speed-dial. Deacon answered with characteristic charm. 'Well?'

Brodie sighed. 'Jack – I think Adam Selkirk may be telling the truth.'

CHAPTER TWENTY

She rang off to find Daniel literally gaping at her. 'Were we just in different kitchens?' he asked, his pale eyebrows askance. 'Did you meet the Marianne Selkirk from a parallel universe?'

Brodie expected this. 'No. But I went in there with an open mind. You decided weeks ago what kind of a situation this family was embroiled in. Who was the saint and who the sinner.'

'I suppose I did,' he acknowledged slowly. 'I thought it was pretty obvious. I still do.'

'Of course you do. You saw a big man and a slight woman, and bruises on their child's face, and you jumped to the obvious conclusion. And she's an attractive, intelligent woman, easy to talk to and easy to like. And he, not to put too fine a point on it, is a bit of a thug.'

She'd lost Daniel totally. He spread a helpless hand. 'Then…?'

'Obvious isn't the same as accurate. I know – Oswald's Razor: the probability is always that what appeared to happen did in fact happen. But there are exceptions to every rule. I think this is one of them.'

'Occam's,' said Daniel absently. 'Occam's Razor. But – *why* do you think that? That boy thinks the world of his mother! It's as plain as the…'

'…Bruises on his face,' Brodie finished dryly. 'Of course he does, Daniel – she's his mother. It goes with the territory. And because he loves her he wants to protect her. He's old enough and smart enough to know that what she does to him isn't acceptable – that if people find out they'll put a stop to it. At best that'll be deeply embarrassing for her, personally and professionally. At worst it may mean keeping them apart. He'd rather go on getting his teeth rattled.'

Daniel tried again. 'But it's his father doing that. You heard him: he loves spending time with his mother. That's been the only problem between them – she's been too busy for them to be together. And she's obviously determined to change that.'

'Obviously,' said Brodie, expressionless.

He was peering into her face, mystified, his brow corrugated under the yellow hair. They had known one another too well for too long for him to dismiss any conclusion she came to. But mostly they agreed on important issues; or failing that, at least they could see one another's point of view. This time, though, she had entirely left him behind. 'What did you see, what did you hear, that I didn't?'

'Nothing. It just meant different things to me.'

'Explain.'

She thought for a moment. 'Suppose that had been Paddy we'd been talking to. Suppose you'd given her the opportunity to list all my faults. What do you think she'd have said?'

'She'd have said that she loves you,' Daniel answered immediately.

'Of course she would. And then?'

His eyes slid out of focus as he pictured the scene. 'And then she'd have done that sneaky little grin – you know the one – and spilt the beans. All of them. Every bean she could remember from the last six years.'

'Even the has-beans,' nodded Brodie slyly, earning a little grin in return. 'She'd have kept talking till bedtime, recounting every stupid thing I'd ever done, and everything I'd ever done that displeased her. We'd have had to gaffer-tape her mouth shut to get some sleep. And if you'd asked if I was ever moody…!'

Daniel was nodding too, slowly, beginning to understand. 'You don't think he was just being loyal?'

'Secure kids don't feel the need to be loyal in that particular way. The very fact that he thinks he has to defend her suggests there's something to defend her against. Look,' she said with a self-deprecating shrug, 'I'm not a child psychologist, if you want chapter and verse you'll have to ask an expert. But there's a recognised pattern in families with one abusive parent. Contrary to what you might expect, the child will often side with the abuser.

'It's a survival mechanism – keep the violent parent happy or God knows what'll happen. If you see them together you'd think that parent was the child's best friend, that there's nowhere in the world the child would rather be than with him or her. If you put him on the spot he'll criticise the non-abusing parent rather than tell the truth. Kids are unsophisticated but they aren't stupid. They know what comes of angering a violent parent. The non-abusive parent won't beat the crap out of him for lying. The abusive one *will* beat the crap out of him for telling the truth.'

It wasn't that Daniel didn't believe her, or thought she was wrong. He was genuinely struggling to relate this new information to a family he thought he'd got to know. 'But – Marianne? She's not much bigger than Noah is! She works for a charity, for God's sake! And you're telling me she beats up her child, and headbutts her husband when he tries to stop her?'

Brodie knew she could be wrong about this. But she really didn't think so. Daniel might have taught a lot of children but he'd never lived with one so his experience of the normal family dynamic was limited. Perhaps he wasn't aware that the behaviour he expected of children in the classroom situation would be positively sinister if repeated at home. That they don't routinely sit quietly and listen, and put their hands up before speaking, and always address you politely, and there's no earthly reason they should. That it's cause for concern if they do.

'I think that's what's happening, yes. I don't know why you're *so* surprised. Because she's small? You're the last one to see that as a limiting factor! Or because she's a woman? Don't know how to break this to you, Daniel, but we're a lot tougher than we look. We live longer than you. In a survival situation, we last longer than you. We might not have your speed or muscle mass – well, most men's muscle mass – but we make up for it in endurance. Whatever your grandfather may have told you, we are not the weaker sex.'

'I never said you were,' said Daniel quietly. 'For the record, neither did my grandfather. But violence is linked to testosterone, and even I have more of that than Marianne Selkirk does.'

'All men do. Not all of them are violent, least of all to their own children. The reason they aren't is self-restraint. They learn to inhibit the urge to violence in circumstances where it isn't appropriate. Violent men lack the ability to inhibit that urge. So do violent women.

'In a situation like this, everyone assumes it's the man throwing the punches. Statistically, it usually is. But modern women are different to their mothers. We too were born into a man's world, but we took the conscious decision to grab it by the balls and make it our world too.'

She took a brief moment to enjoy the twinge of discomfort in his expression before pressing on. 'We've succeeded. Some people feel we've succeeded too well, over-compensated for generations cross-tethered between the crib and the stove. But the success came at a price. Most women who've done well in what were traditionally men's roles have done so by adopting male characteristics. Ambition, drive, aggression. It's not that the female virtues of insight and cooperation have finally been recognised, it's that – as the supremely adaptable creatures we are – we've learnt to take other tools out of the shed. Today we can argue, shout, plot, undermine and hold grudges as well as any man.

'And, like any man, we can get home at the end of a long day – in Marianne's case, at the end of a long fortnight, fighting tooth and nail for vitally important causes – with the dog-ends of all those emotions still washing round in our brains. Tired, and tetchy, and now trained to fight for what we want. Is it so surprising if some tired, over-stretched woman who's been told she can have it all if she just works hard enough now finds herself having the same problems with violence inhibition as the man who was doing her job thirty years ago?'

Behind his glasses Daniel's mild grey eyes were wide with revelation. 'No,' he managed after a moment. 'No, I don't suppose it is. Brodie...'

She knew what he was going to say, brushed it away impatiently. 'Concentrate on the Selkirks for a minute. We can't leave them here. Maybe I'm wrong, but I don't think so and I'm not willing to take the risk. We have to get them back to town. At least, we have to take Noah with us – he isn't safe alone with her. He asked me if his father was coming. When I said no, I wondered why he didn't sound more relieved. Well, the reason is he needs his father to protect him from his mother. I'm not leaving without him.'

She flashed Daniel a brittle grin. 'You may be less robust than a woman but you've a good brain when you use it. Think of an excuse.'

He was still trying a minute later when they heard the front door of the cottage open and close. They exchanged a puzzled look, then Daniel got out of the car to see what was happening.

Noah Selkirk was coming down the path, carrying an overstuffed rucksack and dragging his feet. He mumbled, 'Mum wants me to come back to town with you. She says she'll pick me up later from your house. If it's not too much trouble.'

'Of course it isn't,' Daniel said quickly. 'But...'

He looked at Brodie but Brodie looked away. She started the car. 'If that's what she wants.' Noah and his luggage climbed onto the back seat and they drove away.

At the corner, where Brodie had to slow, suddenly Daniel

shot her a startled look, and ripped off his seatbelt and threw open the car door.

'*Daniel?*'

He was already running back the way they'd come, shouting a kind of an explanation. 'I...forgot something. I'll...come down with Marianne later. Don't wait for me. Don't come back.' Then he was gone.

He didn't even wait to see if Brodie had done as he asked. He didn't think there was time. He ran down the path to the front door and, finding it already barred against him, round the back of the cottage to the scullery.

A moment sooner and he'd have got there first. He saw the shape of her through the dusty window, the quick turn of her head as she sensed him there, then he heard the lock turn and his heart stumbled.

He cried her name. 'Marianne! Let me in.' But she turned without another glance and vanished back into the house.

The grandfather who raised Daniel had put a high value on good behaviour. Saying please and thank you, and not breaking windows. Even this long after Daniel felt a stab of guilt as he searched for a weapon. But if he was right there was more at stake than a pane of glass, and he made himself swing at the window with a baulk of firewood.

If he'd spent some of his youth as a vandal he might have made a better job of it, and broken the glass without driving a spear of it deep into his upper arm.

The pain, and perhaps even more the shock, stopped him in his tracks, left him gasping. He stared at the glass dagger in appalled disbelief.

There was nothing he could do until he got it out. He tried brushing it with feather-tipped fingers: waves of nausea crashed through him. He leant against the wall. He knew he was close to fainting, and if he did that he might as well have stayed in the car and gone back to Dimmock with Brodie.

He clenched his teeth and set about making himself angry. 'You're useless,' he hissed. 'You're like a little girl. A drop of blood and your knees bend both ways. Get a grip, will you? Just for once, act like a man.' And with that he grasped the crystal dagger and yanked; and it came free, and the blood spurted, and the pain went off the graph. Daniel sank to his knees in a red mist.

Only the knowledge that time was a luxury he didn't have got him to his feet again. Awkwardly left-handed he reached through the broken pane and felt for the key; and felt a weak surge of gratitude when he found it still in the lock. A moment later he was inside the house.

She knew he was there so there was only one place she'd be: the bathroom, probably the only internal door with a bolt. Daniel had been here when Mr Turnbull showed her the house and knew where to go. He tapped politely. 'Marianne, please come out. Don't let's talk through a locked door.'

Her voice was sharp. 'I don't want to talk. Go home, Daniel.'

'I can't. Brodie left without me.'

A pause. 'Noah?'

'He's with her.'

'Then just – go.'

'I can't. Marianne, I know why you sent Noah away. I know why you want to be alone, and I'm not going anywhere.

Whatever you decide – whatever you do – I'm going to be right here.'

'I don't know what you mean,' she said roughly.

'Yes, you do. There's only one reason for getting Noah out of the house.' He wanted her to hear the anger in his tone. 'I just hope he hasn't worked it out too.'

He heard an intake of breath, almost a sob, behind the shut door.

The thing to do with an advantage is press it. 'He's an intelligent boy,' Daniel went on brutally. 'Clever enough to fool me. Clever enough to keep you safe, though you know better than anyone what it cost him. How's he going to feel when he realises it was all for nothing? That he lost you anyway. That if he'd spoken up sooner he mightn't have.'

He could have got it wrong. He knew she was desperate: if she was desperate enough he could push her over the edge. But he also knew she was a fighter: he was gambling on her wanting to come out and box his ears before killing herself.

He held his breath. But the silence stretched too far: he had to draw another breath and hold that.

When finally he heard the bolt slide back he could have wept with relief.

He knew what he'd interrupted. He didn't know how she intended to do it – with a gun, a knife, a bottle of pills – but he knew what she intended. Someone arriving now, though, would never have guessed from the indignation on Marianne Selkirk's face as she threw the door back hard enough to bruise the wall.

'How *dare* you say that to me?' she spat. 'Do you think I don't *care* about Noah? That I'm doing this to make him feel bad? Noah is the *only* thing that matters to me, and this is the only way I can protect him. Now go away and let me do what I have to.'

Daniel clung on to his anger, which was serving him much better than empathy would have done. 'Maybe you do care about Noah, but you're not the only one. He's the reason I'm here. You've put that boy through hell – and still he thinks the sun shines out of your left nostril. Beats me why, but he does, and he's willing to forgive you everything because of it. Except this. He won't forgive this.

'At least, I hope he won't. Because the only way he'll convince himself it wasn't your fault is to tell himself it was his. Is that what you want, Marianne? Is that really a burden you want him to carry for the rest of his life?'

'I don't want to hurt him any more!' Distress made her voice climb like a wailing cat's.

'I know that. But this can't possibly be the best way.'

'It's the only way!'

Daniel wasn't sure she'd noticed, but they were talking about it and they weren't talking through a shut door any more. It was progress. 'There's never only one way. I know – I *know* – right now you think you're out of options. That your life's a bad joke, and you can't change the punch-line – all you can do is deliver it and get off the stage. Marianne, I've been there – I know how it feels when you're scared of the dark but the day's even worse because you don't know what it's going to bring. When what scares you most is *you*. When you know you're out of control and you have no idea how to make some sense of your life, and you think probably the only way is to end it. When you honestly can't wait to be quit of the whole damned business.'

She was staring at him, her lips a whisper apart, her brows gathered in a tiny frown. 'Yes, you do, don't you?' she said softly. 'Know.'

'You thought you had a monopoly on pain?' he demanded. 'Marianne, there's more than enough tragedy in the world for everyone to get their share. You know that. You've *seen* the way some people have to live. Compared with that, nothing you or I have had to deal with is worth a damn.

'All over the world people are dying who desperately want to live. In wars, in famines, in natural and man-made disasters. They fight for every last day, every last minute, and still they die. You *can't* decide your life isn't worth living. You betray every one of them if you do.'

'I can't carry them all!' she cried out in despair. 'I can't care for them all.'

'You don't have to,' promised Daniel. 'You've worked for them, you've saved a lot of them, you don't have to feel for them as well. They're not your children. Noah is. Care for him; feel for him. Live for him. That's a life worth fighting for.'

'I've tried,' she wailed. 'I've tried so hard. I can't... I can't...'

'You're exhausted,' he said. Suddenly he felt very tired himself. He slid down the wall and sat on the flag floor with his arms across his knees. After a moment Marianne followed suit. 'You're all used up. You've no energy left for yourself and your family. But you can fix that today. Take a leave of absence. It's somebody else's turn to save the world. Concentrate on saving yourself.

'I know you can do it. We'll get you some help to make it

easier. It's like an addiction – like alcohol or drugs. It's hard to change something that's become a big part of your life. But you have the best motivation anyone could have, and you'll succeed. Two years from now you'll look back and this'll seem like a bad dream.'

'Do you think all this is news to me?' she demanded, furious with desperation. 'That it never occurred to me that hitting my little boy wasn't a great idea and I should stop doing it? I can't. I've tried, and I can't. The only way he'll be safe from me is when I'm dead.'

Daniel shook his head. 'You think it's harder than quitting drugs? Than stopping drinking? But people manage. They *do* find it hard – murderously hard – and sometimes they slip and have to start again. But they succeed. They take their lives back. And I bet every one of them, standing where you are now, thought they couldn't do it – that it would be easier to die.

'There are high buildings, fast trains and cheap guns everywhere,' he went on fiercely. 'Do you know why they went through the misery of detox? Because their reasons to live were stronger than their reasons to die. They had families and friends, people who wanted them to succeed and helped them when the going got tough. The lucky ones had families like yours – people who cared so much about them they were prepared to pay whatever it cost to hang onto them.

'Your son loves you so much he puts up with being hurt to keep from losing you. Your husband loves you so much he let himself be suspected of child abuse rather than explain what was actually going on. You have two people who love you that much, and you want to throw it away? Marianne, most people would *kill* for a family like yours!'

She gave a little snort that was half a sob, half a chuckle. Daniel winced. It hadn't been the most felicitous choice of phrase. He hurried on. 'The hardest part is already over. The bit where you were trying to do everything that was asked of you and not let on it was too much. The bit where the house of cards was tottering and all that was keeping it up was the love of a twelve-year-old boy. Well, the secret isn't a secret any more. Now you can talk to people who can help and concentrate on getting better. You've had a breakdown. It wasn't your fault. Noah knows that, Adam knows that. Everyone's going to understand.'

Her head came up at that, her eyes wild. 'That I beat my child rather than admit I couldn't do my job? I don't think so, Daniel!'

He tried to put an edge back on his voice. It was getting harder. He was running out of arguments, and he knew she wasn't persuaded. A lot of potential suicides are looking for an excuse to back out: telling them their hamster will miss them will do. But Marianne Selkirk had never backed away from a challenge in her life. She was used to taking hard decisions and then acting on them. He couldn't hold her either by strength or by entreaty. She believed, passionately, that the course she was set upon was best for all concerned.

All Daniel had left to fight with was the fact that she hadn't planned this. It might have been a last resort somewhere in the back of her mind, but she hadn't meant to do it today. She hadn't meant to do it when she took this cottage. She'd believed, or at least she'd hoped, that time with Noah and away from her job and her marriage would help her regain control. Only when she learnt that her secret was out – that rather than leave his son and his wife alone together Adam Selkirk had finally told the truth – had the last resort come to look like the least worst option.

Perhaps that made it Daniel's fault. When he had time to think about it that might well be the conclusion he reached. But right now he was still trying to salvage the situation, and it was like running in treacle. Marianne didn't want to be saved. She wanted out.

But if she hadn't had the chance to rehearse her reasons, he might still find one that wouldn't stand up under pressure. If he did that the whole edifice of her intent might crumble.

'Do you know what they won't understand?' he said harshly. 'That you let a child share your load and then refused to share his. It's cowardly, Marianne! I know there are difficult times ahead. But you have no right to walk away from the mess and leave your husband and your son to sort it out. The least you can do is stay around and help.

'You think it'll all be over when you're dead? It won't. There'll be mountains to climb. The only one who'll be spared is you. I wouldn't have thought it of you, Marianne. I never saw you as a woman who'd take the easy way out and leave others to struggle with the consequences. I thought you were stronger than that.'

'I'm strong enough,' she gritted. 'This is the right thing to do, and I'm strong enough to do it. And if you're not strong enough to watch, you'd better leave now.'

He shook his yellow head. 'I can't.'

'Daniel, you must.' There was something like compassion in her voice. As if she knew he'd put his heart and soul into saving her, and it would be like another little death when he failed. 'This is my decision. You have to accept it. Accept that I don't want you here, and go.'

'I can't,' Daniel said again, pale and stubborn.

Marianne's eye kindled at him. '*Why* not?'

'Lots of reasons,' he mumbled. 'The most immediate one is I can't get up. I'm bleeding.'

CHAPTER TWENTY-ONE

'Oh, dear God!' exclaimed Marianne impatiently, as if he'd done it to annoy her. 'Where...? What...? How long?'

'How long have we been talking?' Daniel countered weakly. 'I got some glass in my arm when I broke in. I didn't realise it was still...' He shrugged, one-shouldered, helpless.

Marianne was bending over him, peeling his jacket back. 'Lord almighty, you're soaking!'

'Can you – I don't know – tie it up with something?'

'Daniel, I moved in here yesterday! I don't have an operating theatre – I don't even have a first aid kit.' But she was on her feet, gathering towels from the bathroom, scissors from the kitchen. 'I suppose we can tie you together long enough to reach hospital.'

He went to ease out of his shirt but Marianne shook her head. 'Don't disturb it. I'll bandage over the top.'

She cut a bath towel into three strips. The first turned an instant vermilion with his blood. The second, bound tightly on top, held out a little longer before the blood soaked through. Marianne tied on the third and sat back on her heels, watching intently. For perhaps a minute neither of them spoke. Then Marianne gave a disappointed little cluck. 'It's no good, it's not stopping. We'll have to get you to A&E.' She stood up again, looking for her car keys.

Daniel said nothing and didn't look at her. He was wondering how long it would be before she saw the snag with that, and what she would do when she did.

She took his good hand and pulled. 'On your feet, Burglar Bill.' And then she froze.

Here it comes, thought Daniel.

'You have to promise me something,' said Marianne, her voice an odd mixture of command and supplication. 'You have to promise me you won't send the police here. To...you know...stop me.'

'Don't ask me that,' he whispered.

'I have to,' she said doggedly. 'And you have to promise.'

'I have to promise to let you die? Or you'll let me die?'

'No!' she said indignantly; then, on second thoughts, 'Yes. Yes, I will, Daniel. That's how desperate I am. I'll watch a good man bleed to death if it's the only way I can be sure of putting an end to this tragedy. Don't think I won't. Don't count on me to come over all sentimental at the last moment. You have a choice. I can have you at Dimmock General in fifteen minutes and they'll sort you out in another five. It's that easy. All I want in return is the freedom to make the right choice for me and my family.'

'You're asking me to keep quiet while you kill yourself,' Daniel said baldly. 'Knowing the hurt that's going to cause to people who don't deserve it. Knowing that today you're desperate – but you weren't desperate enough to kill yourself yesterday, and the chances are you won't be desperate enough to do it tomorrow. Give yourself a chance, Marianne. Wait till tomorrow and see.'

She shook her hair, tendrils the colour of winter sunshine escaping the scarf. 'Tomorrow they'll be watching. Tomorrow I'll be the new fish in the aquarium, and every eye will follow my every move. All the ologists you ever heard of will be queuing outside my door. When I said I wanted this finished, Daniel, that's one of the reasons. To avoid the ologists.'

'Even ologists have a purpose in the grand scheme of things,' suggested Daniel. 'And as purposes go, saving the life of a young woman with a devoted husband, an adoring son and a million strangers' lives to her credit is a pretty good one. Me, I'm with the ologists.'

'Then let them analyse you,' she said briskly, 'because I think they'd find it quite rewarding. More than the odd paper to be written on you, I imagine. But I don't want to be studied. I just want peace. I want out. And I want your word – your *word*, Daniel, and I know what that means to you – you'll do nothing to stop me.'

'That's blackmail,' he said weakly.

'Maybe it is,' she allowed. 'I don't care what you call it. I don't care what you call me. This is the right thing for me and my child, and I don't care what anyone else thinks. Your word, Daniel.'

He shook his head. 'I can't.'

She stared down at him as if she couldn't believe what he was saying. As if she wanted to slap some sense into him. 'What do you *mean*, you can't? This is your *life* we're talking about! You're bleeding a river. You need to get it stopped, quickly. You don't have any choice.'

'It's your life we're talking about as well,' he pointed out. His voice was growing breathy. 'I'm not going to help you die.

I don't think you'll let me die either.'

'Don't bet your life on it,' she shot back in anger, and Daniel gave a little chuckle that ended in a cough.

'I have to. It's all I have.'

Brodie Farrell had known Daniel Hood for two years. She knew him intimately. Not by virtue of sharing her body and his bed: that was something she'd never wanted and even now, knowing what it would mean to him, knowing how much she too stood to gain, she couldn't make herself want it. She could pretend, but she knew in her bones it would be a terrible mistake, not a beginning but an end. She wished with all her heart that this was something she could give him, but it wasn't and she wasn't going to lie. Not to him. She had too much to lose.

But whatever the tabloids tell you, sex is a comparatively small part of most people's lives. Sometimes it's entirely incidental. Twice in her student days Brodie had found herself heaving and sweating with someone she didn't know well enough to put a surname to. She wasn't proud of that. These days, unlike in the early days of her marriage, she wasn't particularly ashamed of it either, but it did serve to underline that sex and intimacy are not the same thing. She knew Daniel as well as she knew herself. She knew – even if she didn't always understand – how he thought, how he felt, what mattered to him. Even when he managed to surprise her it was in entirely predictable ways.

And one of the very first things she'd learnt was that there was a reason for everything he did. It wasn't always a good reason, but at least in his own head, in that moment in time, it made sense. He did nothing for effect. If he hurled himself out of a moving car and hared off back down the road, he had a pressing reason. Brodie spent the next minute working out what it was.

When she had, the breath caught momentarily in her throat. The question now was what she should – what she could – do about it. One thing she couldn't do was turn and drive back to the cottage with Noah in the car. If Daniel had been successful Marianne Selkirk would be in a state of such distress that, for both their sakes, her son should not see her. And if, despite his best efforts, Daniel had arrived too late it was imperative to keep the boy out of the house.

Brodie needed more information, and she needed to get it without the child – this smart, astute child who knew more about his family's problems than she and Daniel did even now – realising what she was asking. She cleared her throat, tried to keep her voice light. 'Last time I was out this way was for a pheasant shoot. Those woods over' – she hunted desperately, pointed with relief towards a little copse to the west – 'there. Do your parents shoot?'

'No,' said Noah. 'Mum says, once you've seen people shooting other people it doesn't seem much like a sport any more.'

'Mm.' Brodie was still walking on eggshells. 'So there are no guns in the house.'

Noah shook his head. 'My dad says it's asking for trouble, having a gun and a boy in the same house.'

'I can't argue with that,' said Brodie. She felt a little of the tension easing from her muscles. There are a lot of ways to commit suicide. Most of them require a little time, but a bullet in the brain requires only one long moment of desperation. If Marianne didn't have a gun some of the urgency was gone from the situation. If she'd taken sleeping pills Daniel would have an ambulance on the way by now. If she was screwing a hook into a ceiling beam he'd have confiscated the step-ladders. There was time to get Noah off-side and then to get help.

Half a mile closer to Dimmock Noah said, 'What happens if you drop an electric heater in a bath?' and the fledgling sense of relief that had been stirring in Brodie's breast spat out its last worm and turned belly-up.

'*What*?'

'There's an electric heater in the cottage. The central heating isn't very good. There's a heater on a long cord, and you take it wherever you're going to be sitting.'

'Including, if you're sitting in the bath?'

Noah nodded. 'I don't think you're supposed to do that, are you?'

'No,' she said. 'You're not.'

'I think Mum knows that too. But...'

'What?'

'She tried it to see if it would reach from the nearest plug.'

'Reach the bathroom door?' asked Brodie faintly.

In the rearview mirror she saw Noah shake his head. 'Reach the bath.'

Brodie stopped the car and turned round in her seat. Immediately she saw from his grave, guarded, intelligent expression that her subterfuge had been entirely wasted on him. He knew what she was thinking. He'd known what Daniel was thinking when he leapt out of the car. He'd known what his mother was thinking when she made him stuff a bag and hurry after them. He'd known, and he'd said nothing.

Brodie said softly, 'I'm not fooling you, am I, with all this talk of shooting parties?' The boy shook his head. 'Sorry. I guess, in the desire to protect them, grown-ups forget that kids are as smart as them and sometimes see more. You know what I'm afraid of, don't you?' This time Noah solemnly nodded. 'How about you? You know her better than anyone. Are you afraid?'

Again he nodded.

Brodie decided. 'OK. I'm going back there, and you're not. I'm going to park a hundred yards from the cottage, and you're going to stay in the car. Come what may. Do you understand?' Another nod. She spun the wheel past the protuberance of her bump. 'Come on then.'

'Oh come on, Daniel,' said Marianne, wheedling, as if it was past his bedtime and she was desperate for a vodka and tonic. 'You're just being stubborn. Let me take you into town and get your arm seen to.'

'Great idea,' mumbled Daniel. 'Let's do it.'

She squinted at him. 'And you'll keep your mouth shut.'

Daniel gave a little scowl like a wince. 'Damn. I knew there was a snag.'

All the time she was getting closer to hitting him. All that stopped her was the fear of making him bleed faster, bringing forward the moment when an irrevocable decision would have to be made. 'I can't believe you're doing this,' she hissed, impatient and mystified. 'What business is it of yours? What gives you the right to say I'm wrong?'

'Nothing,' he freely acknowledged. 'If you're sure you're right, do it. Whatever the cost.'

'The cost is your life!'

'The cost is both our lives, Marianne. You'd better be damn *sure* you're right.'

This was a woman who'd spent half her adult life fighting to save lives. She was never going to sit there and watch him bleed to death. She might have thought she was – for a moment, *he* might have thought she was – but she wasn't. It would have made a mockery of everything that had gone before. She'd spent her career taking risks and making sacrifices for other people: this time she was going to have to sacrifice her own needs for Daniel Hood. So today she would live. Tomorrow was another day. But today she would live.

She reached out her hand. 'Come on, hero. You win. But if you think I'm carrying you to the car, think again.'

They had trouble getting him to his feet with both of them trying. His head swam and his legs felt like rope well-chewed by a bored donkey. 'Sorry,' he mumbled.

He knew Marianne was stronger than she looked. All he could hope now was that she was strong enough.

Marianne Selkirk had carried half the world on her back, she wasn't going to be defeated by a pocket-sized maths teacher. She crouched beside him and took his good arm over her shoulders, and – snarling at him to help, trembling with the strain – she straightened up, bringing him with her. She pinned him against the wall to stop him slumping while she got her breath back. 'Jesus, Daniel,' she gasped, 'you must have rocks in your legs.'

'Sorry,' he said again.

Still pinning him to the wall with one hand she unlocked the front door with the other.

As she did it burst inward in a manner quite inexplicable by the normal laws of physics. Marianne recoiled, letting Daniel go in the process. He slid down the wall uncomplainingly. 'Hi, Brodie,' he said, unsurprised.

Imagine an avenging angel in an advanced state of pregnancy. She filled the open doorway, her eyes burnt and electricity crackled about her. The blast of her gaze cauterised the narrow hall. Then, by degrees, the adamant of her expression softened and a puzzled little frown gathered between her eyebrows. She wasn't sure what kind of a situation she'd walked in on, but it wasn't the one she'd been expecting. 'Daniel – what are you doing down there?'

It would take a fairly long explanation or a very short one. He settled for the short one. 'Bleeding.'

'*What*?' Then she saw the makeshift bandage dark with his blood and fury worked on her like adrenalin. She spun on Marianne Selkirk as if she meant to deck her. 'What have you done to him?'

Daniel shook his head wearily. 'It wasn't Marianne. I cut myself breaking in and it won't stop bleeding.'

Brodie stared at him. 'We have to get you to hospital.'

'I was trying,' Marianne said pointedly.

They took an arm each and hauled him to his feet, and walked him outside.

'Where's your car?' asked Marianne. And then, her tone sharpening: 'Come to that, where's Noah?'

'Just up the lane.' Brodie made Marianne meet her gaze. 'I didn't want to bring him because I didn't know what I'd find.'

Marianne dipped her head in acknowledgement. 'Shall I take Daniel? My car's closer, and faster.'

'OK,' nodded Brodie. 'Noah and I will follow you in. Oh…' She dropped Daniel's hand and, startled, her eyes round, clutched at her belly. 'I'm having a baby.'

Marianne looked at her bump. 'Actually, I'd guessed.'

'No.' She shook her head, the dark hair dancing. 'I mean, I'm having a baby *right now*.'

Daniel peered at her through the miasma of his weakness. However frail he was feeling, he could always do math. 'It's too soon.'

'Don't tell *me*,' gritted Brodie, 'tell The Blob.'

It *was* too soon – six weeks too soon. But The Blob wasn't listening. The last hour or so had been enough to persuade it that things were more interesting on the outside and it was time to join the human race. The contractions raked at her as if it was trying to claw its way out. She bent double, gasping, then dropped to her knees on the grassy path.

Unsupported, once more Daniel slid down beside her.

Marianne lifted her head in disbelief and raged at the sky: 'And now there's *two* of them!'

A small figure was standing in the open gateway. 'There's two of us too.'

You heat the steel in a fire, then you quench it in a bath. You'd think treatment like that would be enough to destroy anything. But it makes a sword strong, and it makes it sharp. Noah Selkirk was not only an intelligent boy, he was a resilient one, and he was used to dealing with crises. Daniel bleeding, and Brodie in the throes of parturition, unable to help one another, found themselves at the mercy of a suicidal woman and a twelve-year-old boy.

In the event, they could have done a great deal worse.

The boy smiled gravely. The mother smiled back. 'So there are. You think we can do this?'

'I think we can do anything,' Noah said stoutly.

'When we're on the same team.'

'We were *always* on the same team,' insisted the child.

'I kicked some own goals,' admitted Marianne.

'Don't know a striker who hasn't,' said Noah matter-of-factly.

Brodie was rolling her eyes. 'Any more of the homespun philosophy,' she grated, 'and this baby's going to be born in your garden.'

She was right: there was no time for philosophy, and no time for debate. 'We won't all get in my car,' said Marianne. 'Where's Mrs Farrell's?' Noah pointed. 'Will you stay with them while I fetch it?' He nodded.

She hesitated only a moment longer. 'I am so proud of you.' Then she was running.

It wasn't born in a garden, it wasn't even born in a car. It was nearly born on a trolley in Dimmock General, about half way between A&E and Maternity. But then unaccountably it changed its mind. The contractions stopped as if it had all been a mistake, there wasn't a baby in there after all, it was a bit of wind and too much pasta.

So after a few minutes Brodie, who had been lying prone on the trolley, clutching the sides and yelling unrestrainedly at shorter and shorter intervals, sat up cautiously and looked round at the porter and demanded, '*Now* what?'

* * *

'They're safe?' repeated Adam Selkirk. 'You're sure?'

'Yes,' said Deacon. 'They're in the waiting room at Dimmock General. You can pick them up there.'

'Both of them?'

'Both of them. They're fine, Mr Selkirk. Nobody got hurt. Well,' he amended in the interests of honesty, 'Hood managed to stab himself – don't know how; must have gone off as he was cleaning it – and Mrs Farrell nearly had her baby in the middle of all this, but there's nothing for you to worry about. Your son and his mother are both unharmed.'

The lighthouse beam of Selkirk's gaze swept Deacon's office until it came to rest on DS Voss. 'No thanks to you.'

It wasn't the first mistake Charlie Voss had made, wouldn't be the last. It might be the one that gave him most nightmares: the one that brought him closest to being responsible for an avoidable disaster. 'I was wrong,' he agreed in a low voice. 'I'm sorry.'

Selkirk feigned a look of surprise. 'That's it, is it? You accused me of abusing my twelve-year-old son. You accused me of beating him and lying about it. I'm a *solicitor*, Sergeant Voss. Have you any idea how much damage your mistake may have done me?'

Deacon waited for DI Hyde to say something. When she didn't, and Voss didn't, he cleared his throat and favoured Selkirk with a bleak little smile. 'Damage? I thought lying was what you were paid for. It'd be a damn sight more damaging professionally if it got about that you couldn't tell porkies to save your life.' And before Selkirk could object he added, 'The other thing to remember is, if you'd told us the truth at the start we could have done a better job of protecting all three of you.'

They were old adversaries; out of court they were almost friends. Selkirk was angry but he wasn't stupid. Some of this he'd brought on himself. He could accuse Voss of harassment but he couldn't make the accusation stick, and he wasn't going to start any proceedings that were doomed to failure. But nor was he going to forget.

'If you're waiting for me to say this was all my fault,' he growled, 'bring a packed lunch. On the basis of a flawed assumption – an idea you only picked up and ran with because it would have suited you down to the ground if it was true – you people have put my son in serious danger. If you think we're going to shake hands and forget that, Superintendent, you're living in cloud cuckoo land.'

'It was an honest mistake,' said Deacon. 'Which could have been rectified in a minute if you'd taken us into your confidence.'

'Maybe it was an honest mistake,' agreed Selkirk tersely. 'Detective Sergeant Voss is a young man, he's entitled to make the occasional honest mistake.' He was on his way to the door. 'And to pay for them, Superintendent Deacon. And to pay for them.'

Daniel spent four hours on a drip, replacing the blood he'd spilt standing between Marianne Selkirk and the abyss. He passed much of the time in a daze, neither sleeping nor awake, in limbo, feeling exactly what he was – drained.

And sadly disappointed. By the time his vital signs were sufficiently improved that the intravenous needle could be removed – painfully: he yelped – it was late in the evening. Hours had passed since Marianne stall-turned Brodie's car in front of Dimmock General and Noah went running for help. Almost his last clear memory was Brodie saying she was about to give birth, so he expected it was all over by now: that he'd missed the event the last months had been building up to, and he'd find the pair of them tucked up and glowing like a kind of NHS nativity. He was devastated. He doubted he'd ever have the chance now to be present at the birth of a baby.

He was wrong. When he was detached from his tubing he followed directions to her room but there was only Brodie, still lumpish and bad-tempered, sucking ice-cubes and plotting a lurid revenge on the man responsible for her condition.

'Should I call him?' asked Daniel. 'I'm sure he'd come.'

'What would I want to see *him* for?' she demanded irascibly. 'This is all his fault.'

It wasn't strictly true but Daniel knew better than to argue. 'Have they said when…?'

'Nope,' grunted Brodie. 'When it's ready. When it feels like it. Some time in the next two months. The little sod isn't even born yet, and already it's giving me the run-around.'

'It's probably better that it stays in there a bit longer,' said Daniel, hoping to mollify her. 'Seven and a half months must be awfully early.'

'Don't blame me,' she snapped. 'I wasn't trying to evict it – it *said* it was coming. It said it was coming right there and then, and never mind how inconvenient and downright undignified it was going to be. It was urgent, it was imminent, and everyone had to drop everything to get it safely delivered.

'Only *then*,' she went on, her voice thick with fury and frustration, 'it got distracted. Called away. More important things to do. Just remind me: whose child is this?'

Daniel risked a careful smile. 'Yours. That's why it's doing things its own way and making the rest of us fall into step.'

Brodie snorted a little laugh, and a stab of pain caught her. Not a contraction: just a pain.

Daniel saw her wince. 'Do you want me to leave?'

She shook her head fiercely, and he pulled up a chair with his good hand and sat down. 'Then I'll stay.'

'So now I'm stuck here overnight while it decides what it wants to do,' said Brodie. 'You're right – it'll be better if it goes to term. It may have been a false alarm. If the contractions haven't started up again by morning they're going to send me home.'

It had been a hard day for Daniel too. After ten minutes Brodie noticed him drooping. Her first instinct was to shake him, make him keep her company. But his body craved rest, and actually there was nothing he could do for her awake that he couldn't also do asleep. He was there if she needed him. She'd have no compunction about rousing him if the contractions started again, and if they didn't she'd be fine on her own. When she saw his head tipping forward she pulled out one of her pillows and padded her knee for him; and like that, in a casual intimacy that was a cypher for their entire relationship, they both slept.

At ten to six in the morning Brodie woke with a gasp and the sensation of a vice clasping her innards, and drew herself up in the bed so convulsively Daniel almost fell off his chair.

He hadn't taken his glasses off before he slept so they were skew-whiff over one ear. His pale eyes were foggy and alarmed. 'Is it…?'

'Yes,' said Brodie tightly.

Stupidly, he asked, 'You're sure?'

'*Yes!*' insisted Brodie.

'What should I...?'

'GET HELP!' yelled Brodie.

She was in labour for thirteen hours: long enough to go through all the possible outcomes, especially the bad ones. The baby was coming too soon – it would be stillborn. It would live just long enough for her to hold it. It wasn't *a* baby at all: it was twins, or triplets – they'd heard the ultrasound coming and carefully lined themselves up like soldiers. All sorts of improbable scenarios racked her through the long, unproductive hours.

Daniel stayed with her. Twice more he offered to call Deacon: both times Brodie refused. At four in the afternoon the midwife ushered Daniel out of the delivery room and he thought they were on the last lap. But it was another two hours before the baby was born, time in which he paced the waiting room and spun every time a door opened, for all the world as if the child was his.

Finally, at five past six, a doctor came. He was new to Dimmock General or he wouldn't have said what he said. 'Congratulations, Mr Farrell. Your wife's had the baby and she's recovering well.'

Daniel felt a curious urge to hand out cigars. But the truth mattered. 'She isn't my wife.'

'Oh.' That was hardly unusual these days. 'Sorry. Your partner. Give her a minute to get her breath and then you can see her. And your son.'

The air caught in Daniel's throat. But... 'It – he – isn't my child either.'

This was slightly more unusual. 'Ah. Er...'

Brodie always said, when Daniel smiled it was like the sun coming out, it dispelled anxieties for fifty metres all round. 'We're friends. And of course I want to see them.'

The doctor nodded. 'Good. But there's something I need to explain first.'

CHAPTER TWENTY-TWO

Two middle-aged men sitting on a park bench, so wrapped up against the cold their own mothers wouldn't have recognised them. Nor, and this was important, would anyone else.

One of them said, 'With the image of a brass monkey coming irresistibly to mind, I do hope you've got a good reason for this, Johnny.'

'Don't call me that,' growled the other. 'Nobody calls me that.'

'Det…'

'Don't call me that, either!' snarled the second. 'Jesus, why don't you make a video on your phone and send it to Division?'

The first smiled into his muffler. 'When did you get so paranoid? Keep looking over your shoulder like that and folk'll think you've got a guilty conscience.'

The second and larger man shrugged himself deeper into his overcoat, fighting the urge to look round again. There was nobody close enough to hear, and nobody further off was paying them any heed. 'I need you to tell me something.'

'OK.'

'What do you know about the death of Achille Bellow?'

The narrow strip between the muffler and the cap blinked at him in surprise. 'About as much as I knew about his life. What the Sunday papers told me. That he was a small-time Balkan gangster until the easing of European border restrictions gave him the urge to travel. That he was found dead on a French beach last summer, and the world has not in any real sense mourned his passing.'

'Did you kill him?'

Bushy eyebrows climbed in the visible strip of face. 'What kind of a question is that?'

'An important one,' growled the second man. 'If you didn't, I need to hear you say it.'

The first gave a little snort that was half a chuckle. 'That's easy. I didn't.'

'You didn't take him out into the Channel and chuck him off *The Salamander*?'

'Ah.' The first man gave his scarf a secret smile. 'That's actually two different questions.'

The second man stared at him. '*How*?'

The first man thought for a moment. 'OK,' he said again. 'I'm going to tell you a story. Like all the best stories, this one isn't true, and anyone who thought it was, let alone tried to prove it was, would be laughed out of court. To coin a phrase.

'Once upon a time there was a nasty little Serb who knew there were girls in his own country who would pay him to get them jobs at the wealthy end of the continent, and men there who would pay him to provide them with girls. He thought there was a tidy profit to be made. He didn't tell the girls exactly what kind of work he'd got them, or what was generally considered a fair rate of pay, and he kept them in conditions you'd think were rough for a dog, but he did make a lot of money.

'Of course, he wasn't endearing himself to the local business community whose trade he was poaching. But what were they going to do – call the police? They turned a blind eye. The nasty little Serb with his half-starved amateurs was never going to cream off the profitable end of the business, and they thought it was only a matter of time before the local CID got wind of him and solved the problem for them.' He rolled his eyes. 'It's true, isn't it? You can never find a policeman when you need one. The local Detective Superintendent didn't even know the Serb was working on his manor.

'What happened next was that some of the local toms met some of the Serbian girls. You might think that would be a recipe for a cat-fight, but no. When they saw the state the foreigners were in, and found out what they were having to do and what they were getting paid – and they didn't even want to be in the business, they wanted to go home, but they weren't allowed to, and some of them were beaten for asking and some of them had actually disappeared…well.'

He gave a little shrug. 'A tom's pretty much like any other girl: she's got a heart, and she's got a sense of fair play. A couple of the locals started helping the Serbians get away. They took up a collection and sent the youngest ones home. Some they found other work for. And a couple left the nasty little Serb and threw their lot in with the local toms.'

An elderly woman walking a King Charles spaniel took a minute to pass the bench. The first man fell silent until she was out of hearing-aid range. Then he continued where he'd left off.

'You can imagine how cross the nasty little Serb was. With his own girls, but even more with the locals that he couldn't intimidate in the same way. So one day him and a couple of associates grabbed two of the local toms and cut them. They cut their faces with a razor blade.

'At which point,' he said as if it were self-evident, 'something had to be done. People who thought it wasn't strictly their concern when one foreigner was mistreating some other foreigners couldn't take the same view when it was their own girls who were getting hurt.

'One of the more prominent local businessmen offered to deal with the problem. He invited the nasty little Serb out for a day's sailing – sun, sea, a good lunch, a decent bottle of Chablis and a little chat. Well – maybe *invite* isn't the right word. Actually he didn't have the option of saying no, and the two large friends he wanted to bring were unavoidably detained round the back of the shower-block, but still...

'After lunch, the prominent local businessman explained to the nasty little Serb the error of his ways. That, in this country, prostitution and slavery are two different things. That you treat the girls as employees, not a product. And you don't – you really don't – nobble somebody else's stable.'

There was a long pause. Then the other man on the park bench said, 'So you did. You took him out into the Channel, shot him and chucked him overboard.' The tone was almost expressionless. There was nothing recognisable as censure in it. Perhaps because it was what he'd suspected all along, and he'd had time to come to terms with it. To work out what he had to do next.

The first man clucked in mild disapproval. 'This isn't about me,' he said patiently. 'It's a story, Johnny. A work of fiction. And every good story needs a twist in the tail. You don't just shoot someone in the middle of the Channel, however much they deserve it. Where's the wit in that?

'No, when you've finished the last of the Chablis you explain to your guest just how unhappy you are about recent events. Now, this is a hard man, yes? Even alone, on somebody else's boat in the middle of the Channel, he's not going to roll over and play dead. To start with he tries to bluff it out. Reminds the prominent local businessman how many large cousins he has back home in Serbia, and how quickly they can get here in the back of a cabbage transporter. Apparently, this sort of talk goes down well in the Balkans.'

The little dog had left its elderly owner and come to see if the men on the bench would amuse it. The ground was littered with sticks from the beech trees. The first man threw one for it. It brought it back. He threw it again, further, and waited till it was out of earshot before continuing. From habit, presumably.

'You know what it's like when alien cultures meet. It comes down to whose customs are the strongest. He's the outsider, he should be at a disadvantage, but he wouldn't be here at all if he hadn't the strength of will to mould the world to a shape that suits him. You have the home ground advantage, but he's the one who brought the fight to you. He thinks the cousins with the cabbage truck is a winning argument. He still thinks you're going to back down.

'When he realises you aren't, and that any number of large cousins in Serbia are no use to him here, in the middle of the sea on somebody else's boat, he reconsiders his approach.

Even offers a grudging apology. But it's too little, too late. You try to explain to him that it isn't personal. You talk of the need to make an example. Point out that there are a lot of nasty little people around, not only in Serbia, and a lot of poor and hopeful girls, and if they all thought the streets of Dimmock were paved with gold there'd be no work left for the local talent.'

The dog had brought the stick back. The first man took it, and leant down. 'This is the very last time,' he said firmly; and the second man would have sworn he saw the dog nod. The first man hurled the stick and the dog sped after it, ears flying in the wind.

The narrator returned to his story. 'About now the apologies start sounding rather more sincere. The hard man softens his attitude, promises not to do it again, at least not in your town. Offers to take his face where you'll never see it again. And he means it – you know he means it. But then the image of other faces floats before your eyes – familiar faces, pretty faces once, now damaged beyond repair. And you don't really care what he will and won't do in the future. You want him to pay for what he did in the past.'

His tone remained light, almost playful. Except for the fact that the other man knew what he was capable of, there was nothing to suggest he was describing a cold-blooded murder. 'The thing about a boat is, you've always got a couple of beefy crewmen handy. Ignoring his pleas and struggles both, you tie his hands behind his back and produce a length of chain, the last few fathoms knotted into a ball. You shackle the chain round his leg. You drink in his expression like vintage champagne, then you pull a bag over his head.

'By then, the hard man's screaming. Pleading, and screaming. Which is fun,' he remembered with a muffled grin, 'but you can have too much of a good thing so you hit him a time or two to shut him up. Finally you pick a nice quiet spot and heave to. You express the regret that things have come to this, but you don't offer him any last wishes because obviously he'll ask to live till he's ninety. You have your beefy crewmen lift him over the rail, chain and all, and drop him in the sea.'

A leaden silence descended on the park. Fifty yards in one direction some young mothers were playing ball with a gang of pre-schoolers. Fifty yards in the other the old lady was calling the spaniel in increasing desperation – 'Bonny! *Bonny!*' – while the dog carried its trophy off towards Brighton. None of this impinged on the tiny world of the park bench and its sole inhabitants. Their silence may have been limited geographically, but it went all the way to the core.

After perhaps a minute the second man, believing the story was complete, drew a weary breath to speak. But the first held up a gloved finger, indicating there was more to come.

'But you don't sail away. Not for a minute – not when there's entertainment still to be had. You listen to him screaming and yelling, and feeling the weight of the chain drag him down. You hear him choke on a couple of waves. And then things go kind of quiet because, even in the state of shit-scared panic he's now in, finally it strikes him that iron chain heads for the bottom in pretty much a straight line and he shouldn't still be bobbing around.

'It takes him another minute to work out that the chain's already on the bottom, and actually so is he – the reason he hasn't sunk is that he's standing in four feet of water. And the tide isn't coming in, it's going out. An hour from now he's going to be dragging a length of chain up an isolated Normandy beach, wondering how to explain his situation to the first people he bumps into in such a way that they don't immediately call the *gendarmes*. *That's* when you sail away. Chuckling.'

His story was told. The visible strip of the first man's expression was content.

The second man was thinking. Finally he said gruffly, 'And yet Achille Bellow is dead.'

The first man nodded. 'Yes, I know.'

'They found his body on a Normandy beach at the end of June.'

'Towing a length of chain?'

'Shot full of lead.'

'Well, there you go,' said the first man wisely. 'Obviously he'd had time to go home and change.'

The second man hung onto his temper, though the effort dilated his nostrils. 'He was seen boarding *The Salamander* on June 24th. *Salamander* was observed off the Breton coast on the 25th, and Bellow's body was found on the 26th. He didn't have time to go home.'

'He wasn't seen boarding *The Salamander* on June 24th,' the first man corrected him.

'We have witnesses…'

'They're mistaken.'

'You filed a sailing plan!'

'Indeed I did. For the 24th to the 26th, which was the trip my solicitor came on. I believe you know him – big chap, not much of a seaman but useful as ballast.'

'Achille Bellow was *seen*...'

'Tell me,' said the first man, 'and this is just a guess, but the witnesses who saw him board *The Salamander* – they weren't a couple of old guys from down the pontoon, last sailed with Captain Cook?'

The second man was immediately guarded. 'I'm not going to divulge...'

'Because everyone knows,' the first man went on unconcerned, 'that the Hawkins brothers have no concept of the passage of time. Why should they? They do the same things every day of their lives, but with an extra sweater on in winter. If the bunting's flying they know it's regatta week, otherwise they can tell you the wind force and the state of the tide but don't even ask them what day of the month it is.'

There was a pause as he considered just how forthright he could afford to be. Then he said, 'Johnny, I'll tell you straight because I know you need to know. They *did* see Achille Bellow board *The Salamander*. But that was the previous weekend. I didn't file a sailing plan for that trip, for fairly obvious reasons. I put the fear of God into Bellow the way I told you, and I left him on that beach in Normandy, alive. In need of a change of underwear but unharmed. I confidently expected that would be the last I'd see or hear of him.'

The second man was taken aback. And yet he reckoned he knew when he was hearing the truth. 'Well – *somebody* shot him!'

'Do you want to know what I heard?' The second man nodded. 'I can't prove any of this, but I heard it from usually reliable sources and I believe it to be true. When *Salamander* sailed away, Bellow hauled himself out of the water, found a rock to break the padlock, trudged up the beach and started hitching his way home. It's – what? – about six hundred miles from Normandy to Marseilles, he probably got in late the following day. By which time he was very tired and very angry. Way too angry to do the sensible thing, which was put it down to experience and find another bit of Green & Pleasant to set up shop.

'He called his backers together – the people who found the girls, the men who owned the trucks and those who put up money for the passports – and told them they'd all been made fools of by some jumped-up local pimp. That the gravy-train had been derailed, and if they didn't want to kiss their investment goodbye they'd have to deal with the guy responsible.

'They talked it through and agreed there was no point trying to expand further until the man to blame for their current predicament had been disposed of. So they took him back to the beach and shot him.'

The second man stared at him in – not in disbelief, perhaps in amazement. 'His own backers shot Achille Bellow?'

'He wasn't doing much of a job for them, was he?' asked the first man mildly. 'Costing them money, causing all kinds of ructions… They needed someone to do their trafficking quietly and efficiently, not cause mayhem wherever he went. They retired him. With, er…' He'd forgotten the expression.

'Extreme prejudice,' supplied the second man, deadpan. 'Wait a minute, though. They left him on the beach in the hope that the blame would rebound on you. But then, how did the account – even a slightly garbled account – reach…?' He stopped abruptly short of an indiscretion.

The first man was used to this form of conversation. 'Another of your witnesses?' he postulated smoothly. 'That depends who we're talking about. Only two groups of people could have known about Achille Bellow's little voyage of self-discovery – people I told and people he told. The only people I told were those whose discretion I rely on every day. And you,' he added, beaming invisibly into his scarf. 'I imagine Bellow was equally circumspect about who he talked to.'

'You're saying…' He had to stop and work it out. 'You're saying that…' Oh, discretion be damned! 'You're saying Leslie Vernon had it from someone who had it from Achille Bellow himself?'

'*Leslie*?' exclaimed the first man. 'Oh, that explains it. He works for Joe Loomis. You do know that? That's why I dispensed with his services – too many things I said to Vernon were finding their way to Joe. And it was Joe who was handling the girls Bellow brought in.'

'*Loomis*? Joe Loomis ran Achille Bellow's Dimmock operation?' The second man was shaking his head despairingly. It was bad, but not in the way he'd been expecting. It was bad because a more competent investigation wouldn't have left him to hear what really happened from the prime suspect. On the other hand, he wasn't going to suffer the embarrassment of watching his old adversary taken down by the serious and organised DI Hyde.

The first man nodded complacently. 'He needed someone on the ground here, someone with experience in the business, to mind the girls when he was off trafficking. Who better than Joe? The proverbial bad penny. No trade too low for him, no gutter too dank, and there isn't a slum in England he couldn't lower the tone of just by moving in.'

'And it really *was* Adam Selkirk on *The Salamander* that weekend. He wasn't lying. It wasn't a handy alibi run up for the occasion.'

'Of course it wasn't,' agreed the first man, slightly miffed. 'Hell's teeth, Johnny, you're not talking to a two-bit crook here. If I need someone to lie for me, I don't ask my lawyer. The guy who might one day have to convince a judge and a jury that the police have got it wrong, that I'm an honest upright citizen who's been misunderstood. A man like that, his credibility is what you employ him for. You don't compromise it. Not when it would be as easy to pay someone who'd never hold your future in his hands.'

'You're saying, the more dishonest the client, the more honourable the lawyer needs to be.'

The first man laughed. 'No, I am most specifically *not* saying that! Of course, if that's what you're hearing there isn't much I can do about it.'

The second man was still shaking his head in a kind of wonder. 'Joe Loomis. It's time I did something about Joe Loomis, isn't it?'

'Probably,' agreed the first man. 'You don't want to give people the idea this is a town where gangsters run around with impunity.'

The second man said nothing. But if thoughts counted for anything there'd have been a flash of lightning and a smoking hole in the bench beside him.

CHAPTER TWENTY-THREE

Voss tidied up his desk. He tidied up his office. What he couldn't do was tidy up his mind. It was still in a state of confusion at eight o'clock when he headed for home.

By eight-fifteen he was still in the upstairs corridor, physically leaning against the wall opposite the CID squad room (a.k.a. the Bear Pit), mentally on another planet entirely. There's no knowing how long he'd have remained there if Deacon hadn't passed him and, receiving no response to his growled, 'Night, Charlie,' turned back at the top of the stairs to find out why not.

'Charlie?'

Voss blinked. He had the dazed expression of a boxer up on his feet for a count of eight. 'Sorry. What?'

'I said, "Goodnight, Charlie."'

'Oh – yes,' said Voss. 'Sorry. Goodnight.'

Deacon went on standing there, his hands in his pockets. 'No,' he explained with unaccustomed patience, 'you say that *and then you move towards the car park*.'

Voss grinned. But it didn't last. 'Sorry. Mind elsewhere.'

'Apparently,' said Deacon. 'And will you stop apologising? You have nothing to apologise for.'

Voss gave a troubled little snort. 'That's a matter of opinion.'

'Selkirk?' Deacon's tone was dismissive. 'Selkirk's a solicitor. He thinks policemen should apologise for being born.'

Voss appreciated him trying. 'All the same, he has a point. I don't know – I don't understand – how I got it that wrong. I keep going over it – the whole thing, everything we were told – and I still can't see where I went off the rails. But I ended up in quite the wrong place. And the consequences of that could have been…' He shook his ginger head helplessly, unable to come up with a word of sufficient magnitude.

'Could have been,' agreed Deacon. 'But weren't. You made a mistake. It was an easy mistake to make. That kid was certainly being beaten by one of his parents. Forty-nine times out of fifty it would have been his father. You were unlucky – you backed the odds-on favourite and it was beaten by a fifty-to-one outsider.'

'It's not supposed to be a gamble, though, is it?' said Voss. He looked and sounded worried. 'We're supposed to work from what we know to what we can infer to what we can prove, so when we accuse someone of a serious offence we can be pretty sure he did it. We don't go to a jury and say, "There's a strong statistical likelihood this guy did what we say he did."'

'You didn't take it to a jury. You were never going to take it to a jury. That's not what was going on.'

Voss's frown was puzzled. 'The guy was – at least, I *thought* the guy was – beating up on his twelve-year-old son. We had to do something. All right, it turned out not to be the truth…'

'You think that's all that saved Adam Selkirk from prosecution? I wish. What was happening to Noah was horrible, but helping him wasn't the name of the game. The main feature was Hyde v. Walsh, and even Selkirk was only a travelling reserve. You were the guy in the changing rooms cutting up the oranges.'

Voss didn't follow. 'Selkirk was central to both cases – the suspect in one, the main witness for the defence in the other. It seemed reasonable to think that his behaviour towards his son – what we believed was his behaviour – undermined the alibi he was giving Terry Walsh.'

'It *was* reasonable,' said Deacon, 'and the fact that you were wrong doesn't make it any less reasonable. In fact Selkirk didn't do either of the things you thought he had. He didn't abuse Noah, and he didn't lie for Terry.'

Voss's green eyes flared, astonished. 'He must have! Lied, I mean. We have four independent witnesses. All right, Susan wasn't going to stand up in court, but there was no way she and Vernon could have got their heads together and agreed a story. Selkirk couldn't have been with Walsh when Bellow was killed. He had to be lying.'

'What do you know about your independent witnesses?' asked Deacon quietly.

Voss considered. 'Well yes, one of them's a drug-runner. But if you want someone to tell you about the criminal underworld it's no use asking a nun. And one's an accountant.'

'He was Terry's accountant.'

'Which means he should know what he's talking about.'

'And now,' Deacon went on in the same quiet, unemphatic voice, 'he's Joe Loomis's accountant.'

Voss stared at him with his whole rigid body. '*What?*'

'Terry and Joe are rivals. However much you want Walsh behind bars, Joe wants it more. And was prepared to do more to make it happen. Like bribe his accountant to say he'd overheard something he hadn't. Terry *was* seen with Achille Bellow, but that was a week before he was killed. Your Ancient Mariners got the wrong weekend. Bellow was here the weekend of the 17th, and the French police can place him alive and well in Marseilles on the 20th. Terry didn't kill him. Terry couldn't have killed him.'

'Someone's lying,' managed Voss, and Deacon nodded.

'Of course. We knew *someone* was lying. But it wasn't the brief, it was the bookkeeper.'

Voss was struggling to get his head around what he was being told. His expression might best be described as one of God-forsaken shock. 'Leslie Vernon works for Joe Loomis?'

'That's why Terry wanted rid of him. Things he was saying in front of Vernon kept reaching Loomis. When he was sure, he gave Vernon his marching orders. Joe owed him a favour so he put him on his own payroll.' He gave an amused little grunt. 'I never imagined Joe Loomis keeping books.'

'*Why didn't you tell me?*'

'I didn't know either, until today,' said Deacon mildly. 'But then, it wasn't my case. If it had been I might have thought to look rather more closely at a man who claimed to have heard a very clever villain behaving like a rather stupid one.'

Voss didn't even hear the criticism implicit in that. He was still trying to make sense of it all. 'What about Susan Weekes? Are you saying Joe Loomis got to her too – got word to her in custody in Dover and told her what story to tell? It's not possible...'

'I don't think that's what happened. I think she told you what you wanted to hear. I think the questions you asked her suggested the answers you needed. I think, because it confirmed what you wanted to believe, you were more open to what she had to say than you would otherwise have been.'

'She said she heard Walsh threaten Achille Bellow!'

'Well, maybe she did. She was working in his wife's casino when Bellow met his unmourned end. I don't doubt Terry had been muttering about him for a while before he got round to putting the frighteners on him, and maybe Susan heard what she says she heard. But think about that interview you had with her. Can you honestly say you didn't prime her – tell her what you were looking for, the dates you were interested in, the whole line of your inquiry?'

Voss thought hard. And then he shook his head. 'No, I can't,' he said simply. 'She asked me what we wanted to know and I told her. And then she gave it back to me. She hardly even changed the wording. We'd have got the same statement if I'd written it myself.' He squeezed his eyes shut. 'Why didn't I *see* that? That is such a rookie mistake!'

'It's another easy mistake to make,' said Deacon, and in another man you'd have said that was sympathy in his tone. 'One we can all make any time we start thinking our job is proving our theories rather than collecting evidence. And you weren't the senior investigating officer. Maybe you should have realised what was happening. But your SIO should have prevented it happening.'

Bemused, Voss shook his head. 'She – we both – wanted it too much. Thought we had a case when all it amounted to was one con trying to bury another, and a terrified woman willing to say anything that might keep her out of jail.'

'That's about the size of it,' agreed Deacon. 'Oh, cheer up, Charlie Voss. It could have been worse. You could have been right about Selkirk, and had to turn a blind eye to what he was doing at home because that was the price of nailing Walsh.'

Of everything that had been said to him, that shocked Voss most. 'No way! I swear to you, chief, I was never going to do that. There were two approaches we could take and still protect Noah: the discreet way and the see-you-in-court way. But the boy's safety was always paramount. We'd have done what was necessary to achieve it.'

'I know you'd have tried,' said Deacon quietly. 'But I think, if it had come to a straight choice between charging Terry and protecting Noah, the kid would have gone on walking into doors. No one would have said it was a straight choice, of course. But the serious and organised Ms Hyde had a lot riding on nailing Terry. I think she'd have found a perfectly good argument for keeping a watching brief and not breaking up the family if Selkirk had given her what she needed.'

'No…' But a note of doubt crept into the Sergeant's voice. He'd learnt a lot about the big wide world in the last few days. One thing he'd learnt was that Jack Deacon wasn't the worst thing in it.

As if he'd read his mind, Deacon gave a rough chuckle. 'There are more things in heaven and earth, Charlie Voss, than are dreamt of in your philosophy. If you'd been right about Selkirk, the point would have come where you'd have had to walk away knowing there was nothing more you could do for Noah. Be glad you were wrong. For once, the consequences of being right would have been worse.'

He could see from Voss's incredulity that he still didn't really believe it. Of course, Voss was a young man. Perhaps he still thought that law and justice and good were all facets of the same jewel. Perhaps he had yet to realise that the one thing worse than a man without a creed is one who'll do anything for the one he has. 'Go home, Charlie,' he said. 'Things will look better in the morning.'

'Yes,' nodded Voss.

'No,' said Deacon patiently. '*Go home*. The wall will stand up on its own.'

'Oh – yes.' Finally Voss headed for the stairs.

When he was sure his sergeant had gone, Deacon headed for Alix Hyde's office. The door was open. He closed it behind him.

DI Hyde had her briefcase and a cardboard box on the desk in front of her. She was putting things into both.

'Pulling out, then?' said Deacon levelly.

She flicked him a weary smile. 'No point staying. He's had too long to organise his defences – we won't sneak past them now. We'll get him. We just won't get him this time.'

'Can we expect to see you back, then, in another year or two?'

She shrugged. 'Perhaps. Though it might be better if it was someone else. Someone he doesn't know.'

'I think it would be better if it was someone else, too,' said Deacon.

She wasn't looking for a fight with him. She'd spent the last weeks avoiding him as much as possible. But that wasn't something she could overlook, or put down to an unfortunate infelicity with words, or take as a joke. She had either to challenge it or to tacitly acknowledge he was right.

Alix Hyde hadn't got where she was by turning the other cheek. Her eyes flared combatively. 'You blame me for this shambles? For not knowing that the guy giving us Walsh was actually working for his rival? Superintendent, that's exactly why I asked for local support! You said you were giving me your best man. I relied on him to tell me things like that. To know, or to find out. That was a mistake. He's a nice lad, young Voss, but he's not ready to carry that level of responsibility.'

Deacon lowered himself slowly onto the edge of the desk. It was an old desk, solid enough to take him. He considered for a moment before replying.

'You mustn't think,' he said carefully, 'that I don't know what you were doing here. I don't think Charlie does – like you say, he's a nice lad – but I do. I know how you used him. You used him as a flak-jacket. You kept him between you and anything that might blow up in your face. *He* thought you were giving him a chance to show what he could do. I think he still thinks that – that he let you down. But you and I both know, don't we, Inspector Hyde, that actually he did exactly what you needed him to do. He stood up and drew the fire that would otherwise have come your way.'

She considered denying it. Facing anyone else she would have denied it. Deacon was possibly the only person she would have answered honestly. Not because he was a senior officer, although he was. Not because she was reluctant to lie, because she wasn't. And not because she was ashamed, because she wasn't that either. She'd been playing for high stakes. She'd been given the task of taking an important villain off the streets, and if she'd succeeded everyone would have wanted to shake her hand.

She'd used all the tools at her disposal. Sergeant Voss had been one of them. Detective sergeants were put in the world to be useful to detective inspectors, and Alix Hyde didn't acknowledge any fundamental difference between using them for legwork and using them the way she'd used Charlie Voss. Leaving the ranks of the used and joining the users was possibly the best reason, in her opinion, for seeking promotion.

She let a slow smile spread across her handsome features. 'The role of footsoldiers since the dawn of warfare, Superintendent.'

Deacon acknowledged that with a rueful little smile of his own. 'I've always thought that the history of warfare, and its popularity as a sport among the upper classes, would have been quite different if generals had been made to stop shouting *Charge!* and instructed to shout *Follow me!* instead.'

'On the other hand,' said Hyde, 'dead officers can't lead an army. And neither can live privates.'

'You're aware, are you, that this will have damaged Voss's career? That it'll be a question mark on his record every time he's considered for promotion for years to come.'

Hyde shrugged. 'I don't make the rules, Superintendent. We all have set-backs in our careers – I did, you did. We made mistakes, we paid for them, then we worked hard enough to rise above them. That's how the system works. I'd like to think that what Charlie's learnt from this will serve him well in the long run.'

'Not to put too much trust in senior investigating officers? To remember that they may be willing to shaft him in order to use his bloody corpse as a shield?'

'To keep his wits about him,' said Hyde. She wasn't smiling now. 'To do his homework. Not to assume that his SIO will have nothing better to do than keep him out of trouble.'

Deacon showed his teeth in a feral grin that had nothing to do with humour. 'To recognise the fact that not all the ruthless bastards are on the other side. That ordinary decent criminals have a lot to recommend them in comparison to an ambitious police officer.'

'There's nothing wrong with ambition, Superintendent!' retorted Hyde, genuinely surprised.

'Nothing at all,' agreed Deacon. 'Until it becomes the reason for doing the job. *This* job – I've never done any other so I can't speak for them all. But I know this job. I know what it needs. It needs Charlie Voss. It needs Charlie Voss a lot more than it needs you.'

She laughed at that. But the look in her eyes said the nonchalance wasn't entirely genuine. 'That's a touching vote of confidence in a young man who's still wet behind the ears. Have you told him you see him heading up the Met some day?

'No, of course not,' she answered herself, the smile broadening. 'If he knew you had that sort of faith in him he'd have a bit more in you. Wouldn't, for instance, worry that one day he'll open a door and find you in bed with a con.'

She couldn't have come closer to flooring him without using a baton-round. Among the things Deacon had known were going wrong and those he'd suspected were going wrong, it had never occurred to him that the trust between himself and his sergeant had been under strain. He'd thought, because he was happy with the relationship, the relationship was fine. One reason he'd offered Voss's services to the visiting fireman was that he trusted the dog to come home.

Jack Deacon wasn't a man who trusted easily. It had taken time for him to feel sufficient confidence in Voss to relax with him, to acknowledge – if only to himself – Voss's strengths and to make the most of them. And no, he hadn't told Voss he was the best DS he'd had, even better than no DS at all. He'd thought Voss knew. He'd assumed the young detective was capable of drawing the correct inference from the fact that he did less shouting these days. In truth, he'd made an assumption that generations of men had made before him, if in different circumstances: that if it was good for him it was good enough.

So it came as a blinding shock that Voss trusted him less than he trusted Voss. Of course, Hyde could be lying. It would take almost no effort of will for Deacon to believe she was lying. But Deacon held the truth in almost as high regard as Daniel did. He didn't confuse what was true with what was convenient, and he didn't tinker with it for his own comfort. In spite of which, Hyde had somehow stumbled on a truth he himself had not suspected. That Charlie Voss was unsure whether, if push came to shove, Deacon would do his job or help his friend.

Another man would have staggered under the blow. But Deacon had spent nigh-on thirty years showing people what he wanted them to see and no more. And he didn't want Alix Hyde to know she'd bloodied him. He hid the wound behind a slow, cold smile. 'Worry is good,' he said. 'Worry keeps you on your toes. Worry stops you taking things for granted. I *want* my officers to worry that one day I might cross the line – that any of us could. That in the right circumstances, any of us is capable of betrayal. I don't want them to think that carrying a warrant card makes us superheroes.

'I don't want them ever to think that some DI they don't know from Adam – or Eve – has to be honest, decent and trustworthy because she wouldn't be a police officer if she wasn't. I want them to use the same critical faculties, the same standards, to judge their senior officers as they use every day in their work. I *want* them to be aware that I could cross the line. Knowing that keeps them safe.'

Deacon's lip curled with contempt. 'You knew Vernon was dodgy from the start. You came here knowing it – knowing what he was prepared to say, but also knowing it wouldn't stand up to thorough scrutiny. But it *would* serve as a framework on which to hang other evidence. Only, if it came out that was what you were doing, you wanted to be able to show it wasn't you doing it. You steered Voss onto Leslie Vernon like lining up a jet fighter for mid-air refuelling. You knew what Vernon would say when he was asked – all you needed was someone to ask him.

'Which raises an interesting question, Detective Inspector Hyde. *How* did you know what Leslie Vernon would say? If this plot to dispose of his rival was hatched by Joe Loomis, how did you know what to ask? Unless you've been ignoring guidelines and best practice and all that crap and conspiring with one villain to take down another.'

If he hadn't known it before, the way Hyde's expression clamped down told him he was right. 'Say that in front of anyone else,' she said quietly, 'and I'll take it all the way to the top. And it'll be your word against mine – you won't find any evidence. There *isn't* any evidence. But there are people up there waiting for a chance to push the last of the dinosaurs over the cliff and have a fresh start. You're not the face of policing for the 21st century, Superintendent Deacon – I am. You have rank on your side. I have time. And a lot more friends.'

Deacon didn't doubt she was right. He'd always been better at doing the job than working the room. He should probably have put more effort into the politics. If he had…

…It still wouldn't have been a good use of his time exchanging insults with Detective Inspector Hyde in front of a board at Division. Once she left here, his only abiding regret would be the damage done to Voss's career.

He said, 'I don't need to tell anyone anything. Charlie's going to figure it out all by himself. You put on a good act – smart, glamorous. But he's pretty smart too, and he's not going to be dazzled by glamour for long. He'll work out what you did and how you did it, and he won't need my help.

'In a way it's a shame. It's like seeing a child realise that Father Christmas is actually their dad in their mum's dressing-gown. It's a loss of innocence. But hell, he's a Detective Sergeant, innocence isn't necessarily a survival strategy. Next time he meets someone like you, all the alarms will go off at once and he won't end up paying for someone else's promotion. Maybe, all in all, that lesson has been worth what it cost him.'

Deacon lifted the cardboard box off the desk. 'Let me help you down to your car,' he said. 'I wouldn't like you to have to come back.'

They headed down through the building in silence. And the

building was silent around them. It's impossible to say how – Deacon hadn't been shouting – but something of what had passed between them had leached out through the walls or through the floor, and men and women who had time for DS Voss, and even a certain amount for Superintendent Deacon, registered their disapproval of DI Hyde with three minutes of wintry silence. None of those they passed in the corridors or on the stairs wished her well, or even a safe journey home. Those three minutes were among the longest of her life. There was never any danger of her bursting into tears, but she had to clench her jaw to keep from saying something that might come back to haunt her.

When she pushed through the back door that opened onto the car park the fresh air cooled her blazing cheeks, and also her head. She could make a gesture without conceding much. She turned at the top of the steps.

Deacon put the cardboard box into her arms, turned himself and went back inside without another word.

In times of stress the brain acts like a camera, taking shots and filing them for scrutiny at a better moment. When the door closed between him and Alix Hyde, and Deacon was congratulating himself on the extent to which he'd managed to bridle his anger and say everything he wanted to and nothing more, by degrees he grew aware that one of those he'd passed in the corridor had no obvious reason for being there. He looked round. 'Daniel?'

He had one arm in a sling and he looked pale; otherwise there was little to show for his adventure. 'Have you got five minutes, Jack?'

Deacon glowered. This was the perfect end to a perfect day. The fact that he'd managed to get rid of DI Hyde without resorting to violence could not be taken to guarantee Daniel's safety. 'I suppose,' he said ungraciously.

There was an empty interview room: they went in there. 'Well?'

Daniel didn't want to do this with both of them standing in a grubby little room with a video camera and a tape-recorder. But it was important to get it done. He took a deep breath and came straight to the point. 'Brodie's had the baby. It's a boy. You have a son, Jack.'

CHAPTER TWENTY-FOUR

It was the end of a busy day. Busy for him; busier for her. Deacon wasn't sure what protocol demanded. Which would have troubled him not at all if he'd known what he wanted to do, or what Brodie would welcome. He drove out to the ring road, then twice round the roundabout before heading back into town and going home. He thought he'd sleep on it. But he didn't.

Exhausted as she was, Brodie didn't sleep much either. She drowsed, going over events in her mind, waking with a start at each unfamiliar sound. She was caught in a kind of limbo. None of it seemed entirely real.

They'd told Daniel before they told her, so he wouldn't be too stunned to offer the support she was going to need. Then, in the privacy of her room, with Daniel holding her hand, the doctor explained the nature of the problem. Once very simply, and then again with more detail. She gripped Daniel's left hand so tightly her nails drew blood, but he never complained.

'Don't think you have to take all this in right now,' said the doctor. 'We'll go through it again as many times as you need to when you're feeling a bit stronger. For now, all you need to focus on is that your son's in no immediate danger – he's a bit premature but he's doing well and I've no doubt you'll be taking him home before long. There'll be plenty of time to discuss what we do next. You have a lovely baby, Mrs Farrell – enjoy him.'

After they were alone Daniel prised his hand out of Brodie's grip and put it round her shoulders, drawing her to him. She wept, and then she slept.

Or dozed more than slept, waking every hour or so as her body told her to check the baby, to check that he was warm and safe. Awake, though, she knew that while he was both of those things, he wasn't here with her: he was in an incubator in the nursery. But the reproductive process was hammered out millions of years before the maternity ward was ever thought of, and her hormones wouldn't be convinced that right now the baby was better off with the experts caring for him.

It left her without much of a function here now. Apart from feeling sore, and shell-shocked, she was fine. She wanted to be at home. She wanted Paddy more than the baby. Perhaps that wouldn't last. Perhaps when she was able to hold him and feed him, and spend time with him away from the necessarily intrusive trappings of high-tech perinatals, she would feel differently.

The baby. She'd have to give him a name now – he'd earned it. He'd beaten massive odds just getting conceived. Then he'd hung on in there for seven and a half months, and when he couldn't hold on any longer his mother had been busy with the needs of somebody else's child. It wasn't the best start in life. He hadn't been wanted, he hadn't been expected, and his mother had been so ill-prepared for his arrival that he'd had second thoughts about being born at all.

But he was his father's son: the mere fact of not being welcome was never going to stop him going anywhere. He was here now and the world had better get used to the idea. And it would need something to call him.

Brodie drowsed again, and the next time she woke there was someone standing in the doorway. She only knew one person who eclipsed light like that. 'Jack?'

He neither came forward nor retreated, nor even acknowledged his name, just went on standing there, watching her from across the room. With his back to the light she couldn't see his expression. She waited for him to say something. But the slow seconds mounted into minutes and the silence set like concrete.

Finally Brodie decided life was too short to watch any more of it pass away like this. 'Well,' she said briskly, 'it was nice of you to call in for a chat.'

Deacon gave a gruff little snort of the kind usually associated with retired colonels and written as 'Harrumph!' It was half a laugh. It was impossible to say what the other half was.

What it wasn't was the sound of a man delirious with joy over the birth of his son. Brodie nodded slowly. 'Who told you? Daniel?'

Deacon shrugged massively. 'Who else?' It wasn't much of a conversation, but at least he'd graduated to words.

'I was going to call you this morning. I was too zonked last night.'

For a moment she saw something of the old regard in his eyes. 'You're all right?'

'I'm fine,' she assured him. 'For someone who's just had a baby. It was a perfectly normal birth. Early, but normal.'

Deacon was looking round the little room uncertainly, as if embarrassed to ask. 'Er – where…?'

Brodie gestured with her head. 'Down the corridor. I'll take you in a minute. Jack – did Daniel tell you there's a problem?' She knew he would have done. She knew he wouldn't have left it to her.

'I didn't understand most of it,' he said, and his deep voice was soft and rough at the same time.

'Join the club,' said Brodie, heartfelt. 'I think the doctor was a bit taken aback as well – it's a rare condition, and even rarer when it's present at birth.

'Jack, we always knew something like this was a possibility. Before I even knew I was pregnant I was exposed to enough veterinary tranquilliser to kill me and two other people – and a developing baby's at its most vulnerable around eight weeks' gestation. When all the tests they did failed to show a problem I started hoping maybe everything would be all right. But I never counted on it. I'm sorry it's worked out this way, but I can't honestly say I'm surprised. I think, deep down, I knew there was something wrong.'

'You never said.'

'I said something to Marta. She said it was pregnancy neurosis.'

'You never said anything to me!' His eyes kindled at her with a characteristic touch of anger. It was getting to be a while since she'd seen that. They hadn't been close enough recently to make one another angry.

'We haven't talked much about anything,' she reminded him. 'If I'd known there was a problem I'd have told you. I *didn't* know – it was just something I felt.'

Deacon's anger subsided as quickly as it had flared. Finally he came into the room, pulled up the chair and sat down. He breathed out a gusty sigh. 'And how do you feel now?'

'A bit stunned,' she admitted. 'Every rational instinct was telling me I was wrong. I was just about ready to believe I was imagining things. It's like...you try to prepare for the worst, but in your heart you really expect that everything will be fine. You keep thinking, As long as I'm expecting a problem there won't be one. If I'm psychologically prepared to lose this baby, I'm going to be over the moon if all that happens is it comes out with a hare lip.'

'And has he?' Deacon had to clear a frog from his throat. 'A hare lip?'

'No. He's very pretty. Except...'

Brodie saw the dread in his face and wished she hadn't paused. 'Except?'

'He has white eyes.'

'He's blind?' She heard the crack in his voice, wasn't sure if Deacon had heard it himself. Then his heavy brows gathered in a frown. 'How do you know? They don't open their eyes for the first two weeks.'

'I think that's puppies,' murmured Brodie. 'He has retinoblastoma. It's a cancer, and he has it in both eyes. They're going to try to save one of them, but it's hard to know how much vision he'll have. The other one, the safest thing is to remove it.' She managed a mournful smile. 'Don't think he's going to be a freak, Jack. He isn't – he's beautiful. He just rooted around in the genes of one of us and pulled out a short straw. The good news is, ninety per cent of children born with this condition in the UK survive. Ninety per cent in the world as a whole die.'

She'd never seen Deacon look so shocked. She resisted the urge to keep talking, waited for what she'd said already to sink in. Waited for a response.

Finally he said, 'He could die?' His voice was hollow, barely his own.

'It's possible,' she acknowledged, 'but unlikely. He's a racehorse with a ten-to-one chance of winning. Wouldn't you put money on him?'

Distractedly, Deacon ran his big blunt fingers through his hair. He hardly knew what to say. 'And they want to take one eye out?'

'It's a matter of balancing risk against benefit.' Brodie had had fifteen hours to get her head round some of this, to start to understand the implications, for the child and for herself. She found herself in a strange place, knowing this was something to grieve for and not being ready to grieve. She had a live child who had every chance of surviving – for now that seemed enough. She felt no urge to shriek and beat her head against the wall.

She was aware that this sense of unnatural calm might not last, that the diagnosis would bring immutable problems and difficult decisions soon enough. But the rational part of her brain reckoned that was all the more reason to use this quiet time, when even looking after the new baby was being done by other people, to get done those things she most needed calmness for. Like telling the child's father as much as she knew, so he'd know what they were dealing with before he spoke to the doctors, so he could deal with the grief in privacy.

Oddly enough, telling him about it, having to explain carefully, was helping her too. Was making it real for her by manageable degrees, climbing the mountain one rock at a time.

'By removing the worst eye they limit the risk of cancer spreading to the central nervous system. Then they treat the cancer in the other eye in the hope of giving him some vision. He's never going to be a pilot. But he might have some sight. He might at least be able to distinguish between light and dark well enough to avoid walking into things.'

It wasn't a joke. But he looked at her as if she was joking, and the levity was a knife in his heart. His eyes were swimming. She'd never seen that before. With all they'd been through – with all she'd done to him – she'd never seen him cry. In a single movement she swung her legs out of the bed and put her arms around him. They hadn't held one another for maybe seven months. This child was the product of almost the last time they were that comfortable together. So she was amazed at how right it felt to be holding him again. And almost equally amazed that he let her.

'Jack, there are worse things than being blind. It's rotten luck and it's going to make his life difficult – but there's still a whole host of things he'll be able to do if he wants to. He'll learn to read through his fingertips, and if he's smart enough he can go to university. He can be a businessman, a lawyer, a musician, a politician, a teacher. He can be anything that demands more of his brain than his hand-eye coordination. He can't be a surgeon. He'll never be a professional sportsman, but if he enjoys sports there'll be lots open to him. He can enjoy the company of friends as much as you do – well, as much as I do. He can travel, he'll be able to live independently, he'll be able to marry and raise a family. That's a rich life I'm describing, Jack. Don't feel too sorry for him until you see what he can accomplish.'

To an extent she was whistling in the wind. No amount of positive thinking altered the fact that this baby was unlike the vast majority of babies in that his life, and the life of his family, would get harder and more complicated the more he grew. As an infant his needs wouldn't be very different from any other's: food, warmth, keeping clean, being loved. You expect a lot of work, and a lot of sleepless nights, with a new baby. It's what new babies are for. But by degrees they start fitting in with your routine, and when you slot them into the school system you get a bit of your own life back.

But this baby, and therefore also his mother, had extra hurdles to negotiate. There would be hospital visits, and the anxiety that went with them. There could be repeated surgery. There could be vital decisions to take regarding how much risk was justified by how much benefit.

Even if all went well, this child was never going to get what he needed at his neighbourhood primary school. There would be decisions to make about that too – does a child with special needs get a better overall deal at a specialist school or with extra support in the mainstream? Whatever she decided, there would always be extra time, extra work and extra worry involved.

Which held implications for her other child. Perhaps the hardest thing she'd have to do was stop the baby monopolising her, somehow make the space in which her relationship with Paddy, which had been the chief treasure of her life, could go on flourishing. She wasn't yet sure how but she knew she would do that. She had to do that. But she sure as hell couldn't do a full-time job as well.

Deacon was looking at her with raw, glistening, astonished, above all respectful eyes. As if he didn't know her; as if they'd just met. He wasn't a fool – he knew what this meant, to her and to her future. He knew that being positive in the face of tragedy – because it was a tragedy, however bravely she faced it and however well she coped – took real, genuine, accept-no-substitutes courage. And he'd forgotten that was the one thing she had in abundance. She could be sharp to the point of shrewish, she could be selfish, she could be arrogant. She could be stubborn and demanding, quick to anger, quick to take offence. She could make massive, world-stopping mistakes and yet be devastatingly intolerant of other people's flaws.

But with all that, she had the heart of a lion. Where the interests of anyone close to her were involved she seemed to have infinite reserves of physical and moral courage. She would not be beaten. She refused point-blank to even consider the possibility of defeat. She would hurl herself against a brick wall until the bricks fell.

Deacon swallowed. He said, 'Marry me.'

Brodie was so surprised she all but recoiled. 'No!'

'Marry me,' he said again, more forcefully.

He watched emotions flicker across her face like aurorae

flickering across a polar sky. He identified amazement, and amusement, and puzzlement, and for a moment something that could almost have been affection. Each came and went without settling in her expression. She knelt on the bed peering into his craggy tearstained face as if seeking an answer there. 'No,' she said again.

'This is going to be hard work, Brodie. You don't have to do it alone.'

'I won't be doing it alone,' she said. 'Of course I'm going to need you. Of course I'm going to count on you. I don't need a piece of paper to tell me that I can.'

'Raising a child – any child, let alone this one – is a job for a couple. I can help – I want to help. Financially, emotionally, practically. This is something we should do together. I'll buy a bigger house – a family house. We should have done it before. We owe it to this baby to do it now.'

Brodie went on looking at him, seeing the earnestness, the determination in his eyes. She had no doubt it was a genuine offer, not merely a sudden improbable surfeit of sentimentality. It was the first time he'd said it. But it wasn't the first time either of them had wondered about it and thought that was probably where they'd end up. They'd had worse ideas in their time together.

At length Brodie said quietly, 'This is a really bad time to be making life-altering decisions. I'll tell you what, Jack. If you want to, ask me again on this baby's first birthday. Let's see where we are then, where we stand. What we want. Ask me again in a year's time and I might say yes.'

They sat for a long time after that in silence. But it was a different silence. Companionable. Satisfied.

Finally Brodie reached for her dressing-gown. ‘Come on – it’s time you met your son. By the way,’ she added, as if the thought had just occurred to her – which it had, although it arrived fully formed, signed, sealed and delivered as if *someone* had been thinking about it. ‘His name is Jonathan.’

Deacon’s craggy features softened in a slow smile. ‘Of course it is,’ he said.